The
Beginning

Books by Beverly Lewis

The Beginning · *The Stone Wall*
The Tinderbox · *The Timepiece*

The First Love · *The Road Home*
The Proving · *The Ebb Tide*
The Wish · *The Atonement*
The Photograph · *The Love Letters*
The River

HOME TO HICKORY HOLLOW
The Fiddler · *The Bridesmaid*
The Guardian · *The Secret Keeper*
The Last Bride

THE ROSE TRILOGY
The Thorn · *The Judgment*
The Mercy

ABRAM'S DAUGHTERS
The Covenant · *The Betrayal*
The Sacrifice · *The Prodigal*
The Revelation

THE HERITAGE
OF LANCASTER COUNTY
The Shunning · *The Confession*
The Reckoning

ANNIE'S PEOPLE
The Preacher's Daughter
The Englisher · *The Brethren*

THE COURTSHIP
OF NELLIE FISHER
The Parting · *The Forbidden*
The Longing

SEASONS OF GRACE
The Secret · *The Missing*
The Telling

The Postcard · *The Crossroad*

The Redemption of Sarah Cain
Sanctuary (with David Lewis)
Child of Mine (with David Lewis)
The Sunroom · *October Song*
Beverly Lewis Amish Romance
Collection

Amish Prayers
The Beverly Lewis Amish Heritage
Cookbook

www.beverlylewis.com

The
Beginning

BEVERLY
LEWIS

BETHANYHOUSE
a division of Baker Publishing Group
Minneapolis, Minnesota

Published by Bethany House Publishers
11400 Hampshire Avenue South
Bloomington, Minnesota 55438
www.bethanyhouse.com

Bethany House Publishers is a division of
Baker Publishing Group, Grand Rapids, Michigan

Printed in the United States of America

Library of Congress Cataloging-in-Publication Data
Names: Lewis, Beverly, author.
Title: The beginning / Beverly Lewis.
Description: Minneapolis, Minnesota : Bethany House, a division of Baker
    Publishing Group, [2021] |
Identifiers: LCCN 2021023573 | ISBN 9780764237508 (trade paper) | ISBN
    9780764237515 (cloth) | ISBN 9780764237522 (large print) | ISBN
    9781493433810 (ebook)
Subjects: GSAFD: Christian fiction.
Classification: LCC PS3562.E9383 B44 2021 | DDC 813/.54—dc23
LC record available at https://lccn.loc.gov/2021023573

Scripture quotations are from the King James Version of the Bible.

Cover design by Dan Thornberg, Design Source Creative Services
Art direction by Paul Higdon

Baker Publishing Group publications use paper produced from sustainable forestry practices and post-consumer waste whenever possible.

21 22 23 24 25 26 27   7 6 5 4 3 2 1

To
Donna Simmons,
devoted reader-friend
and constant encourager.

Surely goodness and mercy shall follow me
all the days of my life:
and I will dwell in the house of the Lord
for ever.

—Psalm 23:6

PROLOGUE

SPRING

It was that *wunnerbaar-gut* time of year in Hickory Hollow when the earth stirred from its wintry slumber and snow crocuses peeked through the dark soil. The snow had melted more than a week earlier, leaving behind last autumn's leaves, fallen twigs, and mud. The days warmed and stretched ever longer toward evening.

Already I had seen our neighbor Deacon Luke Peachey out with his six-mule team, plowing the land he'd purchased from *Mamma* after my father died in a barn-raising accident fifteen years ago.

It was time now to get busy with spring housecleaning and fulfilling orders for the framed counted cross-stitch family trees I made to bring in extra money. Tomorrow, however, March twelfth, I would take some time to celebrate my twenty-second birthday.

After rising at four-thirty to bake two loaves of bread, I set to work scrubbing the upstairs hallway and the spare room, determined to be a helpful daughter and to make up for the chores Mamma could no longer do because of her worsening health.

That done, I sorted through my drawers of clothing and noticed the small wooden box where I'd saved a few favorite items, including handmade Valentine cards from girl cousins and my sweet younger sister, Britta. Inside was a pinecone, sprayed white and with a dried holly sprig attached to it, a gift from Obie Yoder, my friend since our third-grade year. That had also been the year my brother Eli—ten months older—was struck and killed by a hit-and-run driver not far from our house.

I paused to glance out my upstairs window at the thick grove of willows below, over near the large pond. The lengthy, supple branches swayed gently as a breeze blew through them. *Such a peaceful spot.* I thought back to the many times I'd sat in *Dat*'s old rowboat and cried after Eli's sudden death, missing my close-in-age brother.

So long ago now . . .

Tomorrow, I would mark yet another birthday without my brother or father. Obie was coming to join my family for cake and ice cream, as he'd promised last Saturday at market.

Just like him, wanting to share the day with me.

Next morning, I baked a three-layer fudge birthday cake for myself. Baking and decorating cakes was something I enjoyed doing, as well as tending to Mamma's little shop, open every Tuesday, Wednesday, and Thursday. The small cottage where we sold goat cheese, jams, jellies, and Mamma's famed Amish peanut butter—that fluffy, sweet spread made with marshmallow—was just across the backyard from the house. I also took orders there, as well as at Saturday market in Bird-in-Hand, for my cross-stitched family trees.

For my birthday get-together, Mamma had invited my older sister, Polly, and her husband, Henry, with their three little ones to come for dessert. My brother Allen and his wife, Sarah, and their six children lived way out in Clark, Missouri, having relocated there last summer. The sudden move had taken Mamma by surprise, as well as everyone else here in Hickory Hollow, but available acreage round Lancaster County was becoming as scarce as hen's teeth. Allen and Sarah, hungry for land, had joined an established church district there made up primarily of Amish families from Iowa.

Close as we were, my adopted sister, Britta, soon to be thirteen, was excited about this birthday gathering, even though fewer of us would be present this year. In truth, most of the People didn't make too much of observing birthdays in any case. Focusing attention on individuals wasn't our way. Other days on the calendar were far more significant: Christmas, Easter, Baptism Sunday, and the fasting days prior to twice-yearly communion—days linked to God.

I hurried downstairs to the front room and noticed what a nice job Britta had done polishing all the wood surfaces after school yesterday. Our sister Polly managed to keep her house over in Landisville spick-and-span, even with a babe in arms, an eighteen-month-old toddler, and a school-age son. The last few years, it had fallen to me to take on most of the household chores, since Mamma's once extraordinary get-up-and-go had been affected by asthma, which had worsened this spring with the melting of the snow. Despite being tired much of the time and having occasional shortness of breath, she refused to see a medical doctor, preferring to use folk medicine—most especially, a syrup from comfrey root, mullein, garlic, fennel seed, and apple cider vinegar—as well as other natural remedies her own *Mamm* had passed along.

After Polly and her family left for home that evening, I slipped into my coat to head down to the willows with Obie, while Britta sat on the steps of the potting shed, playing with her three former strays—Tabasco, Lucy, and Daffodil. Britta had been just a toddler when she developed a keen attachment to barn cats. She waved and smiled at Obie and me.

"I'll be back soon," I called as we walked toward the driveway. Obie had worn his Sunday best for my birthday gathering—black broadfall trousers, vest, and coat, with his pressed white shirt. Best as I could remember, he'd never worn his for-good clothes when coming to visit, not even the years he'd spent Christmas evening with us.

What could it mean? I wondered, half hoping I guessed the answer.

"Your birthday cake was delicious," Obie said, blue eyes shining. "You outdid yourself again, Susie."

I smiled. "Glad ya liked it."

"Well, I wasn't the only one," he said as we headed toward the pond side of the willows. "Henry had seconds, I noticed."

He chuckled, and my laughter mingled with his as we strolled around the big pond, talking about whatever came to mind, like we were so good at doing. Like we had always been good at doing.

He mentioned his fourteen-year-old sister Hazel's friendship with my younger sister, and I agreed that it was a real blessing they'd recently forged such a strong relationship.

"Both of them love cats . . . and book learnin'," I commented, not mentioning that, more recently, Britta had been rather quiet and pensive at home, especially around Mamma. Britta was sometimes prone to moodiness, though, so I didn't think it was anything to fuss over.

"Hazel sure seems fond of her. When Britta comes to visit, they hurry off to the barn to visit the new kittens, talking a blue streak," Obie said, admitting to having overheard them.

"It's great to see Britta breakin' out of her shell. She still prefers her cats, I think, but I'm glad she's including people in the mix."

Obie laughed once more and then fell quiet as we circled back around toward the side of the pond where the willows grew more densely.

Then, under the delicate covering of budding leaves and greening branches, he slowed his pace. His expression softened as his eyes searched mine. "You know," he began, "all these years, we've been such *gut* friends."

I studied him, still surprised he'd dressed up like this in his church clothes today.

He shuffled his feet and glanced at the sky, and back at me. Then he said in his deep and mellow voice, one I knew as well as my own, "Here lately, I've been thinking 'bout something, Susie. Something important." His expression seemed so hopeful as he paused to draw a breath.

"*Jah?*" I encouraged him along, curious.

"We've always been comfortable tellin' each other most anything. . . ."

I nodded, my heart pounding now.

"So, what would ya think if we—"

"Susie!" Britta's voice burst through the willows. "Allen's callin' for ya."

Obie's eyes registered surprise, and we turned to see Britta running toward us. Then, stopping abruptly, she said, "*Ach!* Sorry, I—"

"What's goin' on?" I asked, doing my best to hide my annoyance.

Britta leaned over, hands on her knees as she caught her breath. "Allen and the whole family want to wish you a happy birthday . . . on the stable phone."

I glanced at Obie, dying to know what he

was about to say. "I'll call them back," I told her.

Britta jerked her thumb toward the stable. "Okay, but they're waiting."

"Go an' take your call," Obie said. "It's all right."

"Are ya sure?"

He nodded. "We'll talk another time."

I apologized for the interruption, but he waved it away. "*Denki* for comin' over to celebrate with me," I said, watching my sister hurry back up the hill.

"Wouldn't have missed it." Obie smiled again. "Not for anything."

Like you say every birthday, I thought.

Disappointment made my throat dry as I rushed to the stable. I was happy Allen had called, yet I couldn't help wondering what was on Obie's mind. *"Something important,"* he said. . . .

PART 1

A flagstone walkway led to the long front porch of the old stone house where Susie Mast lived with her widowed mother, Aquilla, and younger sister, Britta. The path curved past a small white gazebo in the side yard near two sugar maples, then around to the back door, which opened into the outer room, where, before he moved away, Susie's brother Allen had been known to clomp indoors with dirty work boots.

Now, three days after her birthday, Susie stood in the driveway waiting to welcome her auburn-haired sister home from the one-room schoolhouse a half mile away. She recalled the times when Mamma had stood in this very spot, awaiting her return each weekday afternoon.

Silently, Susie thanked God for this pleasant afternoon and for the customers who had purchased two dozen jars of Amish peanut butter spread at Mamma's little shop earlier, as well as some fresh goat cheese. *A gut day*, she thought, thankful as well for the money Mamma said Allen pitched in each month to help make ends meet.

Squinting into the sunlight, Susie heard the sound of schoolchildren talking and laughing just around the bend in the road.

It wasn't long before Britta and the girls who walked with her came into view. Some wore dark green and plum dresses beneath their black coats, while others wore brighter hues of maroon and blue. Each also wore a dark blue bandanna. As usual, the schoolboys hung farther back, all of them in black broadfall trousers and coats, their straw hats snug on their heads.

Britta was nearly half a head taller than the other girls her age. They looked toward Susie and waved, then called their good-byes to Britta, who turned and dashed up the driveway.

"Hullo!" Susie said, happy to see her. "What did ya learn today?"

"More than my head can hold," Britta replied.

"Well, you're a *gut* scholar. You'll be fine."

Britta's dark eyes revealed momentary pride. "Just doin' my best." She shrugged, then added, "Oh, and Hazel Yoder an' I are competing in grammar lessons."

"*Des gut, jah?*"

"Keeps us both on our toes, even though she's a grade ahead."

Susie smiled as they walked into the house together. "Want a snack before chores?"

"Applesauce, maybe, but I can get it," Britta answered.

"With cinnamon, of course." Susie beat her to the gas-powered refrigerator and opened the half-full Mason jar of sauce.

"*Ach*, you spoil me, sister," Britta said as she removed her black coat and hung it on the wooden hook on the far wall of the kitchen, near the walk-in pantry. "How would I ever manage without ya?" she teased.

Susie laughed. "You'd do just fine."

Britta shook her head, her face suddenly serious. "Well, it wouldn't be nearly as much fun."

A knowing look passed between them. Susie nodded, touched by the sentiment, but Britta turned pensive and glanced out the window. Then, walking toward the front room, she turned and asked, "Where's Mamma?"

"Over at Ella Mae's."

"Prob'ly needed to get out of the house."

"She seems to be feelin' better, so that's *gut*," Susie said. "Ella Mae's grandson Paul came and picked her up not long ago, and I took over workin' at the shop till just now." Susie glanced out the window, looking to see if any customers had come.

Britta sat down and leaned one elbow on the table, a thoughtful look on her oval face. "Paul's a newlywed and a busy farmer," she said. "Where does he find time?"

"Maybe that's why he walks so fast," Susie joked.

Britta nodded.

Susie spooned an ample helping of the homemade applesauce into a bowl and set it in front of Britta, whose cheeks were still rosy from the walk home. "In an hour or so, I'll go an' get Mamma, after she has tea and time to visit."

Britta brightened. "Did ya know that Ella Mae once told me she was as spunky as me when she was young?"

"Some of us just are."

Britta grinned. "Were *you*?"

"Not really, but from what Mamma's said, Allen certainly was."

"And still is!"

They shared a laugh as Susie went to get the cinnamon from Mamma's spice rack.

"Wouldn't it take *Schpank* to do what he

and Sarah did, goin' to Missouri?" Britta asked. "Or do ya think that shows more grit?"

"Definitely grit . . . and ambition. It must be awful hard to uproot and start from scratch like they did."

"Well, I wish they'd stayed here." Britta momentarily looked sad as she sprinkled cinnamon over her applesauce.

Susie opened the fridge to take out some milk.

"As much as Allen liked Hickory Hollow, I'm still surprised he left." Britta sighed.

This gave Susie pause. Sometimes she worried her younger sister might decide to leave Hickory Hollow as well, or at least dip her toe into the world during her *Rumschpringe*. After all, she adored books and learning new things. Even so, Britta had never so much as inquired about her biological family and whether or not they were Plain. But there were times when she seemed to be deep in thought, which wondered Susie. Thankfully, the season of running around was still a little more than three years away. Susie comforted herself with that thought.

"Allen was practically a father to me," Britta said quietly.

No wonder she misses him, Susie thought sadly, remembering that Britta had never had the opportunity to know Dat.

Once again, Susie tried to explain their older brother's reasoning—his quest for land, and how he'd unsuccessfully searched all over Lancaster County and the surrounding area for a plot large enough to farm and then parcel out to his sons later in life. "Mamma says he's been teachin' his youngest children to fish and hunt and gather huckleberries out there, learning nature's lessons. Sounds like a *wunnerbaar-gut* place to raise a family."

"Do ya think he misses Hickory Hollow?" Britta stirred her applesauce, which she had yet to taste.

Does he miss us, she means. "Would ya like to write a letter, maybe?"

Britta shook her head. "What I'd like is for them to come back."

Just then, Susie heard the gentle sound of the wind chime on the back porch. "Allen won't be doin' that. He believes he was led to go to Missouri, remember?"

Britta stared at her applesauce, still for a moment. "S'pose I'll have to ask God 'bout that," she murmured. "And about a few other things."

Susie wondered what that meant as she poured fresh goat's milk into a glass and carried it to the table.

"If I wasn't adopted, I wonder where my

home would've been," Britta said, finally eating now. "I think a lot on this, honestly."

"Well, if I knew, I'd tell ya." For whatever reason, her sister seemed to be struggling today.

Britta sat quietly and asked no more questions. The silence felt ever so awkward.

After a time, Susie asked, "Would ya like to go to the farm sale over on Hershey Church Road this Saturday?"

Looking up, Britta nodded. "Hazel wants to go, too, so let's all go together, if that's okay."

"*Wunnerbaar*," Susie agreed.

"Who knows, maybe Obie will come along," Britta added, brown eyes alight.

Susie smiled. "I'm sure he'll attend with his father and brothers, like usual."

Later that day, while hitching the buggy to Brambles, one of their two dark bay horses, Susie spotted the first robin of the season, hopping in the grassy area near the hitching post. The pretty red-breasted bird chirped merrily as it searched for worms, and Susie wished Mamma were there to see it. *She loves the first sighting of spring*, she thought, though she was pleased Ella Mae had invited Mamma for tea. The elderly woman had a winning way about her, listening without giving advice, unless requested, which drew folk—women especially—to unburden themselves while sipping her famed peppermint tea.

People don't call her the Wise Woman for nothing, Susie thought as she climbed into the buggy. Picking up the driving lines, she signaled the mare to move toward the road. The horse trotted gracefully, black mane floating up and down with each stride.

Eventually, they came up on Preacher Benuel Zook's dairy farm, where his wife, Linda, was out pinning quilts to the clothesline for their seasonal airing. As Susie turned into their lane, Linda waved and grinned, her deep dimples appearing.

Opening the carriage window, Susie said, "I brought some freshly made peanut butter spread from Mamma."

"Well, ain't that nice." Linda came over to accept it. "Tell your Mamma I'll bring her some pickled beets real soon."

"Oh, she'll love that."

Farther up the road, Susie signaled the mare to turn left into David Beiler's farm, where the district's covered bench wagon was parked near the house. Inside the wagon, piles of *Ausbund* songbooks were neatly stacked, along with many benches for this Sunday's

Preaching service, as well as plates and utensils for the fellowship meal to follow. David and Mattie Beiler were quite adept at preparing ahead, having hosted church numerous times throughout the years, and they would have plenty of help rearranging the living areas in their home to make room for everyone in their large church district.

Susie parked the carriage close to the *Dawdi Haus* and, looking over, she saw Ella Mae and Mamma walking leisurely toward the back driveway, arm in arm, both wearing gray dresses and black aprons beneath their short black coats. Susie observed the sweet friendship.

Mamma looks fairly well today, she thought, hopping down from the buggy to go and fetch her.

"We've had us a real nice visit," Ella Mae declared, her blue eyes almost shut as she peered into the bright sunshine. "And plenty-a tea."

With a nod, Mamma glanced at Ella Mae. "She just kept servin', and I kept drinkin'."

"We had scones and biscuits with jam and honey, and some with apple butter, too." Ella Mae winked at Susie. "'Tis best to wash all of that down with delicious tea, ya know."

Susie nodded, delighted to see Ella Mae again. She'd never known the dear woman to be anything but cheerful, and today was no exception. She just wanted to bask in the woman's presence. But Mamma seemed tired.

"Looks like you're ready to go," Susie said to her.

They waved good-bye to Ella Mae, who planted herself at the end of the walkway and smiled sweetly.

"*Gut* visit?" Susie asked her mother as she backed the horse and buggy out of the parking spot to head toward the road.

"Ella Mae has a way of helpin' me forget myself," Mamma observed before sighing deeply. When she spoke again, it was soft and wistful. "'Twas just what I needed."

Susie glanced at her mother, grateful she enjoyed such a friendship.

"By the way, Ella Mae said that Delmar Petersheim's older sister plans to drop by the shop soon."

Susie's ears perked up. "Del, who sometimes worked with Allen before they moved to Missouri?"

"*Jah* . . . from over in Gordonville."

"Must be his *married* sister Ella Mae was talking 'bout, then."

"Might be." Mamma leaned back against the seat. "I don't keep up with the folk in Gordonville so much."

Just then Susie remembered her earlier stop at Preacher Zook's. "Before I forget, Linda Zook seemed mighty happy for the peanut butter spread. Said she'd come with pickled beets sometime for ya."

"*Ach*, now my mouth's watering."

Susie chuckled a little. "Didn't ya eat your fill at Ella Mae's?"

"Well, there's nothin' quite like Linda's beets, that's for sure." Mamma paused. "Kinda like how Obie talks 'bout your baking, ain't?"

Susie smiled, hearing Mamma say that. "True, he's never been shy 'bout compliments when it comes to food." She hurried the horse.

"Are we in a rush?" Mamma asked.

"Well, chores are waitin'."

"Aren't you the Little Red Hen?" Mamma reached over and gave her hand a gentle pat.

Two days later, Susie gathered up the letters Mamma had written the night before to Allen's wife, Sarah, as well as letters to two Pennsylvania relatives who lived over in the community of Willow Street. Susie carried them to the mailbox at the end of the driveway while her mother assisted customers in her shop.

In the distance, she could hear the sound of a tractor, as well as the *clip-clop-clip* of a road horse. *Fancy and Plain alike*, Susie thought, opening the mailbox and sliding the letters inside.

She raised the red metal flag and turned to see a wagon coming into view. Del Petersheim sat high in the driver's seat and waved as he slowed his gleaming black horse to a halt. She remembered what Mamma had said about Del's sister wanting to drop by the shop. Not having heard about Del or his family since Allen moved to Missouri, it was kind of a surprise to see Del there now, smiling at her.

"Hullo, Susie." Beneath his straw hat, his dark bangs ruffled in the breeze.

"Makin' a delivery?" she asked, glancing at the wagon box filled with mulch.

"Just up the road to your deacon, *jah*." He bobbed his head in that direction, a grin still on his tan face. "Say, I've been curious 'bout the family trees ya make," Del said. "Do ya have a sample I could see? I might like to order one for my parents' anniversary."

"When is it?"

"Late November, but I wasn't sure how long it'd take you to make one."

"Well, not *that* long." She laughed softly. "Where'd ya hear 'bout them?"

"Oh, one of my aunt's friends received one you made. Her daughters ordered it as a gift recently. She's mighty pleased . . . has it hangin' in her front room to show it off."

"I'm glad she likes it," Susie said, realizing how nice looking Del was. It had been such a while since she'd seen him that she'd forgotten.

"When's a *gut* time to stop by?" Del asked, his brown eyes dancing.

"The shop's open Tuesdays through

Thursdays—nine to four. But I could show ya right quick, if you'd like."

"*Denki*, but I really need to be on my way. I'll come back a different day." He tipped his straw hat and offered another smile. "Say . . . now that I'm here, I've been wonderin'—how would ya like to go to the farm auction with me this Saturday?"

At that moment, Susie noticed Obie's mother, Kate, coming toward them in her gray family buggy. Kate turned her head to nod as she approached, and when Susie waved to her, Kate waved back with a pleasant expression. *I've always liked Kate.* Susie wondered if the woman ever hoped her son might ask Susie out. So far, though, it looked like Obie wasn't going to, and here was Del, showing interest right now.

If I ever hope to marry, I'd better start accepting dates again, she thought, not having done so for several years in the hope that Obie just might make a move.

She thought back to her birthday, five long days ago. She hadn't seen or heard from him since then. *Be patient*, she'd told herself. *You've waited this long.*

Yet what if Obie never asks me out? another part of her argued.

She became aware that Del's focus remained on her, his eyes questioning.

"*Jah*, I can meet ya at the auction," Susie said at last, mentioning she'd already made plans to take her sister and Britta's friend Hazel along.

"That's fine," Del said, brightening. "Let's meet at the food stand."

Susie nodded.

"I'll see ya Saturday."

"Okay." She felt a little awkward that Kate had seen her with Del, though she really shouldn't. Surely Kate knew better than most that Susie and Obie were merely friends.

"Well, have yourself a nice afternoon." Del picked up the driving lines and pulled away from the shoulder back onto the road.

"Tell Deacon Peachey hullo," Susie called, eyeing the big load of mulch again. She remembered how Dat would haul wheelbarrows full of dried compost to spread around Mamma's flower beds every spring. *Helping her was his greatest joy. . . .*

Missing those days, Susie made her way back up the driveway toward the house to cook the noon meal for her and Mamma.

Britta awakened a few moments before daylight that Saturday and slipped out of bed to raise her dark green shades. She stood yawning and waiting for the first pale washes of color across the sky—that cherished moment of peace each morning while she was still hazy with sleep.

She prayed a silent blessing over the day like Mamma had taught her to do. *"Give your first thoughts of the day to God."*

Britta had always enjoyed the solitude upon waking, just as she loved being outdoors at sunset, listening to the earth's music as the violet shadows lengthened. In summertime, whenever she felt sad, she liked to lie in bed and listen to the birds chirp their goodnights, her windows flung wide open as she said her rote prayers.

Another of her favorite things was milking their goats. That, and spending time with the stable cats. She loved the contented purr of her pretty black cat, Lucy, and paid such close attention to its changes in tone and tempo that she was almost sure she knew what the cat was saying.

Britta turned her thoughts to the day's local farm sale. As much as anything, she enjoyed going to the auctions around Lancaster County, including the springtime mud sales in Gordonville, Kinzers, Strasburg, and other nearby towns. She particularly liked to look through the old books and the carnival glass and Anchor Hocking sets, though she couldn't possibly afford to bid on the latter.

Despite their cost, they still appealed to her, while Susie preferred admiring the quilts. It was so much fun going with Mamma and Susie, who always made her feel included as they stopped to talk with their many kinfolk and friends. Mamma had taught all of her children to pay close attention to the people in their lives, learning truths and gleaning wisdom from them. But Mamma didn't talk about the woman who'd birthed Britta, and she wondered why.

Britta's stomach rumbled, and her thoughts turned to the loaded chili dog she'd eaten at the last auction, her mouth watering at the memory. *Today will surely be another wunnerbaar-gut time,* she thought while brushing her long, wavy auburn hair. Quickly, she pulled it into a thick bun and dressed for the day.

Downstairs, she helped Susie make scrambled eggs, German sausage, and toast to serve with the strawberry jam Mamma had put up last summer and the raw honey Susie liked to purchase from their beekeeping Amish neighbors, Jonathan and Liz Ebersol.

Mamma was already sitting in her rocker near the back window overlooking the yard and horse stable. Despite the early hour, she looked rather spent. "You girls are spoilin' me, doin' all the work." Mamma glanced their way, hands wrapped around her coffee mug.

"It's *our* work, too," Susie said as she fried up the sausage, her white half apron tied over the waist of her long black apron to keep it clean. "Besides, cookin' makes us happy."

"And it's your turn to be looked after." Britta turned the gas burner down under the scrambled eggs. "When's Polly comin' with the children?" she asked.

"Oh, about eight-thirty, I 'spect." Mamma pushed her white *Kapp* strings back over her lean shoulders.

"It's nice of her to keep ya company while we're gone," Susie said. "Our big sister always has interesting things to share, 'specially when it comes to her little ones."

"Next farm sale, I want ya to come with us, okay, Mamma?" Britta left the gas range to go and give her mother a kiss on her cheek. "Ain't the same without ya."

"*Denki*, but I'm not feelin' up to it today." Mamma reached for the hem of her black apron and began to fan herself.

"If Polly wasn't comin', one of us would stay home with you," Susie said from across the kitchen. "Wouldn't think of leavin' when you're under the weather."

"*Ach*, yous can't always be here." Mamma's expression changed. "And I don't expect it." She gave them her sweet, familiar smile, with all the love it represented.

"I love ya, Mamma," Susie said, her light brown eyes glistening.

"*Jah*, me too—even more than books," Britta added with a grin.

"Well then," Mamma replied, chuckling, "I must *really* be loved!"

They laughed merrily.

But Britta, feeling a prick of concern for Mamma's health, knelt to rest her head on her mother's knees.

At the Yoder farm, Britta was happy to see her friend Hazel coming out the back door just as Susie halted Atta-Girl, their main driving horse. Hazel wore a salmon-colored dress with a black apron, her silky blond hair bun hidden by her heart-shaped head covering. A quick smile spread across her pretty face.

Susie got out and folded down the front seat so Hazel could get in back with Britta.

"Whose eye are ya hopin' to catch today?" Britta teased as Hazel sat down next to her.

Hazel blushed, then whispered, "I'm too young to think 'bout fellas." Despite her words, a smile dimpled her cheeks.

"And pigs can fly, *jah*?" Britta replied.

Hazel giggled. "Okay, *sometimes* I think about boys."

"Well, it won't be long an' we'll both be going to Sunday Singings," Britta observed.

"Just two more years for me," Hazel said, eyes alight.

"So, is there a fella you're sweet on?" Britta glanced at her friend. "There must be someone, considerin' how nice ya dressed for the auction."

Hazel shook her head. "*Ach*, must ya ask so many questions?"

Britta blushed, embarrassed. "Sorry. Guess I'm more used to talkin' to cats."

"Don't feel bad," Hazel said quickly. "And I talk to cats, too. Well, cats and cows," she added with a smile.

They laughed about that, and even Susie joined in the gaiety, mentioning that animals were good listeners.

Soon, the conversation turned to the items they were looking to purchase for their individual hope chests with money they'd earned. Hazel was a part-time gardener for her grandparents, and Britta was an occasional babysitter for the Ebersols.

"Are you searchin' for anything special, Susie?" Hazel asked, leaning forward.

"Not really. Just goin' for the fun of it,"

Susie told her, glancing over her shoulder at the two of them.

"I'd love to surprise Mamma with a big cast-iron skillet," Britta said, knowing Susie would get the most benefit from it.

"Those usually go fairly high, though," Hazel pointed out. "How much money did ya bring?"

"Only thirty dollars." Britta shook her head. "Maybe I'll look for some baking molds for my hope chest instead."

Another half mile, and Susie directed Atta-Girl to turn into the long lane. As her sister halted the mare, Britta noticed the many gray buggies and some spring wagons parked along the side yard.

"Lookee over there," Britta told Hazel. "It's your *Bruder* Obie."

Hazel nodded. "He was asked to help lead the horses to the feed wagon over yonder. See?"

Britta glanced but didn't want to stare. *Good thing Susie's here*, she thought, having seen her sister talking with Obie in the willow grove on her birthday. She knew they were close friends but suspected they could possibly be more. And she secretly hoped so, too, although she didn't dare speculate on that with Obie's sister—and Susie—nearby.

The farm sale had drawn perhaps hundreds of Amish folk, though Britta couldn't be sure. Nevertheless, there was a cluster of yellow straw hats wherever men took interest in items such as the hunting gear lined up on what looked to be an old barn door set up on two sawhorses. A good many young men were also examining the hand tools and a drill press set out on some other tables, while a few couples inspected a wringer washer and double wash stands. Out of the corner of her eye, Britta noticed several teenage fellows over near the silo, perhaps sneaking away for a quick smoke.

"Other than at Preachin', have you ever seen so many people in one place?" Hazel asked Britta as they strolled along together after Susie went her separate way.

"Only at horse auctions."

Hazel laughed. "There's something here for the whole family."

Britta sighed. "Now that Allen and Sarah live in Missouri, Mamma and Susie are the only family I have left, 'cept for Polly and Henry."

"I know ya miss your brother and his family."

Britta nodded. "But I'm not as lonely for them as Mamma seems to be sometimes," she admitted.

Hazel seemed to study her. "I can't imagine I'd like it if anyone in my family moved away."

Britta stopped walking and poked her wavy hair back into its bun. "*Ach,* I wish my hair was straighter, like yours—then I wouldn't keep havin' this problem." She removed her *Kapp* and took out several bobby pins to fix her hair, then pushed the bobby pins back in, hoping they would hold the most unruly strands. "I wonder if my hair's like my first *Mamm*'s."

"Could be," Hazel replied. "Wavy hair looks so nice, I think."

"But you know it's nothin' like anyone else's round here. More red."

"Why's that matter?" Hazel smiled and motioned for her to come along. "You are who God meant ya to be."

Britta followed, surprised at herself, since she'd never shared any of her private thoughts about her birth parents, whoever they might be. But hearing Hazel say this made Britta realize again what good friends they were becoming, and why. *If only my own shyness hadn't held me back for so long.*

Just then, Britta spotted a large collection of kitchenware and went to take a look. Hazel seemed equally excited, saying she'd also like to stock up for her hope chest, which her father had built and given to her on her twelfth birthday to store household items till she was married.

A while later, as Britta and Hazel waited in line to pay for the items they'd bid on, Britta noticed Susie strolling around with Delmar Petersheim. They were talking and smiling at each other, and it made her wonder how Obie Yoder might feel about that if he knew.

A few minutes later, Obie himself came over with red licorice for Britta and Hazel

"*Denki*, Bruder! You know what we like," Hazel said.

Britta nodded her thanks, as well.

"Have ya seen Susie?" Hazel asked. "She's round here somewhere."

"*Jah*, with Del Petersheim," Obie said, answering Hazel but giving Britta a little look of disappointment. "Have they been goin' out?"

Britta wished the ground could open up and swallow her. Truth was, she didn't know, but then again, it wasn't her place to. So she said the only thing she could think of. "I can't say, really."

Obie nodded graciously. "Well, from what I've heard, he's a fine fella. I shouldn't have put ya on the spot." He seemed to force a smile before heading on his way.

Britta glanced at Hazel and shrugged.

This is Susie's doing, not mine! she thought, feeling a little sorry for Obie, even though he'd clearly tried to take it in stride.

Some time later, Britta spotted neighbors Josh Miller and his wife, Becky, with four of their children. The youngest had been adopted at birth and given the name Martha. Seeing the petite brunette girl who resembled neither her blond parents nor her siblings made Britta curious about her. Did the little girl know how she stood out?

With her own auburn waves and her fancy, English-sounding name, Britta never could quite forget how she must stand out to the Amish families around her. Her name particularly made her wonder. No one else among the People had the name Britta. She wondered if her first mother had named her before she was adopted. And if so, why had Mamma Aquilla chosen to keep it?

I should ask someday, Britta mused, but she felt shy about bringing up a past she knew nothing about.

CHAPTER 3

Susie relished the sunshine and the pleasant day and even caught herself laughing at times while walking with Del Petersheim at the farm auction. Earlier, she had seen Britta and Hazel near the food stand, though it had been a while since. She couldn't help but notice Britta's surprised look when she'd spotted Del with her.

I should've told her ahead of time, Susie thought, despite not being one to talk much about the fellows she'd casually dated through the years. Only Obie Yoder was privy to who she'd gone out with, because of course he'd seen her leave Singings with other young men from time to time, although not recently. She actually wondered now if Obie had noticed the way she'd backed away from other fellows, hoping to give him a chance. *Likely not.*

"What're ya interested in bidding on?" Del asked, drawing Susie's attention back to him. He'd been scrutinizing the driving horses and field mules up for sale and had just finished admiring a large hay rake and plow. "You've been so patient while I look around."

"Well, I'd like to poke around in the house, if ya don't mind," she replied, motioning in the direction of the old farmhouse.

"Need some extra kitchen gadgets?" Del asked as he quickened his pace with her.

"Without 'em, there'd be no delicious meals . . . or baked goods," she teased.

He chuckled. "From what I've heard, you know your way round the kitchen."

She was curious where he could have heard that, then remembered Allen had sometimes hired Del. Could it be Allen and Sarah had put in a good word for her?

Have they been playing matchmaker? she wondered, waving to two of her cousins, Laura Ann and Miriam Mast, as they came down the back steps.

On the way inside, Susie asked Del if he'd ever tried his hand at cooking.

Del chuckled. "Should I count the one and only burnt omelet?"

She smiled. "My Dat used to make chocolate chip waffles for breakfast. And plain ones, sometimes, for supper, too, with chicken and gravy. I don't know where he learned how," she said while navigating her way through the crowded kitchen.

"One of my uncles likes to help his wife with the cooking, 'specially during the winter months when the field work's done," Del said, following her. "He tinkers around in the kitchen, even makes noodles from scratch."

"His wife must be real happy 'bout that," Susie said, spotting a bin of small kitchen tools in the corner.

"Lookin' for anything specific?"

"*Jah*. Bulk packages of cheesecloth would be nice, and Mamma could use another carrot grater."

"Yous still makin' goat cheese to sell?" Del asked, standing near.

Susie nodded. "And we sell the milk, too. Along with peanut butter spread and jams and jellies."

"I'll have to take a look when I stop by to order that family tree."

"Sounds *gut*." Susie smiled.

When the household items were finally auctioned off, Susie won the bid for the carrot grater she'd found, which was in a box with some other kitchen gadgets. She and Del wandered back out to the barn, where Susie happened to see Obie with his younger brother, Jerome, and their father. They and some other men milled around near the log splitter, mowers, and manure spreader as the auctioneer geared up to start the bidding.

Before she could turn her head, Obie caught her eye. Her face warmed, but she smiled. Obie waved in response before turning back to his family and the farming equipment.

Guess I was wrong about whatever he wanted to ask me on my birthday, she thought, *before we were interrupted.*

She wondered now if he'd just wanted to inquire if she was coming to today's farm sale, just maybe. Nothing earthshaking, and certainly not the question she'd longed for.

Upon returning home that afternoon, and while Britta was making goat cheese in the kitchen, Susie read to her mother from the old German *Biewel* in the front room. Mamma embroidered a yellow pansy design on a pillowcase as Susie shared from the first chapter of the book of Job, slowing when she came to the latter part of verse twenty-one. "'The Lord gave, and the Lord hath taken away; blessed be the name of the Lord,'" she read. When Susie finished, she closed the Bible gently.

"*Ach*, what Job had to suffer," Mamma said softly, looking up from her embroidery. "We can learn a lot from his response to being faced with ever so many sorrows. 'Tis wise not to let our troubles turn us toward bitterness." Mamma returned to her stitching. "Easy to say, but hard to do."

"God permitted Job to be tested," Susie said, a part of her wondering if Mamma's struggles with her health, and maybe even losing Dat and Eli, had been similar tests. "Do ya think God allows the same for us?"

Mamma tilted her head and smoothed the fabric under her stitching. "Maybe so. But remember: Job lost *everything*, yet he continued to trust the Lord. Havin' that kind of trust . . . well, that's what I focus on."

Susie considered that. She'd felt the loss of her father and brother greatly—some days it was still all too fresh. She listened now as Mamma continued to talk about God's sovereignty and why it was important not to question His will.

When there was a lull in the conversation, Susie said, "You might find it interesting that

Del Petersheim and I walked around together at the farm sale today."

Mamma's eyebrows rose. "Del . . . not Obie?"

"Well, Obie's never asked me out."

"Honestly, it wonders me. I've always thought there was somethin' special 'tween you two." Mamma shook her head. "You've been friends for years."

Susie had always assumed her mother approved of Obie. "I really can't speak for him, Mamma."

"A solid friendship is the best foundation for a relationship, ya know, and dating takes things a step further—tells ya if there's a spark."

"Obie'd have to pursue me, though," Susie said. "And he hasn't."

Mamma studied her. "*Jah*, well, if he *did* have feelings for you, I'd be truly happy."

Thankfully, Mamma changed the subject before Susie could grow any more embarrassed. She held up her embroidered piece to display it. "I've thought of givin' something to Ella Mae Zook for her many years of kindnesses toward me. This set of embroidered pillowcases would be nice, don't ya think?"

Susie nodded, liking the idea. *We all need a trustworthy friend like the Wise Woman*, she mused, thinking again of Obie.

Susie preferred to work on her cross-stitches in the small, sunny sewing room just off the front room. Sitting by the open window, she could hear Britta near the house, talking to the cats. Of the three felines, Daffodil and Lucy angled for the most attention, which was unusual compared to most cats, who were, as a general rule, fairly independent. But even the more standoffish Tabasco was drawn to Britta. As for Susie, Daffodil was her favorite—such a pretty golden coat, and with a sweet way about her.

Susie set aside the sketch pad where she kept all of her designs, as well as the names and dates for each of the family trees her customers had special ordered. She prioritized them by which customers needed them soonest, since she worked on more than one at a time.

Going outside, she found Britta sitting on the potting shed steps, cuddling black-furred Lucy. Meanwhile, Daffodil was rubbing against Britta's leg and purring loudly, competing for attention. Across the way, Tabasco had pushed his head under the lilac bush while the rest of his orange body soaked up the warmth of the sunshine.

Britta pointed this out to Susie, who

laughed at the sight. "Too bad we can't have cats in the house," her sister said.

"Not with Mamma's allergies. Besides, I can't think of anyone among the People who has an indoor cat, can you?"

"*Nee.* Awful as that is," Britta said comically, scratching Lucy under her chin.

Susie remembered when Britta was little and liked to pretend that tiny Lucy was her doll baby. Surprisingly, the kitten would stay put while being rocked in the little handmade cradle, beneath a doll quilt Mamma had sewn.

"I didn't have a chance on the ride home today to show ya what I bought for my hope chest. Hazel found some things, too," Britta said, but then her expression turned tentative. "Her brother Obie stopped to talk with us." Britta let the last words dangle.

"I saw him, too," Susie replied.

Britta looked surprised, but Susie didn't feel the need to share more.

"Honestly, I think he might've wished you were with him 'stead of another fella." Britta put Lucy down and reached now for Daffodil.

It didn't seem like it.

"Obie's always been so nice." Britta snuggled Daffodil, then tilted her head at Susie, looking at her. "*Ach,* you're usually so happy when you talk about him, but you don't seem that happy now."

After Mamma's seeming disappointment over hearing about Del, Susie wasn't sure what to say. "It's hard to explain," she said, walking toward the back porch.

"I hope you're not upset with me," Britta said, getting up with Daffodil still in her arms. "I couldn't bear it."

"I'm pretty sure you could, *jah*?"

Britta laughed. "Okay, but I'd hound you till you forgave me. After all, the Good Book says you *have* to forgive me."

Susie smiled at her teasing. "Aren't you the clever one! But my chores and yours are waiting. We should prob'ly get busy."

Britta nodded. "Mamma doesn't call ya her Little Red Hen for nothin'."

Susie ignored the remark and headed inside, where she went back to the sewing room to finish sketching out a family tree she'd been commissioned to create, the fifth of seven current orders. She wanted each cross-stitched tree to be uniquely special, and this one, a fiftieth wedding anniversary gift for Mattie Beiler's uncle and aunt, would have extra curlicues and flourishes stitched around its four corners.

After a while, she went to the kitchen, where Mamma was writing a letter at the table. Susie opened the gas fridge and noticed a five-bean salad chilling.

"You didn't have to make anything," she told her mother, glancing over her shoulder.

"Just doin' my part." Mamma offered a smile. "I made us some meatloaf, too."

Susie placed seven large potatoes in the deep sink. Turning on the faucet, she let the water pour over them before picking up the first potato and the paring knife, making a peel that grew nearly as long and wavy as Britta's hair.

But Susie's mind was not on the chore at hand. She realized that no matter how much she cared for Obie, he was probably never going to be anything more than a friend. Going forward, she might as well accept further invitations from Del, assuming he asked her again.

4

The jeering of crows in the tree outside her window roused Susie from her slumber. Stretching, she rose to read from *Rules of a Godly Life*, an early eighteenth-century book used by the People to guide them along the right path. She liked to read it first thing in the morning, before her day began. And since she was awake, she might as well make use of the extra time.

Reaching for her brush, Susie began to work through her hair as she read. When her tresses were completely smoothed, she wound them into a low bun near the nape of her neck and secured it by feel with bobby pins.

Then, going to the narrow closet in the alcove of her room, she ran her fingers over the sleeves of her two best blue dresses, one darker than the other. A glance out the nearby window revealed Britta heading to the stable to water their two road horses and the pony and to milk the goats. The sun already shone bright, and Susie remembered what Mamma had read in yesterday's newspaper about the mild springlike forecast for today.

So Susie chose the pale blue dress and removed a black apron from the hanger to wear over it, but only till after breakfast. Before leaving for church, she would don her crisp white organdy apron, making sure she looked neat and tidy. She had spilled a time or two at breakfast and didn't want to risk doing that again. Besides, wearing her best and cleanest clothing to Preaching was an act of reverence to God.

When they arrived at David Beiler's for the Preaching service, Susie hurried around the buggy to help Mamma step down from the left side while one of the teenage boy attendants kept the horse still. Then Britta climbed out of the second seat.

Two of David and Mattie's teen granddaughters—Amanda and Rose Hannah— were standing together near the back porch, talking quietly and sometimes greeting people as families strode by. They waved to Samuel and Rebecca Lapp and smiled shyly at Bishop John Beiler's handsome grandsons, identical twins Michael and Jonas. But it was the girls' reaction to the sight of Obie Yoder and his family coming up the walkway that caught Susie's attention. She didn't feel jealous; it wasn't that. Rather, it was the sudden and plain reality that she wished Obie would talk to *her*, tell her what she hoped he'd almost said on her birthday.

Susie walked with Mamma across the backyard and around to the separate entrance for the womenfolk, to Mamma's spot in line with the older women. Then Susie headed toward the end of the line, past many of her older cousins, including Naomi Flaud, who cradled her infant daughter, and took her place behind tall, slender Cousin Laura Ann Mast, also twenty-two.

Across from the women, the menfolk stood respectfully in their own line, every one of them dressed in a black frock coat, vest, trousers, felt hat, and white shirt, and shook hands with one another as they arrived. Perry Stoltzfus, who had been a friend of her brother Eli, nodded at her, and she waved back, wondering what it would have been like for Eli to grow up to courting age like Perry. She imagined her brother smiling as he strolled toward this side of the house, then spotted her across the yard, looking for him. At the time of his death, he'd been so close to fully memorizing the German words of the praise hymn *Das Loblied*, eager to finally walk into church with the other boys his age. Somehow, thinking of Eli dressed in his Sunday best helped to soften the memory of that awful night that had snuffed out his young life, his nine-year-old body crumpled along the roadside.

Forcing the frightful memory away, Susie noticed Obie's sister Hazel behind her, looking ahead. *What might Hazel have on her mind? Does she even suspect I like her brother?* Susie wondered, then stopped. She wouldn't let her mind wander again. It was time to quiet her thoughts for this solemn assembly.

Bowing her head, she tried to focus on God and not her imaginings.

Susie politely declined Mamma's offer to take her to the evening Singing in the family buggy. She wouldn't think of it, not when Mamma looked so peaked. Besides, it was unseasonably warm and easy enough to walk there and possibly rid herself of some pent-up energy after sitting in church all morning. And anyway, walking briskly alone in nature was one of the best ways to ask God for His perspective on her scattered thoughts.

As for the route she would take, Susie purposely chose the road where the hit-and-run driver had careered toward Eli fourteen years ago, striking him and narrowly missing her. She had dawdled that day, stopping to pick up a long, white bird feather from the road when she heard Eli's holler before that terrible thud. Some time later, Mamma had read a newspaper article to her about Eli's untimely death and police speculation that the driver may have been impaired. To this day, Susie wondered if that was true. Nevertheless, Mamma had always instructed her children never to hold a grudge, even after something as terrible as this. Scripture admonished them to be quick to forgive, so Susie had done her best to follow that practice, hard as it was.

Coming up on the accident site, she paused as she always did, pushing down the sorrow, trying not to blame the location. What had happened there still tormented her, yet it was also the last place she'd seen dear Eli alive.

The familiar dread made her feel breathless as she glanced at the white horse fence, the spot where a cluster of flowers tied with a blue ribbon mysteriously appeared every year on the anniversary of the accident. Closing her eyes, Susie could picture her brother's golden hair, deep blue eyes, apple cheeks, and the single dimple on his left cheek as they'd walked together that last evening. *His features so closely resembled Dat's.*

Images of that long-ago evening hung heavily around her. A mistlike rain had been falling as she and Eli walked together along the side of the road at twilight. They'd been chattering about trivial things, especially the big chocolate whoopie pie *Aendi* Emmalyn had surprised them with before they'd left for home. Mamma's sister had given them a treat to take with them, too—a large tin of rhubarb cookies, still warm from the oven. And then Susie had spotted the bird's feather, silky and white, like a dove's. . . .

Sighing now, she hastened her pace. Even after the loss of their father, she'd never questioned why God had taken Eli at such a tender age. Yet the grief had left her with something amiss. She sensed it regularly but didn't know how to describe it even to herself. One thing was sure: Eli's death might not have happened if she had done things differently that night. And even though just eight at the time, she remembered every painful detail of that day.

The rising moon touched a cloud, then vanished behind it. Susie stared at the sky, thankful she'd be able to spend time with her many cousins at the Singing. Tonight was not a night to be alone.

Susie had gone nearly halfway to David Beiler's farm when she spotted two of her close cousins, Verena and Marnie Mast, coming down the hill from their house toward the road. Susie waited, then fell into step with them at the end of their lane. "Was hopin' ya might be walking to Singing, too," Susie said, glad for the company.

"Well, Dat's still over at the bishop's, so we had no way to get to Singing 'cept on foot," said Verena, the older of the two at nineteen.

"Must've just slipped his mind," said seventeen-year-old Marnie, matching her stride to her sister's and Susie's.

"We get to spend more time together this way," Susie commented as the spring peepers began their reedy-noted song from a nearby creek. She and Mamma used to walk this road at the close of the day, especially in summer, soaking up the sounds of evening. Sometimes Eli had come along, too, and Mamma would tell stories of her childhood, growing up on a big dairy farm. Susie missed those strolls and how, nearly every time, her brother had found a walking stick along the way.

At the Beilers' farm, Susie pushed open the door to the hayloft and noticed how tidy everything looked in the bank barn. The familiar scent of stored hay and the sound of lowing cattle from the level below greeted the three cousins as they crossed the wooden planks to sit with their other Mast relatives on the side facing the young men, most of whom were still standing around talking. Like many young women, Susie usually spent her time at Singings with her girl cousins, other than the handful of fellows whom she'd dated, of course, rarely going out with any more than once or twice.

Susie folded her hands in her lap and noticed that several other girls had worn a pastel blue dress like hers. *We all love this nice weather*, she thought with a smile.

Out of habit, she looked for Obie but tried not to be obvious about it. She was well aware of which fellows he often talked to prior to the start of the actual singing portion of the evening. But she didn't see him, so she wondered if he was running late.

Soon, David and Mattie, their hosts for the evening, arrived carrying two plastic bins of cookies to set out on the refreshment table. Now that he was in his late sixties, David's hair had turned somewhat gray on the sides in the last few years, but Mattie's was a blend of washed-out blond and a whisper of white, which made her look more youthful than she was.

David walked over to Perry Stoltzfus and a few other fellows and talked briefly, and soon they all left the barn together. Susie guessed they would help bring in the coolers of ice and canned pop. But more than refreshments, she looked forward to singing the gospel songs from a different hymnal than the one they used for church. She wondered again what was keeping Obie, late as he was. Had he gone to a Singing in a different church district, maybe?

In the past, he'd dated at least two girls outside the Hickory Hollow district, something Susie knew because Obie had asked what she thought about dating outside their district. But so far tonight, there was no sign of him.

During the break, while Susie ate chocolate chip cookies with her cousins, she noticed Obie's eighteen-year-old brother, Jerome, not far away, chewing the fat with a few other young men. Jerome's chestnut bangs had been recently trimmed straight across his forehead, most likely by his father, known to cut both his sons' hair.

At one point, Jerome caught Susie's eye and bobbed his head toward the refreshment table, as if wanting her to meet him there. Susie excused herself from her cousins and headed over to the table to see what Jerome wanted.

"Did ya wanna talk to me?" she asked as Jerome approached.

"Oh, just thought I should say why Obie isn't here." He stuffed his hands in his pants pockets.

"He's well, I hope."

Jerome nodded halfheartedly, and Susie felt a flicker of concern.

"All right, I guess. He made an unexpected trip." Jerome shuffled his feet and glanced toward the hay bales stacked clear to the rafters. "Sounds like he's got a chance to work as a farrier for a blacksmith who needs some assistance."

"That's *gut*, *jah*?" She thought of Bishop Beiler, the Hickory Hollow blacksmith, and the many years he'd worked in the trade.

Jerome ran his hand through his thick hair. "Well, the job ain't in Hickory Hollow."

She felt the air catch in her throat. Where was it, then? And why was Jerome telling her before Obie did?

Glancing uncomfortably toward the group of fellows, Jerome said, "Well, I should get back. Obie doesn't even know I planned to say anything, so I've prob'ly said too much already. He'll tell ya more."

"When he decides, ya mean?"

"Oh, he's perty close to that already," Jerome said as he turned to head over to rejoin the other young men.

Susie couldn't believe it. Why on earth hadn't Obie told her such big news? Or had he tried to on her birthday?

Cousin Marnie had been invited to go riding with Jerome after Singing, so Susie and Verena set out walking home together. Verena had recently broken up with her former beau, so, like Susie, she'd only gone to Singing for some fellowship.

"I didn't see Obie tonight," Verena mentioned as they walked. The stars were so bright, they scarcely needed the flashlights they carried to be seen by passing vehicles.

"Oh, he's out of town."

"That explains it, then, 'cause he rarely misses a Singing."

"Not recently that I recall." Susie paused for a moment, then changed the subject. "Say, your sister seemed real happy that Jerome asked her out."

"'Tween you and me, I think he's had his eye on Marnie for a while now."

"They do look cute together."

"I think so, too," Verena said, giving a little spin. "And just think how perty their children would be if they got married someday." She seemed to catch herself. "*Ach*, what am I sayin'? This is only their first date!"

Susie smiled at Verena's remark. She heard a horse and buggy coming up behind them and glanced over her shoulder to see it slowing up. "I think someone might be interested in talkin' to you."

"Or to *you*." Verena stepped back from the road with Susie.

The horse pulled the courting buggy forward and stopped.

"Would yous like a lift?" Delmar Petersheim asked. He looked right at Susie.

"Ain't much farther, really," she said, surprised to see him again.

"Are ya sure?" he replied, leaning over on the passenger side to open the door.

"Why not?" Verena said, going around the buggy and waiting for Susie to get in first.

"*Denki*." Susie was embarrassed, sitting so close to Del, and curious why Verena seemed so eager. "What brings ya to Hickory Hollow tonight?" she asked him.

"Oh, was just over visitin' my uncle and

aunt, and they invited me to stay for supper," Del replied.

Susie found it interesting that he hadn't attended a Singing near his own church district.

"I'll come by to order one of your family trees sometime soon, Susie," Del added out of the blue.

Even though she didn't dare look her cousin's direction, Susie was sure Verena was grinning.

"All right," Susie replied politely. Del was certainly friendly, but he hadn't asked her for another date, if their time at the farm sale could even be considered that.

Susie stared at the starry sky and wondered how long this mild weather would last, considering it was only mid-March.

"See that mailbox up there?" Verena said, leaning forward to show Del. "You can let us off there."

"Both of yous?" Del asked, which brought a little chuckle from Verena.

"*Jah*," Verena said. "*Denki*, awful nice of ya to offer the ride."

"Any time," Del said.

Susie thanked him, as well, before quickly climbing down out of the carriage.

Once his horse and buggy were on their way, Verena elbowed Susie while they stood at the end of her lane. "So, is he sweet on ya?"

"Seems like it."

Verena laughed. "*Seems?*" She said nothing more for a moment. Then, glancing at Susie, she said, "What's it like to have two fellas interested in ya?"

"*Ach*, now . . ."

"You're too modest, cousin. I 'spect Obie's got his eye on ya, too, and has for some time now."

Goodness! Is everyone talking 'bout Obie and me?

Verena frowned. "Wait a minute. Is something off beam 'tween you and Obie? I mean, a fella wouldn't typically miss Singing to go out of town unless it was an emergency or something."

"Obie an' I aren't fussin', if that's what ya mean."

"*Gut.* 'Cause once that starts, believe me, it's all downhill."

"Well, we're not dating, either. Just friends, I'm sure ya know."

Verena snickered under her breath.

"I'm serious," Susie protested.

"Okay, then," Verena said, but there was no mistaking the tone of disbelief.

They were quiet for a time, and then she said, "If you need someone to talk to, remember I care 'bout ya, cousin."

"Same here . . . 'bout you."

"*Gut Nacht*," Verena said, then headed up her lane.

"I'll see ya again soon," Susie called, glad to be alone with her thoughts the rest of the short way home.

While Mamma sat in the next room reading, Britta served a warm brownie to Hazel in the kitchen, topped with a generous scoop of vanilla ice cream and sliced peaches. Britta scooted in next to Hazel on the wooden bench, both of them still wearing turquoise dresses from Preaching service.

Hazel took a bite of the brownie. "Ooh, this is delicious."

"Susie made them yesterday. All I did was warm them up in the oven for a bit," Britta told her. "She's much better at baking than I am."

Hazel took another bite. "Wanna know what Obie says 'bout Susie's baking?" She was grinning now.

"What?" Britta was all ears.

"That no one else's can hold a candle to it."

Interested, Britta turned to look at her. "That's really something, since you and your Mamma are practically blue-ribbon bakers."

Hazel laughed a little. "If you ask me, he's

fallin' for her." She paused to take a sip of milk. "And finally, ain't so? Honestly, Obie thinks Susie is the best at everything."

Britta recalled her short conversation with Obie at the farm sale. "Well, she is, don't you agree?"

"Oh, definitely." Hazel paused a moment, observing her. "There's only one problem."

Britta stiffened. "What do ya mean?"

"I'm worried Obie might take a job workin' for our blacksmith uncle a hundred miles from here."

"Wha-at?" Britta felt like she'd been sloshed with a bucket of cold water.

"Well, it's not for sure yet."

Why would he leave? Britta wondered, puzzled by this.

"Mamma doesn't want him to work so far away. And I don't, either."

That's how Mamma felt when Allen and his family moved away, thought Britta. "I don't blame either of ya."

Hazel forked up another piece of her brownie and dipped it into the melting ice cream. "It wonders me how Obie will break the news to Susie. They're such *gut* friends and all."

Britta wondered, too. Evidently it seemed poor Susie knew nothing about this. Suddenly, Britta wished she were in the dark about Hazel's unsettling news.

It's mighty strange to know something about Obie before my sister. . . .

While Britta and Hazel were playing another game of checkers, Mamma walked into the kitchen and said she was turning in early. Cordial as always, though, she encouraged them to enjoy the rest of their time together, so they continued their checkers game and even managed to talk between moves about the books they had been reading.

Hazel mentioned some old Grace Livingston Hill paperbacks her mother had stored away and let her read.

"Mamma and I like those books, too," Britta told her. "Susie used to read them, but not in the last few years. Just too busy."

"She *does* seem that way."

Britta reached for her black checker and jumped Hazel's last king, trying not to smile with victory at hand—her third of the evening.

Hazel grimaced. "You're hard to beat tonight!"

"You should play Mamma if ya think I'm *gut.*"

Hazel smiled halfheartedly. "If you were truly my best friend, you'd let me win sometimes."

"*Are* we best friends?" Britta looked up, holding her breath.

Hazel caught her eye. "It all depends," she said, playing along.

"On what?"

"If you let me win sometimes."

Britta laughed as they finished the close game. *I'll make sure I win fewer games in the future*, she decided.

"You'll have to come to my house next time."

"Okay."

After the fourth game—which Hazel won without any help from Britta—Hazel picked up her big flashlight. "*Denki* for havin' me over." She headed for the back door, carrying her neon green reflective vest, and Britta followed.

"Be sure an' wear your safety vest," Britta said, walking out onto the back porch with her. "My mother always reminds me to if I'm out after dark."

"Okay, Mamma," Hazel called back teasingly as she scampered down the steps.

Britta stood there wondering how long it would be before Susie returned home. And sighing with the significance of Hazel's revelation about her brother, she hurried upstairs for bed, wanting to avoid any conversation with Susie tonight.

Just after dawn the next morning, amidst the sound of birdsong, Susie awoke with a bittersweet memory she'd nearly forgotten. Early one Saturday, she, Eli, and Dat had gone to the creek behind the line of tall trees not far from the northernmost meadow. It was one of the few times Dat hadn't taken just Eli, and lo and behold, young Susie had caught a nice-sized panfish. Even now, Susie remembered the feel of the abrupt jerk on her line and the way Dat had immediately reached for the pole, his strong hands over hers, helping to reel in the flapping fish.

Susie's catch had been a pleasant surprise for Mamma, who let out a little whoop and offered her a big hug. And Mamma had rolled it in cornmeal and fried it up, along with the fish Dat and Eli had caught.

Carrying the recollection close to her heart, Susie slipped out of bed and thanked the dear Lord for all the memories of Dat . . . and Eli, too. She raised the green window shades and looked out over the paddock below. "I miss ya both," she whispered, recalling now how Dat had taught her to whistle while they cracked English walnuts together on the back porch.

Feels like a lifetime ago . . .

Susie carried her laundry to the basement and turned on the water for the wringer washer, preparing to put in the white clothing. Britta had already brought her and Mamma's whites down and piled them nearby on the counter.

After sorting clothes, Susie returned to oversee the whites through the rinse cycle, feeding them one item at a time through the old rollers, which made everything flat before landing in the neighboring rinse tub. She thought again about Jerome's peculiar revelation last evening. Why had he felt the need to share this news with her? Wasn't Jerome happy for his older brother's opportunity? And wouldn't Obie expect that of her, too?

While the second load of clothing was

washing, she occupied herself by watering her potted seedlings. The tomatoes, cabbage, broccoli, and cauliflower were arranged all across a long table in the daylight basement. She was just itching to get her hands in the soil to sow sugar snap peas and carrots and lettuce and Swiss chard next month, once she could borrow the tiller from their neighbor Jonathan Ebersol. Depending on the weather, she would also plant squash, string beans, and cucumbers in three weeks or so. And, knowing how much Mamma enjoyed sun-flowers, she added them to her mental list of things to plant in May, after any chance of frost had passed.

By the time the colored clothes were in the wash cycle, Susie carried the well-rinsed whites upstairs to be pinned to the outdoor clothesline. Mamma's oatmeal was baking in the oven when Susie opened the kitchen door at the top of the stairs. "It's so *gut* to see ya up and perky," Susie said, going to the apron drawer.

"I slept like a rock at the bottom of a pond."

"*Ach*, Mamma!" They laughed together as Susie tied an apron around her waist.

"Britta's already gone to the stable," Mamma said. "Didn't say much. Guess she's deep in thought."

"She does seem to be at times." Susie glanced toward the window facing the stable. "But we can always count on her to get right to her chores."

"Look who's talkin'." Mamma chuckled.

Susie turned on the spigot and poured water into the teakettle in case Mamma had a sudden flare-up of her asthma. Her allergies were worse this time of year, making an attack more likely. The steam from the warm water helped to ease her breathing.

"Britta and I'll pin the clothes to the line. No sense you—"

"Oh, I can help," Mamma interjected. "Besides, you should be busy makin' a family tree for Mattie Beiler, ain't so?"

Susie nodded. "Okay, but let me know if ya change your mind." She poured orange juice into small glasses as her sister came inside to join them.

Together, they ate Mamma's tasty baked oatmeal, topped with apple chunks and chopped walnuts. Britta poured cream over hers, the way she liked it, but said very little during the meal, keeping her head bowed over her bowl. Even a couple of casual questions from Mamma didn't pull Britta out of her thoughts, although she answered them pleasantly enough. Her sister's seeming distraction baffled Susie, who resisted the temptation to probe. *She's never been this quiet at mealtime. . . .*

After breakfast, Mamma went with Britta to hang the clothes before school. Meanwhile, Susie stayed indoors to redd up the kitchen and make Britta's sack lunch. Later, she sat down at the table and chose the embroidery floss for the names of Mattie's uncle and aunt.

As she worked, she glanced occasionally out the window and wondered if Britta would tell Mamma what was troubling her, convinced there had to be something.

During dinner at noon, Mamma mentioned to Susie that Britta had made plans with Hazel to go to her *Haus* after school. "So she'll be a little late comin' home."

Susie listened and waited for Mamma to say more about Britta's unusual hush at breakfast.

"It's *gut* for Britta to have a friend who goes out of her way to include her," Mamma observed while dishing up the scalloped potatoes and cubed ham. "An answer to my prayers."

"Everyone needs a friend like that," Susie replied.

Mamma passed the casserole to her. "That's for certain." She nodded slowly. "Say, did ya notice how preoccupied our Britta was at breakfast?"

"*Jah*, I wondered if you might know something."

Mamma shook her head. "I 'spect she'll tell one of us, sooner or later."

Susie hoped so as she enjoyed the first bite of Mamma's tasty meal, glad she'd made extra for leftovers.

"I have no doubt Britta confides in you at times."

Susie smiled. "Mostly, *jah*."

"That's a blessing to me." Mamma reminded her that she and her own younger sister, Emmalyn Riehl, had always been exceptionally close.

"Aendi Emmalyn was *wunnerbaar* to give so much of her time after Eli died, remember? Stoppin' by with food, cleanin' the kitchen, and you name it."

"She was a real comfort . . . like so many others." Mamma nodded. "I felt so overwhelmed . . . don't know how I woulda gotten through without her. Emmalyn even spent several nights with us, starting with that very first night."

Susie hadn't forgotten that visit. "She sat beside me on the settee and held my hand. Told me it was all right to cry."

"And it surely was," Mamma said, nodding. "Emmalyn must've sensed you were tryin' to be brave for me, young though you were. Such a caring sister, she is."

Eventually, the conversation moved to other things, including the fact that Mamma had cut the amount of marshmallow creme somewhat in the latest batch of peanut butter spread, so it wouldn't be quite so sweet.

"Customers with a sweet tooth can always purchase some jams or jellies," Susie suggested.

Mamma smiled. "Well, Britta likes the peanut butter extra sweet, so we'll be sure an' make some with the original recipe."

As the meal continued, Susie contemplated her sister's quiet mood further. *What's gnawing at her?*

After breakfast the next morning, Susie worked in the sewing room on Mattie's relatives' family tree while Britta washed dishes and Mamma wiped them dry. Susie had made good progress on this cross-stitch and liked the deep blue and barn red colors she'd chosen—quaint and homespun-looking—for the names of the couple's children. If she kept up this quick pace, she would be ready to iron it and get it ready for framing in another day or so.

Around midmorning, Susie poured some lemonade into a thermos and took it out to Mamma's little shop, where plump Mary Beiler, the bishop's chatty wife, had come to pick up an order of peanut butter spread, or "church spread," as she liked to call it.

"Hullo there, Susie. *Wie geht's?*" Mary asked, her round face aglow.

"Doin' all right," she replied.

Mamma nodded. "Grass has no time to grow under our Susie's feet."

"Well, if we keep *too* busy, we can miss out on livin'," Mary said, returning her attention to the four jars of spread. "John's been workin' long hours, too, tryin' to get all the plowing done. He'll be glad for a treat, and goodness, his mouth'll water when he sees this—his favorite peanut butter ever." Mary grinned at Mamma. "A nice surprise, for sure." She opened her purse and held out a wad of ones. "Just keep the change."

Mamma shook her head. "Ain't necessary."

Susie could tell by the set of her jaw that Mary was determined to have the final say. She leaned against the counter and waved her money. "I insist, Aquilla."

"Well, if you're sure." Mamma exchanged glances with Susie.

As Mary bobbed her head, Susie placed

the four jars in an empty box, then carried it out to Mary's waiting carriage. A car pulled up just then, and Susie could see three *Englischer* women inside. It was a good thing Mamma had made a new batch of her famous peanut butter spread, the most popular item among tourists. Britta had also made plenty of goat cheese to stock the gas-run cooler.

"*Willkumm!*" Susie said as the middle-aged women walked toward the shop. "Are ya from around here?" she asked, making small talk.

"We're visiting from Arlington, Virginia," the first woman said, pausing there on the walkway. "We were told we had to make a stop here."

"How'd ya hear 'bout us?" Susie asked.

"People were talking up your place at the bed-and-breakfast where we're staying," the woman said, glancing at the other two.

"Is that right?" Susie smiled. "Well, my mother's behind the counter, and we're happy to help ya. Let me show you inside."

With that, she opened the shop door for them, thinking her stitching might just have to wait a little longer.

Late that afternoon, Susie was surprised to see Obie arrive in his father's spring wagon.

He was still in work clothes and black boots, but his blond hair gleamed in the sunlight. She put down her cross-stitching and walked out to meet him in the driveway, feeling both awkward and tickled to see him.

"I thought of dropping you a line, but since I was passin' by, it made sense to just stop to see ya. Hope that's okay," he said, his look serious. "If you can get away, I'd like to take ya ridin'."

She was taken aback, since they'd never really gone anywhere together before. "Right now?"

"*Jah*, just a short ride . . . as friends sometimes do," he added.

I thought you'd never ask, she mused.

"Or, if it doesn't suit—"

"Now is fine," she said, recalling again what Jerome had told her.

Obie moved back toward the right side of the wagon. Then, stopping, he said, "Listen, what if I bought up the rest of your Mamma's peanut butter spread for the day? It'd save her some time and make my Mamm happy, too." He smiled briefly and glanced toward the shop.

"Not sure how much is left, but you can go an' check with Mamma."

"Maybe that way, she can close up shop

early," Obie said, catching Susie's eye. "At least a few minutes early, anyway."

Susie was moved by his generosity toward Mamma. And yet, she was unable to shake the feeling that he was about to tell her something she didn't want to hear.

While Obie was checking on pea-nut butter with Mamma, Susie imagined how it would be to sit in the spring wagon beside him, in plain sight.

Like a courting couple, she mused, know-ing better.

Quickly, she slipped inside to smooth her hair and to reposition the blue bandanna. It crossed her mind to wear her *Kapp* instead, but Obie had come straight from work, so she didn't want to dress up much. She did remove her old coat and put on a newer one, however. Then, hurrying down the hallway, she found Britta in the sewing room, pin-ning a dress pattern to cocoa-colored fabric.

"I'll be gone for a little while with Obie," she told her.

Britta's eyes widened. "Obie?"

"It's not a date, silly."

Britta shrugged. "Still, goin' out riding with him'll be nice," she said, then added, "Guess he's not upset 'bout the farm sale."

Susie frowned. "Farm sale?"

Britta clapped her hand over her mouth. "*Ach*, sorry for speak-in' out of turn."

She didn't press further, but the odd way Britta was acting, like she was privy to something, made Susie wonder. But she let it go.

She made her way back down the hall, through the kitchen, and outside to the porch, where she sat in one of the hickory rockers to wait. She wondered if Obie knew that Jerome had already let the cat out of the bag to her. If so, would Obie reveal more about his plans?

In a few minutes, he came walking across the yard, carrying a large sack of what had to be several jars of peanut butter spread. He paused politely at the sidewalk to wait for her at the bottom of the porch steps, and together, they walked toward the driveway. It struck her as odd that her first ride with Obie should take place in his father's rickety spring wagon.

Brushing the thought aside, she hoped God would calm her rattled nerves.

Obie placed the sack in the back of the wagon, then returned to offer his hand. "Here, I'll help you up," he said with a smile.

"*Denki*," she said softly, dying to know what was on his mind.

Obie untied the horse from the hitching post, got into the driver's seat on the right side of the wagon, reached for the driving lines, and directed the horse forward. When they were out on the road, Obie glanced her way. "You okay?"

"Just haven't seen ya around is all."

He nodded. "I apologize for askin' spur of the moment like this. It's just that this morning, Jerome said he'd told ya about my job offer. I'd wanted to be the one to talk it over with ya first."

This surprised her but also made her feel warm inside.

Obie continued, "I know what my family thinks about the opportunity, Mamm 'specially."

"I'm sure they want ya to stay round here," Susie said. *Like I do.*

Obie nodded. "It would be different, bein' gone so long, but my smithy uncle needs help after the corn harvest this fall. That is, if I agree."

He'd leave in October, she thought, her heart beating faster. "What do ya mean by *long*?"

"*Onkel* Leon wants me to commit to at least two years," Obie said, his eyes straight ahead as he held the reins steady. "Could end up as long as three, since it takes a while to learn the smithy trade."

He turned to look at her just as Susie's mouth dropped. "*Ach* . . . that *is* a long time. It sure wouldn't be the same without ya round here." Flustered, she wasn't sure what to do now, and she fidgeted with her coat as Obie held her gaze, as though surprised at her reaction.

It was the first she'd ever let on that she cared for him—she had for a long time—so now she'd have to be extra cautious, since he seemed to see her only as a friend.

"I've been offered *gut* pay, as well as room and board, in exchange for my work as a farrier. I'd become an apprentice in his blacksmith shop, too."

Susie remembered back years ago, when Obie first shared his keen interest in becoming a smithy someday. "This must be a dream come true," she forced herself to say.

"*Jah* . . . and quite possibly my best chance to learn the trade." Obie paused. "Besides, I've always liked Onkel Leon."

Susie realized her hands were clenched in her lap.

"What do you think . . . that is, *if* I accept?" Obie's voice was thin in the chilly air.

"It sounds like a great opportunity," she said, her mind spinning. "But wouldn't you miss everyone . . . I mean, your family?"

"I would." He let out an audible breath. "I'd still like your opinion."

She felt befuddled. *Does he hope I'll try to change his mind?*

"To be honest, it would be strange not seein' ya," she said, careful not to reveal just how much she'd miss him. Then she was struck by a thought. *But that's bound to change no matter where he lives and works, once he meets someone and marries. And Del will probably ask me out again. . . .*

Obie slowed the horse. "If I take the job— and I'm leanin' toward it—I'll try to keep in touch with you, Susie."

He'd write to me? Something welled up in her, and she suddenly wanted to share her heart. But she couldn't do that, not when he had always treated her more like a special sister. She refused to make a fool of herself. It could ruin their friendship for certain, and then how would she feel?

Finally, she said, "I would be glad to hear from you, when ya have the time." *Thrilled is more like it. . . .*

Obie gave a nod before hurrying the horse to a trot.

They rode on in complete silence, and Susie knew that now was her chance to speak up, ask him not to go.

She noticed they were coming around the next bend to the spot where she and Eli had been walking the evening he was hit and killed. At that moment, being there—at that place of great loss—felt like too much.

"You all right?" Obie slowed the horse.

She felt an urgency to tell him why she sometimes took the family carriage to haul a rake and a broom in order to tend the place alone—something she hadn't really shared with anyone but Mamma and Britta. Yet she held back, struggling with what, exactly, to say.

"Are ya ill, Susie?" Obie frowned and directed the horse to move onto the side of the road and halt.

She pointed ahead. "Up yonder's where Eli and I were—"

Obie slapped his forehead. "*Ach*, I forgot. I'm awful sorry."

"Ain't your fault." She pulled her scarf out of her coat pocket and wrapped it around her neck, tears threatening. "I go there often on my own, but mostly on foot. I'm not sure why it's such a problem right now." She hugged herself to try to settle down, like she did sometimes when sweeping the side of the road or raking leaves from the grassy ditch. "I've tried and tried to block that night out of my mind."

"I can't imagine what you went through, seein' your brother . . ."

Sitting there with Obie's full attention, she felt conflicted, at once comforted and uncomfortable and strangely vulnerable, and tempted to tell him something she'd buried since childhood and never told a soul. *If anyone would understand, Obie surely would.*

Susie shuddered suddenly, recalling how stubborn Eli had been before they began their walk home from Aendi Emmalyn's that day. *If only I'd stood my ground with him*, she thought, tears welling up.

"Susie . . . you're crying," Obie said, fishing for something in his coat pocket.

"Still thinking 'bout Eli." Sighing, she uttered, "And what happened before he was hit."

Obie offered her his blue paisley handkerchief, concern on his handsome face.

She accepted the handkerchief, wishing now she hadn't brought this up. *Such bad timing*, she thought.

"I'm a *gut* listener, ya know," Obie said, a faint smile appearing.

That she knew, but she'd been caught off guard by her emotions. "I thought I could talk about it, but I guess I can't. It's just too much right now."

He was quiet for what seemed like a long time, and when he spoke, his voice was muffled. "I've said this before, Susie, but you can tell me anything."

Inhaling deeply, she exhaled slowly before admitting, "It's the same awful grief, rearing its ugly head whenever I least expect it."

"I'm sorry you still suffer so," he said. "But I think it's normal. My Dat said he felt that way after his uncle died. Never knew when the sadness would overwhelm him."

"*Jah*, I feel like I might drown sometimes."

"I wish I could help; I truly do."

She nodded, glad she was able to confide at least that much. "You're a help, believe me," she managed to say.

"*Gut*, then." He picked up the driving lines, checked over his shoulder for traffic, and directed the horse to move forward.

What came over me, crying in front of him? It wasn't something she'd done before.

Obie turned onto the side road and drove clear around to avoid the accident site, a gesture she appreciated. This ride was longer than she had expected with suppertime approaching, but Obie had moved on to talk about some of his favorite memories from their many years of friendship, as though he'd already made his decision to leave Hickory Hollow. She couldn't bring herself to interrupt that, not for the world.

He reminded her of their first time out in the rowboat Dat had built. "To try it out, remember?" Obie asked.

"*Jah*, and it nearly capsized, both of us yellin' for dear life." She gave a small smile.

"It would've, too, if your brother hadn't been there to right it."

Susie remembered full well. "We got plenty of use out of that rowboat. In fact, Mamma said we went out in it more than she and Dat ever had."

A while later, as they returned to the house, Obie offered his hand as she stepped out of the wagon. He walked with her over the long walkway, past the gazebo, and up the porch steps to the back door, where, for the first time around Obie, she felt incredibly self-conscious.

The tinkle of the wind chimes filled up the silence.

Quietly, she said, "*Denki* for comin' by."

"Remember what I said 'bout you bein' able to tell me anything." He smiled thoughtfully, his eyes serious. "I mean it."

For a brief moment yet again, she experienced something different between them—a spark or deeper sense of connection, perhaps? Or was it just her imagination?

"Well, *Gut Nacht*," he said and turned to leave.

"*Gut Nacht*, Obie." It didn't make sense to say good-bye when October was still months away. If he committed to going to Sugar Valley, that was.

Hopefully we'll talk again soon, she thought as she opened the back door and stepped inside.

>>

After supper, Susie listened closely as Mamma read in the front room from Isaiah, chapter twenty-six. When she'd read verse three, Mamma paused to reread it a second time. "'Thou wilt keep him in perfect peace, whose mind is stayed on thee: because he trusteth in thee.'"

With a sweet smile, Mamma commented softly, "Always remember this verse, my dear girls."

Susie glanced at Britta, whose gaze was intent upon *her*, of all things.

Her sister looked away suddenly, as if sheepish.

What's going on? Susie wondered yet

again, thinking she might try to talk with Britta soon.

"'Trust ye in the Lord for ever: for in the Lord Jehovah is everlasting strength,'" Mamma continued, and Susie asked God to soothe her mind and heart about Obie, and to give her wisdom regarding her sister.

Following a night of steady rain, Susie rose very early to finish work on the fiftieth-wedding-anniversary gift for Mattie's uncle and aunt. When this piece was done, she was looking forward to starting the next cross-stitch, this one for an *Englischer* customer. And maybe sometime this week, Del would be placing his order, too. Creating these projects gave her joy, as did witnessing the delighted smiles on customers' faces.

After breakfast, Susie and Britta redded up the kitchen for Mamma, then walked out to the stable so Britta could check on her cats.

"I'm a little curious," Susie said, trying to sound casual, "did Hazel happen to say something 'bout Obie's chance to work in Sugar Valley?"

Britta suddenly looked sheepish.

Susie prodded, poking her sister's elbow. "C'mon now."

Britta blew out a breath. "I didn't think it was my place to tell ya, partly 'cause I prob'ly wasn't s'posed to know." She grimaced. "But mainly 'cause I didn't know if *Obie* wanted to keep it a secret."

"Is that why you've been so quiet here lately?"

Britta nodded. "I felt like frosting in a whoopie pie, stuck between you and Hazel."

Susie had to laugh. "Well, I'm glad we got this cleared up. Obie told me yesterday, so you can be yourself again." She glanced at Britta. "It must've been *kitzlich* for ya."

"Ticklish, for sure." Britta opened the stable door, and Lucy came running right to her, while Tabasco hung back near the pony's stall.

"Obie says if he *does* accept the job with his Onkel, he'll be gone for at least two years," Susie told her.

Britta's eyes widened. "Wha-at?"

"I thought ya knew."

"Not for how long. Hazel didn't share all that much." Looking pensive, she said, "I've been wonderin' . . . well—" Britta shook her head, as if having second thoughts.

"Tell me." Susie leaned down and reached for cuddly Lucy, picking her up and carrying her like a baby.

"I prob'ly shouldn't." Britta hesitated. "But . . . I've always wished Obie might be part of our family someday."

"Aw, Britta." Susie shook her head.

"Ain't my business, I know."

Susie snuggled Lucy's furry little head as she recalled Obie's thoughtful smile last night before they'd said good-bye. "For a while, I thought there *might* be something between us, but I'm very sure he thinks of me as a sister."

"Well, having an older Bruder is real nice," Britta replied. "In that way, he *is* sort of in the family."

There was a slight pause before Britta continued. "Speakin' of that, have ya ever noticed that Mamma never talks 'bout Eli? 'Least, not to me. Does she ever to you?"

"*Nee* . . . I guess not, now ya mention it."

"Why not, do ya think? She'll mention your Dat, from time to time."

Susie wondered why Britta was asking this just now, of all things, as if it somehow weighed on her. "For one thing, it's ever so painful—just ain't the right order of things. Parents aren't s'posed to outlive their child." She paused. "I believe Mamma's still heartbroken."

Nodding her head sadly, Britta seemed to ponder that. "I think you're right, and for *gut* reason."

"We've had losses, *jah* . . . but many happy moments, too. For one thing, you brought great joy into Mamma's and my life when ya came along." Susie put Lucy down gently. "I'm glad we could talk like this."

"Me too." Britta smiled.

Gut, at least Britta's all figured out, Susie thought, going over to the first stall to groom Brambles.

The next morning, while Susie worked in Mamma's shop, Del Petersheim arrived in his father's family carriage. He smiled broadly as he entered the shop, looking all scrubbed and smart in his black broadfall trousers and black suspenders against a pressed white long-sleeved shirt. He removed his straw hat and walked directly to the display counter. "Mornin', Susie."

"*Wie geht's?*" she asked, wondering where he was going, all dressed up.

"I'm just fine. How are you?"

"Doin' all right."

Del looked at the jars lined up on the counter. "Well now, first things first," he said, pointing toward them. "I'll have some of that grape jelly, please."

"How many jars?" Susie asked, noticing his frequent glances her way, as if trying to catch her eye.

"Two. That might last for the next couple of weeks." He chuckled.

Sounds like he plans to be back for more, she thought, amused. She reached beneath the counter for some newspapers to wrap them in, and a sturdy paper bag. She placed the jars carefully in the bag before setting it aside.

"Now, about the family tree." He pulled a piece of paper from his trousers pocket. "Here are the names of my parents and everyone in the family . . . so far."

Accepting the paper, Susie could see how neat and methodical he was. "This is helpful. *Denki.*"

"Look on the back, too, if you'd like a possible idea for the basic layout."

She turned the paper over and was again impressed with the care and thought he'd put into this. "Do ya want your family tree to look exactly like this?" She tapped the paper.

"It's just one option." He shrugged. "Feel free to plan it however you like."

Nodding, she assured him she would do her best. "Wedding anniversaries are so special," she added. "I feel honored you picked one of my cross-stitches to be your gift."

"My mom has commented on how beautifully done yours are. She and my father will be so pleased," he said, lingering as though he wanted to talk longer. He glanced around, his gaze falling on the small shelf Dat had built years ago, where Mamma kept a few small lanterns, a rustic birdhouse, and a quilted potholder hanging from a hook, just to decorate the shop a little. "Has my sister come by yet? I know she'd enjoy this little nook."

"She may have," Susie said, explaining that she, Mamma, and Britta took turns helping customers. "But if not, she's certainly welcome to."

He glanced again toward the display of jams and jellies. "Just curious, do yous ever sell rhubarb jam?"

"We do, once the rhubarb comes on." She laughed a little. "It's still early, and we sold the last jars of that before Christmas. Ours is extra special, so it always goes fast."

"What makes it special?" he asked, stepping closer to the counter.

"Three secret ingredients."

"How secret?"

She shook her head, laughing now. "Mamma'd never let me tell."

"*Ach*, guess I'll just have to taste it to know, then."

She wasn't sure if he was pulling her leg. "Honestly, you can tell ingredients by taste?"

"S'pose it's a family trait. My Dat and sister can do it, too. Mamm makes a little game of it sometimes—tries to see if she can stump us."

"Okay, then. I guess you *will* have to taste it."

"When will there be a sample?"

"Oh, in another six weeks or so."

"Sounds *gut* to me." Del paid for the jam, thanked her, and was on his way.

Susie had noticed how hard he'd tried to be matter-of-fact and not too obvious. But she was quite sure he was interested in getting to know her better. After all, not many young men came into their shop.

Suddenly, the door opened again, and Del poked his head in. "Would ya like to have dessert with me, say a week from Sunday night?"

"I have a Singing at Deacon Peachey's that evening," she said, figuring he'd be attending his in Gordonville.

"What 'bout afterward?"

She couldn't help but agree. "That'd be nice, Del."

"All right with you if we double with another couple—*gut* friends of mine?"

"Sure."

Again, he grinned. "I'll see ya after my Singing, then."

"In the meantime, I'll get busy on your cross-stitch."

Del waved and closed the door behind him.

He must've dressed up just to come here, she thought, smiling to herself.

CHAPTER

9

It was still dark that Saturday morning when Susie sat up in bed, breathing hard, hands clammy. She trembled, trying to push away the bad dream, in which she had been trying to reach Eli, warn him that a car was coming. . . .

After a time, she eased back onto the pillow, her heart still pounding as she took deep breaths and tried to calm herself so she could return to sleep. But sleep was far from her now.

Hours later, all wrung out, Susie stood in her room, staring at the farmland calendar and at today's date, March twenty-sixth. *One month till the anniversary of Eli's passing,*

she thought, brushing away a tear. "I miss ya so," she murmured. "Not a day goes by that I don't think of you, Bruder."

She often wondered how different her life might have been if Eli—and Dat, too—were still alive. Yet there was no sense in pondering that right now. Lest her sadness get the best of her, she began to brush her hair and make a fresh bun for market day with Mamma and Britta. It wouldn't be good for her to have puffy red eyes, so she tried to dismiss the nightmare and set her mind on positive things, like the wonderful years she'd had with Eli—very special ones, indeed.

One summer getaway came to mind, their family trip to Cape May, New Jersey, where Dat had rented a small cottage by the sea for a full week. Oh, the sight of the morning mist rising off the waves, and six-year-old Eli standing on the beach beside her, carrying his plastic spade and bucket. *"I wanna live here!"* he'd declared. And off he had gone to find the perfect spot to dig and build another sandy structure.

Susie smiled at the memory as she finished dressing for the day.

After breakfast, she rode with Mamma and Britta to the local market with Rachelle Good, a young woman driver who had recently met Mamma while purchasing goat cheese from the shop. Susie could scarcely suppress her rising feelings of delight for Mamma, who sat up front with Rachelle, talking cordially while Susie and Britta sat in the seat behind them. Susie couldn't help noticing the brown leather New Testament on the console.

Rachelle mentioned that she and her husband had been brought up in the Old German Baptist Brethren church but were no longer members. They did, however, continue to embrace much of the Plain life, which was apparent from Rachelle's conservative attire. Not many *Englischer* women Susie knew wore skirts with hems at mid-calf or blouses with high necklines.

She's so pleasant and conscientious, Mamma will want to ask her to drive us again, Susie thought as Bird-in-Hand Farmers Market came into view on the south side of Route 340.

Unexpectedly, she recalled another market day years ago, some time after Eli's tragic death. Susie had gone to get coffee for them as a surprise, and she'd come upon Ella Mae and Mamma whispering at the market booth, their heads together, ever so serious. Mamma had seemed startled, if not alarmed, to see her suddenly standing there, cups in hand. *"I best not say more,"* she'd told Ella Mae—rather abruptly, Susie had thought.

The memory troubled her now. *What were they discussing?* Susie wondered to this day.

In the first two hours after arriving at market, Susie received five new orders for her cross-stitched family trees. Carefully, she wrote down all the essential information—correct dates and name spellings, as well as thread color preferences. Mamma, too, was having a successful sales day.

As usual, Britta didn't interact much with customers, shy as she was around strangers, but she helped bag up purchases for Mamma. She also went to get brats and potato salad for them for lunch from the deli two aisles away.

Midafternoon, Obie's mother, Kate, dropped by the market table. Susie tried not to let her emotions overtake her and put on her best smile, listening as Kate talked adoringly about her newborn grandson. But Kate said nothing about Obie possibly going to Sugar Valley come fall, which baffled Susie.

Is it too upsetting to talk about?

After hanging out the Monday washing, Susie called Rachelle Good to schedule a ride to Landisville to visit her sister Polly and Henry, primarily to have the anniversary family tree she'd completed for Mattie Bieler stretched and framed. Henry was skilled at making custom frames using leftover wood and had kindly offered his woodworking services to her without charge for a number of years now.

When Susie arrived, her sister was in the kitchen, rolling out dough. Polly sprinkled flour on her hands and all over the rolling pin, preparing to fit the dough to the large baking pan.

"I'm makin' deep-dish pizza for the noon meal," Polly said. "There'll be plenty for us and you, too. I hope you'll stay."

"Sure," Susie told her, smiling at little Joey over in the corner babbling in *Deitsch* while playing with building blocks. Susie went over and tousled his hair, the color of butter, and he grinned up at her. "Is your baby sister asleep?" she asked.

"*Jah*." He bobbed his little head and held a block up in his chubby fist to show her.

Polly glanced over at them. "Joey has been busy building nearly all morning. He'll be a big help to his Dat someday."

Susie agreed, happy to spend time with them both again.

A while later, when two-month-old Nellie Ann awoke crying, Susie walked into the next room and reached down to pick her up from the cradle. She carried her into the kitchen, swaying back and forth. "She's so petite, like a fragile flower."

"Such a difference 'tween her and Joey at that age," Polly said.

"Well, wasn't he nine pounds at birth?"

Polly nodded and began to set out the ingredients for pizza toppings. "Junior was a *gut* size, too."

"Is he still doin' all right in school?" Susie asked as she stroked Nellie Ann's soft cheek.

"*Jah*, but he's a *rutchey* one. We've been workin' closely with his teacher, who's just twenty but real bright and so helpful." Polly came over and kissed tiny Nellie Ann's forehead, then lifted her out of Susie's arms to nurse her.

Susie went over to sit on the floor and play with Joey, who seemed to delight in knocking down each of the structures she made. And as she did his repeated bidding—"Again, Aendi!"—she realized how very happy her sister was as a wife and mother.

Will I ever have such a happy future?

After supper back in Hickory Hollow, Susie hitched Brambles to the family carriage and prepared to head over to David Beiler's to deliver the beautifully framed family tree to Mattie. Britta had already gone on foot to babysit the neighbors' two youngest children for the evening, so Susie invited Mamma to come along. "Maybe you'll have a chance to visit with Ella Mae, too," she suggested.

"Well, she might be havin' tea with someone. You just never know."

"Oh, I would think she expects to see ya. After I called over there, Mattie surely told her I was comin'."

Mamma got up from her chair at the table to get some water at the sink. "I believe I can see right through ya, dear."

Susie couldn't hide her smile. "Wouldn't want ya to feel left out."

Mamma's expression grew thoughtful. "You really don't wanna leave me here alone, do ya?"

"So, you'll come?"

Mamma drank half the water in her glass and set the tumbler on the counter. "All right, then."

"Since they're ready, you can bring the pretty embroidered pillowcases along, too," Susie suggested.

"*Jah, gut* idea." Mamma went to find them, then wrapped them in some plastic for protection before she and Susie made their way outdoors to the carriage together.

A bird was singing stridently in the large tree behind the Beilers' farmhouse as Susie and her mother carried in the neatly packaged family tree and the wrapped pillowcases. They walked to the back door and knocked, and Susie glanced down at her package, glad Henry had framed it with pine wood and a dark stain, ideal for the thread colors she'd chosen.

"*Kumme* in." Mattie opened the door and ushered them inside. "I'm so eager to see how the finished tree looks."

Susie set it on the long table and let Mattie unwrap it, eager to watch her reaction. At that moment, they heard footsteps and turned to see Ella Mae coming through the connecting hallway from her little *Dawdi Haus*.

"You're just in time," Mamma said, welcoming her to observe the unveiling.

When Mattie removed the wrapping, the oohs and aahs made Susie blush, though she was pleased with the response.

"My Onkel and Aendi will love it," Mattie said, shaking her head in obvious admiration. "What marvelous workmanship, Susie."

"Well, I sure enjoyed makin' it," Susie told her.

"She always prays before she starts stitch-in'," Mamma said, smiling as she looked Susie's way.

Again, Susie felt her face warm. "I just want it to be a blessing to the family that receives it."

"Oh, believe me, it will be." Mattie's eyes glistened just then, and she pulled a hankie from beneath her sleeve. "It truly will." She walked over to the cookie jar and began to remove chocolate chip cookies by the handful, placing them on a plate. "I made these earlier, so why don't we all sit down and enjoy a sweet."

Ella Mae brightened. "I'll go an' get some freshly brewed peppermint tea, too." She started toward the hallway.

"Have Susie help ya, Mamm," urged Mattie, signaling Susie with her eyes.

When they returned, Mattie poured the tea into yellow butterfly teacups with matching saucers, and the four of them gathered around the table for Ella Mae to pray the silent blessing, as she liked to do for even desserts or snacks.

After the prayer, Mamma presented the pillowcases to Ella Mae. "These are for you."

"Is it my birthday?" Ella Mae said, a smile spreading across her wrinkled face.

"Just a small gesture of my appreciation for our many decades of friendship," Mamma told her.

"Well, I'm honored, Aquilla." Ella Mae looked fondly at Mamma. "And my old set's wearin' mighty thin, too."

"Perfect timing, then," Susie said.

As they continued to sip their tea and munch on the delicious cookies, Mattie began to share her anticipation for a new buffet David was making. "It'll give me more space to display my best dishes and knickknacks."

"Do ya still have the original set of dishes your parents gave as a wedding gift?" Mamma asked.

"Oh *jah*, but some are chipped awful bad," Mattie replied, her teacup close to her lips.

"Every chipped plate has a story behind it," Ella Mae said, stirring more sugar into her cup.

Susie caught herself bobbing her head and realized she didn't yet have a single plate or piece of china in her own hope chest. Britta, on the other hand, already had a large set of teacups and saucers.

"Do *you* have a story to tell just now, maybe?" Mamma asked her longtime friend.

"About old plates?" Ella Mae asked, her smile mischievous.

"Any story, really," Mamma said, taking another bite of her cookie, clearly enjoying herself.

"Here's a quick one: I'll never forget the

day Mattie brought David home to meet us." She paused and looked around. "Right here in this kitchen."

Mattie's face turned pink as Ella Mae continued. "The weather had taken a nasty turn that washday, and I'd lost track of the hour, but I knew Mattie planned to come sometime later with her beau. Anyway, when it started makin' down rain real heavy, I ran out and snatched as many clothes as I could off the line and hung them over near the old cookstove." She pointed to the stove. "Not this fancy gas one, mind you.

"To make a long story short, Mattie arrived with David before I was ready for them."

Mattie covered her mouth with her hand and nodded.

Ella Mae took a sip of her tea, then asked her daughter, "Why don't you tell the rest?"

"Well, since it's just us womenfolk . . ." She glanced at her mother, shaking her head but also smiling a little. "David and I walked into this big kitchen from out of the rain and saw two nightgowns . . . and a row of Mamma's underclothing hanging up to dry."

This struck Susie as funny as it did Mamma, and soon everyone around the table had joined in the laughter, Mattie included.

"I don't know why I've never heard this story before!" Mamma exclaimed. "What on earth did your mother say when her future son-in-law walked in, Mattie?"

"Let me answer that," Ella Mae said, grinning. "I was embarrassed, but David was ever so nice 'bout it, acting like there was absolutely nothin' whatsoever out of place. But Mattie, now, she nearly had a fit."

Mattie chuckled. "I was mortified, *jah*, as you can imagine. Poor David told me later that he'd never seen anything like it, since his own Mamm always hung the clothes in the basement when it rained."

"He must've wondered what sort of family he was marryin' into," Ella Mae said, fanning her face with a hankie.

This brought yet another round of merriment, and Susie was glad Mamma had agreed to come along, seeing what a wonderful time she was having today.

That family story led to another, and another, which Ella Mae and Mattie took turns telling, and it was apparent to Susie as she listened that both of them cherished the act of sharing them.

As the hour grew late and Susie and her mother were preparing to leave, Mattie mentioned that Kate Yoder was having a Sisters Day gathering at her house a week from tomorrow. "She wants some company," Mattie said, her expression serious now. "You're both invited."

"She's not under the weather, I hope?" Susie asked.

Mattie shook her head. "It's just that Obie's made a decision to go ahead and work for his Onkel in Sugar Valley come fall."

Susie's heart dropped, though she'd assumed as much, the way he'd talked during their ride. *The one and only ride I'll ever have with him*, she thought sadly, the reality hitting hard.

10

Things were muddled in Susie's mind in the days following her and Mamma's visit to Beilers'. The house seemed strangely quiet when Britta left for school each morning. Mamma, thoughtful as she was, did not inquire about the cause of Susie's downcast mood any more than she had on the ride home last Monday night.

Truth be known, Obie's decision to leave Hickory Hollow had shaken Susie to an extent she'd never thought possible. She tried to shrug the sadness away while working on a new cross-stitch and running errands. Yet the busyness of daily life wasn't enough. Once, in the wee hours, Susie awakened and whispered into the darkness, "Why did I encourage Obie to go?"

This wasn't something she wanted to talk

about, especially with Britta, who surely had heard this recent news from Hazel by now. Susie had considered visiting Cousin Verena as she liked to do, but Saturday at supper she realized she'd see them tomorrow night at Singing, and Mamma reminded her of Kate Yoder's Sisters Day get-together in just three days for a big farm breakfast. *Sounds like I'll see Verena and Marnie soon enough.*

Presently, she examined the sketched layout for the names and dates of this latest cross-stitch as she sat alone in the sewing room, trying to plan how best to fit in the names of the twins who had been born just a few days ago. Sunlight fell over her shoulders and onto the long table Dat had built years ago. Typically she didn't mind the solitude, but today it pressed in on her. She wasn't ready to lose anyone else from her life, even if Obie was only moving away. *But it's not for me to determine Obie's choices,* she thought. *Why wouldn't he be enthusiastic about having a chance to work with his uncle? It's time for him to get on with his life.*

Yet Susie couldn't help dreading October, usually her favorite month.

The next day brought the first Singing of April, which was especially well attended.

Susie was happy to see Obie was present this time, and when refreshments were served, he walked directly over to her.

"You've prob'ly learned through the grapevine that I'll be takin' that job I told you about," he said, his eyes searching hers as he cupped popcorn in his hand.

"*Jah* . . . I heard the other night at Mattie's."

"I would've liked to tell ya myself, but things have a way of slipping out round here. Sorry 'bout that."

She nodded. "It's all right, Obie." She smiled, though she didn't much feel like it. "So, you'll leave after the corn harvest, then?"

"Dat needs me to help him and Jerome, so I'm honoring that. I'm planning to leave mid-October."

"Who'll take your place?"

"We're still discussin' that, which is another reason why I decided not to make a hasty exit." He explained that his uncle wished he'd come sooner but was willing to wait.

It's just like Obie to be so dependable, she thought. *Doesn't quit till the work's done.*

Her neck and shoulders felt tight with all she was holding in, but it was too late now to speak up, to tell him she wished he would stay put here. *Where he belongs . . .*

Once the singing commenced, Susie went

to sit with her cousins, and Obie joined Jerome and their own male cousins clear down at the end of the table, on the other side. Susie wanted so badly to look his way, wanting to memorize these times they were sharing. After all, memories would soon be all she'd have of Obie.

Except for letters . . . if he writes, she remembered. *Until someone else captures his heart.*

———

Susie had been talking to Verena and Marnie for a while and was getting ready to leave the Singing and walk down to the road to meet Del Petersheim when Verena discreetly poked Susie on the arm.

"Looks like your date's here," Verena whispered.

Sure enough, Del had appeared, stepping into the barn as he looked around for her.

"Okay, I'll see ya," Susie said, then made her way over to Del, who gave a friendly wave to a group of fellows.

Susie glanced toward the refreshment table, where Obie was talking with the deacon who'd hosted the Singing. She felt awkward yet also relieved Obie didn't appear to have seen Del standing by the barn entrance.

She smiled at Del as she headed outside with him to walk to the enclosed carriage he must have borrowed from his father. "Our Singing ran a little overtime," he said.

"Ours too," she replied.

"Glad I didn't put you out waitin'." He accompanied her to the left side of the buggy.

Stepping in, she saw that the couple they were doubling with were seated in the second seat. "Hullo," she said, and they smiled and greeted her as Del got in on the driver's side after untying the horse.

"Susie, I'd like ya to meet Mervin Allgyer and Cindy Jane Esh, longtime friends of mine," Del said, making introductions.

"Nice to meet ya," Susie said. "Did yous have a nice ride over?"

Cindy Jane nodded. "It's another beautiful evening. Perfect for a night out."

Susie agreed, then turned around as Del reached for the driving lines and clicked his cheek to signal the horse forward.

The conversation was pleasant enough as they rode and during their pie at Cindy's cousin's house, but in the back of Susie's mind was how disloyal she'd felt meeting Del while Obie had been standing a few yards away.

The morning of Tuesday's gathering, Susie hitched up Atta-Girl, their older driving horse, to the enclosed gray carriage. Before leaving, Mamma told Britta she was sorry she had to eat breakfast alone on a school day, but Britta assured her it was all right. "You an' Susie have yourselves a *gut* time at Sisters Day."

"Well, s'pose we should get goin'," Mamma said, pulling a hankie out of the pocket of her best black dress and placing it over her nose as she and Susie left the house to walk to the horse and carriage. As they rode together, Susie holding the driving lines, Mamma sniffled and kept clearing her throat. "*Ach*, my allergies are especially bad today."

Susie glanced at her. "Well, aside from Preachin', you rarely get to see many of the other womenfolk, so I'm glad you're goin'."

"Bein' round people is a blessing, indeed," Mamma replied, going on to say it was particularly nice that so many relatives with sisters would be coming. She gave a little cough, but thankfully it settled right away.

"Did ya take time for your warm tea this mornin'?" Susie asked, wishing she'd made certain.

"My fault," Mamma said. "Hopefully Kate'll have some brewing. Even coffee would help. Or just some boiling water in a cup."

Arriving at the Yoders', Susie recognized several of the road horses tied to the hitching post in the side yard and tried to guess who'd come besides Aendi Emmalyn and Mattie Beiler. "Looks like Kate's sister Lena is here. And Mattie's sister Rebekah Glick."

"Ella Mae's sure to be here, as well," Mamma said, a lilt in her voice now. "She wouldn't miss it, even though her sisters are all gone to Jesus."

"Well then, *you* and Emmalyn can be her sisters for today," Susie suggested, getting out to go around and wait for her mother to step out of the carriage.

Inside Kate's roomy kitchen, there was so much cheerful chatter and rushing around to get the hot breakfast on the table, Susie wished she could help, too. But, seeing Verena and Marnie already seated toward the foot of the table and waving her over to join them, Susie headed there.

The minute the food was set before them, everyone else sat down and bowed their heads for the silent blessing. Susie prayed the usual rote prayer but also asked God to help Mamma feel well enough to enjoy the get-together.

After the prayer, Kate Yoder thanked all of them for coming. "I thought today we could just enjoy some *gut* fellowship together.

There'll be plenty-a time for canning and baking soon enough. *Jah?*"

Different ones agreed out loud as others nodded their heads, and there were smiles all around.

Kate began to pass the food, a large breakfast casserole with eggs, sausage, cheese, and bread. There was also a basketful of warm maple muffins, fresh from the oven, as well as orange juice and coffee, and tea was brewing, thanks to Ella Mae. As each one dished up and chose a muffin for her plate, Kate shared that Obie was going to work for her husband's brother Leon. "In case a few of yous haven't heard," she added. "The hardest thing is knowing that he'll be gone for quite a while, and so far away in Sugar Valley."

"How long?" Rebekah asked, glancing at her sister Mattie.

"A minimum of two years," Kate replied.

The room grew silent, and Susie assumed this *must* be news to some of the women, sober as they now looked. Susie felt compassion for Kate and glanced at Ella Mae, planted between Mamma and her sister Emmalyn and right across from Susie and her cousins. What did the Wise Woman think about all this?

In the quiet, Ella Mae leaned forward and

looked kindly at Kate. "I daresay your son will return for visits, dearie. And sooner than ya might think."

"Oh, I hope so," Kate said, still looking glum.

Mattie spoke up next. "I believe I understand what you're feelin', Kate. It was hard to let my children go when they were ready to fly the nest."

"Well," Kate replied, "we'll trust that Obie will be ready when October rolls around."

Susie wanted to add that Obie most certainly was a responsible and hardworking young man, but that was a given. The thing Kate hadn't addressed aloud was the fact that no Amish community was ever ready to lose one of their youth to another church district. Even two years was a long time, and if Obie formed attachments elsewhere, there might not ever be a homecoming.

Britta left the one-room schoolhouse with Hazel, each waiting for her girl cousins at the edge of the fenced schoolyard as usual. Once they were all together, they made their way along the same stretch of road, some leisurely swinging their lunch thermoses as they walked along.

Hazel mentioned the Sisters Day breakfast that had taken place that morning. "Wish I could've been there."

"Me too," Britta said with a glance at Hazel.

"Mamm says once I finish eighth grade, I'll be able to go to all the Sisters Day gatherings."

"School will be out for summer soon enough, so hopefully there'll be more comin' up," Britta reassured her.

"And canning bees," Hazel said. "I love those."

"Putting up jam with Mamma and Susie is my favorite, too."

Hazel moaned. "To be honest, I'm gonna miss school when I graduate the end of this school year," she admitted.

Britta felt the pang of knowing how much she would miss her friend. "It won't be the same come next fall, that's for sure."

Both girls were quiet for a moment.

Then Hazel said more softly as they walked together, "Say, I saw Aaron Kauffman with his brother at the General Store the other day."

Britta winced.

"Isn't he the boy who used to tease ya at recess?"

Britta nodded. "He was always throwin' trouble around."

"Well, he seems nicer now."

"Not to me," Britta replied. "He still thinks I don't belong here with the People."

"How do ya know?"

"Well, every time he sees me, he scowls or rolls his eyes."

Hazel shook her head. "Some boys just like to pester girls they secretly like. Could be that's behind it."

Britta huffed at the idea. "Not Aaron," she scoffed. "He said I wasn't Amish and never would be."

"Well, it's not true, so don't believe it." Hazel glanced over her shoulder at the younger girls walking with them. "You're just as Plain as I am, Britta."

I hope you're right, she thought.

Days passed, and Susie and Mamma were at the table sketching a plan for the garden while Britta made bread dough at the counter. "I've got some more ideas for things to sell in the shop and at market," she said.

"More?" Susie glanced at Britta, whose hands were deep in the dough.

"What about popcorn balls?"

Mamma's head lifted suddenly. "Sounds *gut*, an' I'm sure they'd sell like hotcakes."

Britta grinned. "Hotcakes too?"

Now Susie was laughing. "Sure, why not? Maybe homemade pancake mix in Ball canning jars."

"And while we're at it, maybe homemade soup mix, too," Britta added.

"Now, girls, let's not get ahead of our-selves," Mamma said, pencil in hand as she looked down at the sketch she and Susie had been working on.

"Well, the more we make and sell, the better, *jah*?" Britta said.

"True," Susie agreed. "Ain't so, Mamma?"

"And when do ya think yous will have time for all this?" Mamma replied.

Britta nodded. "Okay, let's just start with the popcorn balls and see how they go over."

Mamma agreed, and although she liked the ideas, Susie was relieved. *There's enough to do round here*, she thought.

That evening, after supper and kitchen chores, Susie took the scooter to meet Verena to clean the schoolhouse. It was the ideal time to share their hearts without being overheard.

While she mopped the schoolhouse floor, Susie mentioned not having seen Obie around since the last Singing, ten days ago now. She tried to keep her tone casual, but this both-ered her more than she cared to admit.

"It must seem longer than that," Verena said as she ran a damp cloth over the teacher's desk.

"Oh, does it ever," Susie replied, surprised at how well her cousin understood her.

The mid-April day Susie had been anticipating arrived the next morning with ideal
weather for spring chores. She rose early to
make breakfast, eager to till up the large garden plot, as well as cultivate the smaller pe-
rennial herb garden, where tarragon, marjo-
ram, and peppermint would eventually break
through the soil. She also looked forward to
planting basil, dill, and sage once the weather
warmed a little more.

So, while Britta was at school and Mamma
was meeting customers, Susie hitched up
Brambles to Dat's old spring wagon and
headed over to Jonathan Ebersol's to borrow
his tiller. He loaded it for her and even rode
along to haul it down for her when they arrived back at home. "If ya like, I can stay and
till the plot for ya," he said, but Susie politely
declined, saying she had always managed fine
before.

"No sense not doin' it again this year,"
she said, wiping her brow with the back of
her hand.

Jonathan chuckled and volunteered any
other help she and Mamma might need, as he
always did, then headed back on foot through
the pasture to his own farm.

Meanwhile, Susie set to working the large
plot that had been mulched with compost
from last fall and into the winter. The soil

was dark and soft enough to take a footprint, and Susie could hardly wait to get her hands dirty planting the flourishing seedlings. *The wonder of new life*, she thought as she pushed the tiller forward.

The morning sun broke through a thin layer of clouds and glimmered off the edge of Mamma's silver whirligig near the gazebo steps. *A wunnerbaar-gut day*, Susie thought as she moved slowly along, making careful rows. As she worked, she thanked the Lord for their blessings, including kind neighbors like Jonathan and Liz, who gave them extra honey whenever Mamma bought a new batch. Susie was also grateful for a close friend in Cousin Verena, and for her growing friendship with Del, too. In fact, she wondered when he might ask her out again.

By midmorning, Susie went to sit on the rustic wood bench near the potting shed for a little while. She had gone to the house to get a tumbler of cold water and brought it out so she could rest briefly in one of her favorite spots. The white clapboard garden shed had once been her and Polly's childhood playhouse, built years ago by Dat. Then, when she was old enough, Susie had enjoyed playing in it alone. Occasionally Eli would join her, pretending to be the father to the faceless dolls she would line up, but he preferred to work alongside Dat.

More than a decade ago now, Polly's husband had decided to turn the beloved little cottage into something more practical, so Britta had missed out on the opportunity to play there with her dolls or read storybooks on a plump homemade cushion in the cozy reading corner like her older sisters had.

Just then, the shop door opened across the way, and Mamma stepped out and walked toward the stable.

Is she calling for a driver? Susie wondered, leaning back against the step. Mamma seldom visited the stable for any other reason now. She thought ahead to Saturday market and wondered if Obie might be there, then pushed the thought away. *I have to get used to not seein' him*, she thought sadly.

Quickly, she finished drinking the cold water and returned to tilling. All the while, she watched for any new customers, despite the fact it had been slower this morning than yesterday. Yet it was still early in the tourist season, so this was a good day to till the garden and possibly start planting, especially since Mamma felt well enough to work in the shop. It would be another six weeks or so before strawberries were ripe for picking, which would be followed by hours of making jam to sell and to stock their own pantry.

Just when will there be time to make dozens of popcorn balls? Susie wondered, hoping Britta might take that upon herself.

Customers started coming later that morning, and Mamma and Susie took turns working the shop during the noon hour, eating separately at the house. Glad for the business, Susie didn't mind, and as far as she could tell, Mamma was still doing all right.

When Britta arrived from school, she promptly went out and took Mamma's place in the shop to give her a break. Susie, however, kept busy planting her seedlings, one after another, in the freshly tilled soil.

Twice Britta slipped out between customers to talk to Susie, who was determined to get as much gardening done today as humanly possible.

"I told Mamma not to bother cookin' supper," Britta said the second time she emerged.

"We do have leftovers." Susie straightened and stretched her aching back. "I hope Mamma didn't overdo it today."

"She seemed okay when I went to spell her off." Britta paused and glanced toward the house. "S'pose you've been out here all day." She shielded her eyes from the sun and looked at the expanse of garden, dotted by the seedlings and Susie's seed markers.

"Shouldn't waste such nice weather, *jah*?"

"True. And you've always enjoyed workin' outdoors."

"Eli did, too. It was the hardest thing to get him to come inside."

Looking up toward the sky, Britta replied, "I wish I could've known him."

Susie nodded, feeling tenderhearted toward her. "I wish that, too. He'd have loved you."

"It must still hurt awful bad for ya. And Mamma, too," Britta said quietly. "Such heartache."

Susie bobbed her head but didn't speak. At times, the events of the accident still seemed crystal clear. At other times, downright hazy. But she'd never forgotten how devastated she'd felt.

As Britta turned to make her way back across the yard to the little shop, Susie heard the clear song of a bird somewhere high in the oak tree behind the potting shed, not far from the bird feeder. *Does God see me like He sees that bird?* she wondered, her mouth suddenly dry. *Does He see deep into my heart?*

Susie didn't bump into Obie or his mother, Kate, at the weekend market, nor did she run into him at the General Store as she sometimes did. She felt emotionally numb and wondered if this was how she would feel once he left Hickory Hollow.

On the morning of Tuesday, April twenty-sixth, Susie wrote Eli's initials on her bedroom calendar as she had done every year since his death. Doing this felt essential to her: one small way to honor his precious memory. That, and visiting and redding up the accident site. She assumed Mamma had her own way of marking the day. Everyone grieved differently and in their own time, Ella Mae had once shared with her.

Mamma had seemed especially weary following breakfast, and Susie had encouraged her to rest after Britta left for school. As far as she could tell, Mamma hadn't had an asthma flare-up today, but her mother was tuckered out, nonetheless. *Such a day for us both . . .*

After school, while they were walking ahead of the other girls, Britta tentatively asked Hazel, "Say, this might seem strange, but I've been wonderin' . . . do ya happen to know anything 'bout my adoption?"

Hazel looked at Britta and frowned. "What would I know that you wouldn't?" She sounded baffled.

Britta shrugged. "People talk, you know—just not usually around the person they're talkin' *about*. I just thought maybe you might've heard something."

"What would ya like to know?"

"*Ach*, near everything. What my first mother looked like, for starters. And was she Plain or fancy?"

Hazel glanced over her shoulder. "I was only a year old back then." She slowed her pace and was quiet for the longest time.

"So you're saying you've never heard anyone talk about it?"

"All I know is that your Mamma and her husband were foster parents for some years before he passed. Then you arrived," Hazel told her.

They walked a bit farther without saying anything at all.

When Britta could scarcely keep her thoughts to herself any longer, she said, "I just wish I knew more, like why my first family didn't keep me."

Hazel was still, as if thinking. "Why don't ya ask your Mamma?"

Britta sighed. "I could, but I can't bear to bring it up. She's the only mother I know, and I wouldn't wanna hurt her."

"Well, can ya just let it be, then?"

Britta wished now she hadn't said anything. Even so, the questions she'd shooed away for several years now pestered her like so many mosquito bites. And the older she got, the stronger they itched.

How will I ever get any answers?

Later that afternoon, while still in the shop, Susie glanced out the window and saw Britta arriving home from school. Instead of heading to the stable to see her cats as she often did, Britta moseyed toward the house, her shoulders slumped. *Not her usual self*, thought Susie, concerned.

A few minutes later, Aendi Emmalyn pulled up in her gray family buggy and came into the shop. "I'm holdin' my breath for some blueberry jam," she said with a smile. "Hope yous haven't sold out."

Susie was glad to see her again. "How many pints would ya want?"

"Just three for now." Emmalyn opened her shoulder purse and counted out the money.

"It's a *gut* thing we put up more than usual

last year," Susie said cheerfully as she tucked away the money.

"For certain!" Emmalyn glanced toward the house. "How's your Mamma feelin' today?"

"Not too *lebhaft*."

Emmalyn sighed. "I daresay she hasn't been lively for some time."

"*Jah*, sad to say."

"But then, considering what day it is, who can blame her?"

Susie nodded, then reached under the counter for a small box. "Honestly, she hasn't seemed so under the weather on this day other years. If you'd like to go to the house and visit, though, I know she'd be happy to see ya."

"Well, only if she's not resting." Emmalyn zipped her purse shut.

"I'm fairly sure she's up . . . likes to talk with Britta after school."

"Oh, then I'll stop by an' visit another time. Wouldn't want to interrupt."

Now Susie wished she'd kept mum about Mamma typically spending time with Britta, but she couldn't backtrack. Carefully, she placed the pint jars in the box and handed it to her aunt. "I'll let Mamma know you were here."

"You do that." Emmalyn paused, holding

the box just so. "Say, with the way Britta's growin', you might want to know the fabric store has green dress fabric for half price this weekend."

"*Denki.*" Susie nodded and watched her aunt open the door to head toward her carriage, where she placed the box inside. Then, to Susie's surprise, Mamma stepped out onto the back porch and waved Emmalyn over. Susie felt pleased as she watched the two sisters warmly greet each other.

A glance at the red-and-white wall clock told Susie it was time to close up shop, so she tidied up, then adjusted the farmland calendar behind the battery-run cash register. Closing the door behind her, she heard someone talking over in the stable, so she turned to walk toward its open door. Through the entrance, she could see Britta standing there, holding black Lucy and murmuring to her, although she couldn't make out what her sister was saying.

Wanting to make sure all was well, Susie walked inside. "Saw ya head for the house after school, and now you're out here. You okay, Schweschder?"

Startled, Britta looked up at her. "Oh, just a little down. I tried to talk with my friend about somethin'."

"Hazel?"

Britta nodded sadly. "She's the only one I felt comfortable askin'."

Susie went to her and wrapped her arms around her, the cat tucked between them. "Well, *I'm* here," she said. "You can ask me."

Britta pulled back slowly from Susie. "I don't know."

"Go on."

Britta looked even sadder now as she stroked Lucy, whose purring grew louder. "Do you know why I was adopted?" she asked timidly.

Oh dear, thought Susie, taking a quick breath. "I don't know details. Far as I remember, Dat and Mamma wanted another child, so they became foster parents for a time. You must've been available to be adopted after Dat died and Mamma still wanted another child. I never really asked Mamma about it. I was just glad to have another sister."

At that, Britta gave a little smile. "Did you ever meet my first mother?"

Susie shook her head. "Have ya talked to Mamma 'bout any of this?"

"Not yet. Not sure how she'd feel about me askin'."

"Won't know till ya ask." Susie looked out the window, uncertain what else to say, or if she should even be encouraging this line of thinking. "You know what? I could use some help makin' supper, unless Mamma's got something cooking already."

"Okay," Britta said rather reluctantly. "I'll come in soon."

Susie walked past the horses' stalls and outside, pondering Britta's sudden interest in her origins.

After an early supper, Susie and Britta cleaned up the kitchen while Mamma made herself comfortable in the front room with an issue of *Family Life* magazine.

"I'll be heading up the road soon, if ya want to visit Hazel for a while," Susie offered, handing Britta the last plate to be wiped. "I could drop ya off."

Looking toward the front room, Britta asked quietly, "Are ya gonna redd up the spot where the accident happened?"

Susie nodded.

"I could go with ya," Britta offered. "Keep you company."

"'Spect you'd rather see Hazel, ain't so?"

Britta shook her head. "I can see her at school tomorrow. This is more important."

Except for Mamma on a few occasions, no one had gone with Susie to honor Eli's memory on the anniversary of his death, or at any other time. "Okay, then," Susie said softly. "We'll leave right after dishes are put away."

The sounds of Hickory Hollow this time of year were muted—no chainsaws were cutting logs in the distance, and few horse and buggies were out. Presently, the early evening sun cast long shadows through the trees lining the pasture not far from the road where Susie and Britta drove along. A flock of redwinged blackbirds dotted the sky, and Susie could hear the distinct call of the males.

"What was Eli's favorite thing to do?" Britta asked.

"Well, fishin' and goin' turkey hunting with Dat—they did that at least a couple of times together."

"Deer hunting, too?"

"*Nee*, Dat usually went with Allen to get his deer, but I think Eli would've grown up to be a *gut* shot."

"How do ya know?"

"He had a *gut* aim at corner ball during school recess." Susie laughed quietly. "Eli also liked to take me in the pony cart when Mamma asked him to go to the General Store to get odds and ends. She'd give him a list and stick the money in a zipped leather holder, and off we'd go."

"You made some happy memories to-gether, ain't so?"

Susie nodded. "For sure and for certain. Just like you and me."

As they arrived at the destination, Susie directed Atta-Girl toward the side of the narrow road, opposite the location of the accident, and came to a halt. Without speaking, she stepped down from the carriage and went around to the back, opening it to remove the rake and broom.

While Britta was climbing from the carriage, Susie crossed the road and began to rake a long patch of grass, including the sloped area beside the road where wild flowers would soon grow.

Britta wandered over, surprise on her pretty face. "Did ya see the bundle of flowers over yonder?" she asked, pointing.

"They show up here every year in the exact same spot."

Britta walked over and leaned down to look at the bouquet but didn't touch it. "They look fresh . . . smell nice. Must be hand-picked, too," she said, reaching for the broom propped against the horse fence.

"*Ach*, you don't have to sweep," Susie said. "That's my job." *My responsibility* . . .

Britta left the broom where it was. "Who leaves the flowers, do ya think?"

Susie had always found their appearance peculiar, since placing flowers as a memento like that wasn't really something the People did. "I don't know."

"Mamma didn't come earlier today, did she?"

"She rarely comes on the actual day, and I've never seen her bring flowers." Susie stopped raking and paused to look at the pretty pink bleeding hearts, purple creeping myrtle, and white daffodils held together by the soft blue ribbon, its ends tied in a neat bow. "Mamma doesn't even put flowers on Dat's and Eli's graves that I know of."

Britta looked even more melancholy now. "Do ya remember what happened that day?" she asked timidly.

Susie inhaled sharply. *I couldn't even bring myself to tell all to Obie.* "The driver must've lost control . . . was goin' too fast in the rain, then swerved . . ." She couldn't say more. Her stomach was a ball of knots.

"The English do drive fast." Britta tilted her head, arms folded around her middle. "To tell the truth, I don't even like travelin' in the passenger vans."

Susie nodded but stayed quiet.

"Hazel said her Mamma thinks the driver was prob'ly drunk," Britta added. "But that could be gossip."

"A hit an' run is what it was."

"A what?"

Feeling uneasy, Susie said, "The driver kept goin' . . . didn't stop, after hittin' Eli."

"Maybe the driver didn't know anyone'd been hit," Britta said. "Could that be?"

Susie would spare her the horror and not reveal that she'd screamed, over and over . . . nor speak of the low, hollow sort of cry Eli had made as the car struck him and he fell to the asphalt. *The last sound he made.* Oh, how she wanted to end this conversation.

Tears welled up in Susie's eyes as Britta said, "I hope Eli didn't suffer long."

Susie found her voice again. "Mercifully, he went straight to Jesus." She put down the rake, walked over to Britta, and stood next to her. "Honestly, talking 'bout this today maybe ain't such a *gut* idea," she admitted at last, then gently slipped her arm around her sister.

"I'm sorry." Britta leaned against her. "Comin' here's awful hard. No wonder Mamma doesn't want to do it very often."

"*Jah,* who can blame her?" Susie said quietly.

CHAPTER

13

A full week swept by, and while the farmers all over Lancaster County were planting field corn for October harvest, Susie planted even more vegetables and completed two additional cross-stitched family trees, accepting orders for several more. She also helped Britta make plenty of popcorn balls.

Looking back, Susie could see that she was purposely filling up her hours, trying to keep from brooding on Obie's decision to work for his uncle, so far away.

The first Saturday market day in May, while Susie waited with Britta and their mother for their van to arrive, Britta unexpectedly mentioned the wild flower bouquet she and Susie had seen at the spot where Eli had died.

"It was leanin' against the white horse fence," Britta told Mamma. "Real perty."

Nodding, Mamma seemed unsurprised. "Ella Mae and I have both noticed it over the years, too."

Susie wondered why Britta brought this up to Mamma when Britta had already discussed it with Susie. Was she trying to get Mamma to talk about the accident?

"From what I've heard, there used to be lots of flowers and cards or notes . . . even a little white cross," Britta said. She paused, and Susie wondered what Mamma was thinking about all this. "But now it's just this one bouquet," Britta continued. "It's sweet, isn't it, that someone besides us still remembers what happened there?"

"Truly it is," Mamma said softly.

"But *who*?" Britta asked.

Susie shrugged. "S'pose it could be any number of folk." She wondered who Britta had been talking to, to know that there had been other flowers and notes and cards and such years ago.

At that moment, Mamma waved at the van coming down the road. "Lookee there, our driver's right on time," she said quickly.

Mamma seems uncomfortable with this talk,
Susie thought, wishing Britta hadn't mentioned the bundle of flowers.

Susie stood outside with Britta after the
mid-May Preaching service, waiting for the
youth to be called indoors for the fellowship
meal. She couldn't help noticing Mamma
over talking with Ella Mae near a terraced
bed of pink, white, and rose-hued peonies,
both of them looking quite solemn. Ella Mae
was nodding her head thoughtfully, and
Mamma leaned closer, as if to whisper. The
scene reminded Susie again of that peculiar
time at market when she'd clearly interrupted
a private exchange between the women. Seeing them like that now, she sometimes wished
she was privy to their shared secrets.

Susie sat on the back porch that afternoon,
waiting for Britta to finish the late-afternoon
goat milking. Over yonder, she could see the
Ebersols' road horses standing head to tail in
the southwest corner of the meadow. Rarely
one to just sit and twiddle her thumbs, even
on the Lord's Day, Susie enjoyed the cool
breeze, knowing summer weather was just
around the corner.

To the west, the neighbors' dairy cows were drifting into the deep pasture, where they would likely spend the night under the stars and waxing crescent moon. Susie recalled the warm summer night, five years ago, when Mamma had let her pitch a tent in the backyard. Susie and Britta and two of her cats had slept happily beneath a full moon.

Smiling at the memory, she recalled telling stories to Britta—they'd both been too excited to close their eyes and go to sleep. Mamma's own mother, Susannah Fisher, gone to Jesus, had been the subject of one of those stories, as had one particular tree in *Mammi* Fisher's yard when she had been a wee girl. Without her parents' knowledge, Susannah would take her book and climb high into the branches after chores were done. One evening after supper, though, she had fallen asleep up there, worrying her parents something awful as they searched the house and the property for their missing girl.

When Susannah awakened to sharp calls from her father, she realized what she'd done and looked down through the darkness and gasped, realizing she could easily have fallen to her death. Instead, she scrambled down, limb over limb, until she fell into her father's arms, pleading tearfully for forgiveness.

Susie never forgot how Britta had begged

to know if Mammi had learned her lesson, a quaver in Britta's small voice. "Mammi was grateful her Dat had come lookin' for her," Susie had reassured Britta. "It was a blessing everything turned out all right."

I haven't thought of that night in ages, Susie thought as she saw her sister come across the yard toward her.

By taking a little time every day following daily chores, Susie finally managed to complete the Petersheim family tree. She went to the stable to call Del that following Friday to let him know. Sounding pleased and upbeat, he said he would pick it up next Tuesday. "And if it's ready, I can also sample that special rhubarb jam," he teased.

"Oh, that won't be for another week yet," she told him, amused by his enthusiasm.

"Okay, then this time I'll just come by for your handiwork," he said, and Susie wondered if he might stick around and talk awhile.

At noon, Cousins Verena and Marnie brought over a generous picnic of pulled pork sandwiches, homemade potato salad, and fruit cup, just as they'd planned a few days ago. Britta was able to join the other three cousins, since school was out for the summer. It was time now for children to help their parents with the fieldwork and planting going on all over Hickory Hollow. The girls sat and ate together on an old blanket near the potting shed while Mamma had a meal with Ella Mae.

Marnie suggested they all go swimming in the pond in a few weeks to celebrate Britta's thirteenth birthday on July second.

"I'd like that," Britta said, grinning, and Susie agreed that it sounded like fun.

"Since it's a Saturday, how about we have a picnic lunch on the porch here, then change into our bathing suits?" Cousin Verena proposed.

"By that time of day, it'll feel *gut* to get cooled off," Britta said.

Marnie agreed. "Just the four of us."

"Unless there are other cousins or friends you want to invite, Britta," Verena said. "That's up to you, but let me know so I'll have plenty of food for everyone."

"Mamma will eat with us, too, of course," Susie spoke up.

"Oh *jah*," said Britta. "Mamma for certain."

"But no boyfriends allowed," Marnie teased.

Verena rolled her eyes at her sister. "*Jah*, just us girls."

Susie laughed with them, grateful for this lighthearted time together.

As promised, Del stopped by the very next Tuesday to pick up the framed family tree. Susie soon realized that, because there were several customers ahead of him in line and more behind him, he wouldn't be able to engage her in much conversation. As it turned out, he only remarked how *wunner-baar* the cross-stitched family tree had turned out, though he made no attempt to hide his enthusiasm from the other waiting customers. The two Amishwomen behind him exchanged knowing glances, and one gave Susie a little smile.

"I'm glad you like it," Susie said as Del paid. "Hopefully your Mamm will, too."

Later, Susie and Mamma enjoyed the noon meal together, since Britta was visiting Hazel.

"Tomorrow, we should pick rhubarb," Mamma said to Susie. "Ain't so?"

"That's exactly what I told Britta this mornin'—she knows we need her round here." Secretly, Susie hoped Mamma wouldn't insist on helping too much. "Del Petersheim says he's lookin' forward to sampling some of our special rhubarb jam soon," she added.

"Sounds like he's dropped by the shop a couple times," Mamma observed, arching her eyebrows.

Susie nodded. "He's real nice."

Mamma made a small sound as if agreeing, though Susie couldn't really tell. One thing was certain: She really didn't need to hear again that Mamma preferred Obie. They'd already had that conversation, and besides, there wasn't anything she could do to get Obie to change his mind about going now.

After a quick breakfast of sticky buns and coffee, Susie and Britta picked the plump red rhubarb stalks amidst heavy morning dew. Mamma, for her part, helped to hose off the dirt before they carried the stalks inside to make their delicious jam. Bobwhites were calling back and forth in the paddock, and the sweet scent of newly cut hay wafted on the spring breeze.

At nine o'clock, Mamma went out to mind the shop, while Susie and Britta made a big batch of their special rhubarb jam to sell.

Growing up, Susie had often heard the womenfolk talk about the health benefits of rhubarb juice, which many believed improved eyesight and aided digestion. A good number of them, Mamma included, kept rhubarb juice on hand when it was in season. Susie knew, however, that Britta disliked the taste, so she didn't drink the juice, although as long as strawberries were added, she liked the jam and pies made with rhubarb.

"Do ya s'pose we get our tastes from our parents?" Britta asked clear out of the blue as she poured sugar into the large pot.

Susie shrugged. "Maybe so," she replied.

Del stopped by once more on the last day of May to sample the rhubarb jam. Susie was impressed when he guessed the secret ingredients: clementine juice, lime juice, and cinnamon. She enjoyed bantering with him while he paid for two pint-sized jars.

"Both jars are for you, *jah*?" she teased.

He bobbed his head. "We'll just see how long it lasts, considering my parents and siblings like rhubarb jam, too. They really need to try this."

"Well then, maybe you'd like to purchase *three*?"

"You should be in sales," he said, closing his wallet and chuckling.

Before he left, Del mentioned that he had been very busy with the crops, but he wanted to take her out again. "I hope ya understand," he said, looking apologetic.

"It's a busy time for us, too, what with gardening and canning an' all. Time to re-stock the shelves so we're ready for you next time."

He grinned and she smiled in return. "Enjoy the jam," she said as he headed for the shop door.

Susie was in the gazebo watering the hanging plants when she heard the sound of a horse and buggy turn into the driveway the next day. She looked and was surprised to see Obie and Hazel.

Oh, that's right—Hazel's come to bake pies with Britta. She recalled Britta saying as much earlier that morning. The girls planned to take one to the Ebersols and the other up the road to Lois Peachey and family, a neighborly thing to do.

Susie continued watering and wondering if Obie would head on his way with just a wave.

To her surprise, he climbed out of the buggy and walked over to the gazebo steps. "Hullo, Susie," he said, running his hand over his clean-shaven chin.

"*Wie geht's?*"

"Doin' all right." Obie glanced toward the pond. "Say, I was wonderin' if we might take the rowboat out, maybe? I've got a little time before I need to run an errand, and it's the perfect day for it."

Well, that's unexpected! she thought, pleased. She glanced back at the house, where Britta was already occupied with Hazel. Then, looking toward Mamma's shop, where a couple of buggies were parked, Susie decided that her mother would be fine without her. "*Jah*, I can prob'ly slip away for a while," she replied, setting down the watering can.

When they walked out to the far end of the dock, Susie stepped barefoot into the moored rowboat, and Obie followed. The boat swayed gently as she sat down, and he untied the rope, then took a seat facing her. Slowly, he pushed the boat away from the pier, then began to row toward the deeper water.

Susie tried not to grin at how wonderful it was, skimming through the water on such a fine day with Obie. Since it was only the first day of June, it wasn't terribly hot yet.

"I've managed to keep what I'm gonna tell ya under my hat this time," he said, sitting tall as he rowed more slowly now, letting the boat glide gently into the heart of the pond. "I learned my lesson 'bout tellin' my Bruder first."

Susie hadn't the slightest idea what Obie meant, so she waited quietly.

"Onkel Leon has been pressin' me to come sooner than October. I'm plannin' to head down to Ronks tomorrow to talk to one of my cousins 'bout helpin' Dat and Jerome through the summer and into fall harvest. Assuming I can find Dat some help, I'll be free to leave for Sugar Valley sooner than planned."

Once again, Susie didn't know how to react. Here lately, she had seen Obie only infrequently, mostly at Preaching or in the distance at a Singing or two, and with him leaving, she felt uncomfortable letting him know how she felt about much of anything. So she simply nodded her head. *And here I thought there were months yet.*

"Lord willin', I hope to leave this Saturday. Just wanted you to hear it from me," Obie said, studying her expression.

He was observing her so closely that she struggled to keep her expression calm. "You're here to say good-bye, then?"

"Just for now. Nothing's going to change the fact that we're friends." Obie's smile was warm and reassuring.

But with Obie leaving, wouldn't their friendship become something far different now?

"I'll pray for safe travels for you," she said, reaching over the side of the boat to dip her hand in the water, still doing her best to hide her disappointment.

He began rowing faster again. "I can always count on ya, Susie," he said. "For prayer."

"*Jah*," she said.

It crossed her mind to ask how he expected them to maintain their bond into the future when, more than likely, one or both of them would meet the mate God intended, bringing their longtime friendship to an end.

This could be the last time Obie and I talk alone like this, she thought, determined now to enjoy their last few leisurely moments together, the breeze on her face, the sun's rays dappling the water.

As they floated along beneath the willows, she wanted so badly to ask what he'd started to say on her birthday, which seemed ever so long ago now. She even opened her mouth to speak but caught herself, believing that if it was still important, he would bring it up on his own.

As they talked about his plans in Sugar Valley, it became obvious that Obie wasn't going to inquire about Susie's own plans, or Del Petersheim. It seemed a little strange, since before now, they had always been comfortable talking about the different people each of them had gone out with from time to time. But she kept mum on that and let Obie row the boat.

If the auburn-haired woman had been Amish or Mennonite, Britta might not have given her a second look. But the woman at Saturday market was quite obviously an *Englischer* and even gave Britta a sweet smile as she caught her eye.

Britta hoped Susie and Mamma, there with her at their usual market stand, hadn't noticed. It was all Britta could do to stay put there and merely observe the woman.

What if she's my birth mother, just a few yards away? she thought, her breath coming in little spurts. *What would she think if I went over to her and asked some questions?*

"Britta," Susie said, "can you get several more packages of goat cheese from the cooler?"

Jolted out of her thoughts, Britta nodded and leaned down beneath the table to get what Susie needed. More than likely, she was completely wrong about the woman. *Does my first mother ever think of me?* Britta wondered. *Does she ever want to find me and know me now that I'm almost a teenager? What if she is actually fancy?*

When Britta rose and gave Susie the goat

cheese, Britta could see the woman walking with two young boys, one with hair a similar color to Britta's own. Oh, she felt frozen in place, yet she wanted with all of her heart to scurry after her and talk to her.

If I could just hear her voice, she thought, *maybe I'd know.*

Britta smiled at the next customer, who had a question about the ingredients for the peanut butter spread. All the same, she caught herself glancing repeatedly toward the woman and boys until they were out of sight.

Obie had been gone to Sugar Valley for a little more than a week when Susie hurried out to the road to retrieve the mail. Susie sorted through the letters and saw two addressed to her. "For goodness' sake," she said, surprised at how happy she was to see Obie's handwriting. And a letter from Del, too, of all things.

She scurried up the driveway and took her mother's mail into the kitchen, where Mamma was measuring flour to make dumplings. Then Susie walked back to the shop, presently empty of customers. In the stillness of the cozy spot, she opened Del's envelope and discovered a note asking her out for supper this Saturday. *I'll look forward to hearing from you, Susie,* he'd written.

Smiling, she decided to send her reply in tomorrow's mail, expecting he would get it in plenty of time. Del hadn't mentioned double-dating this outing, so she assumed they'd have more time to talk and get to know each other. Either way, she was pleased to hear from him.

Reaching next for Obie's letter, she paused before opening it, feeling a bit giddy since he'd never written to her before, other than the birthday and Christmas cards he'd given her through the years.

Slowly, she opened the envelope and began to read.

Dear Susie,

How are you? How is your Mamma doing, and Britta, too?

It's taken me a whole week to get settled here and into my new routine— Onkel Leon has plenty for me to do and learn, and I'm eager to master all of it. But I find myself wondering how you are and wanting to sit down and write.

You should know that your encouragement about this job helped me make the decision to take it, and I'm grateful,

Susie. You've been a trusted friend to me over the years.

That's why it pleases me to see you happy with Delmar Petersheim—he's not like the other fellows you've gone out with. Del is obviously well-suited and a God-fearing man, so once you start seriously courting, let me know, so I don't interfere with my letters.

Know that I'll keep you in my prayers, just as you've done for me.

Your friend,
Obie Yoder

Susie folded the letter and slipped it into her dress pocket, glad to hear from him, but also thinking that, as accommodating as he sounded about Del, Obie may as well have signed off *Your brother.*

She rose and looked out the window at the sky scattered with cottony clouds. *At least he wants to keep in touch,* she thought, her heart still tender toward him.

A car pulled up just then, and she made her way back to the counter, where she took her spot on the wooden stool, thinking how odd it was to receive Obie's letter on the exact same day as Del's supper invitation.

CHAPTER 15

Mamma's chicken and dumplings supper was so delicious that evening that both Susie and Britta had seconds. Yet as the three of them ate together, Susie noticed how droopy and pale her mother looked, though she was talkative enough.

"You certainly seem cheerful tonight, Susie," Mamma said, observing her.

"Do I?"

Britta nodded. "*Jah*, and right after the mail came." Britta exchanged glances with their mother.

"Goodness, just now you two remind me of certain cousins." Susie looked out the window, not sure she wanted to tell them about the letters quite yet. They'd probably make a bigger deal of it than necessary.

Mamma took a sip of her warm tea, not saying more.

"Which reminds me, I might take the pony cart over to see Cousin Verena after dishes are done," Susie told them. "If that's okay with you, Mamma."

Britta eyed Susie. "I'd be glad to stay here with Mamma."

"Don't you worry over me. A little rest is all I need." Mamma sipped more tea, then ran the back of her hand across her brow.

"*Ach*, you should've let us make supper," Susie said, "'cept that no one makes better dumplings."

"Say, that's another idea: We could sell ready-made dinners at the shop," Britta said. She looked at them as if eager for a response.

"Mamma's a *gut* cook, for certain, but that's too much extra work," Susie pointed out.

"Those syrupy popcorn balls of yours were sure a *wunnerbaar* idea, though— they're nearly as popular as the peanut butter spread," Mamma said. "People have even stopped by just for those and ended up buyin' other things."

"We're doin' all right with the money from my cross-stitch sales and Britta's babysitting money from the Ebersols—and, of course, the check Allen sends each month," Susie mentioned, her gaze on her mother.

"The Lord has provided." Mamma reached again for the chamomile tea she always drank with raw honey. "He's met our every need."

Britta rose and carried the leftovers to the counter while Mamma stayed at the table with her tea.

Susie reached over to put her hand on her mother's. "I think you might need to take a break from cookin' for a day or two."

Mamma's eyebrows rose. "I just wanted to surprise yous."

Susie squeezed her hand. "*Denki.*"

Britta returned to clear the rest of the table. "One of your best meals, Mamma," she said, and Susie agreed.

"You don't have to help clean up the dishes, Susie," Britta told her. "Go an' have your visit with Cousin Verena."

"I'll make it up to you," Susie promised.

"Just glad to see ya so happy," Britta replied mischievously.

Now Mamma was studying Susie again but good.

"I shouldn't be gone long," Susie said as she rose from the table, eager to be heading out.

"Take your time, dear." Mamma gave her a knowing look.

There's no hiding anything from Mamma, thought Susie.

"Ain't one bit surprised to hear it," Cousin Verena said when Susie told her about Obie's letter as they sat on the front porch swing.

"Well, I'd actually wondered if he'd remember to write once he left."

"After all the years you've known each other?" Verena shook her head. "*Nee*, Obie's a loyal friend."

"Del Petersheim wrote, too, inviting me out for supper," Susie mentioned.

Verena nodded. "Interesting."

Susie agreed and changed the subject. "Say, I never told ya, but Obie asked me earlier this spring what I thought 'bout him workin' in Sugar Valley," Susie said. "He really wanted my opinion."

Verena stopped the swing. "What'd ya say?"

Susie decided to tell her everything, including that she'd encouraged Obie to go. "It's the kind of job he's always hoped for— not many chances like that come along. And I figured he might as well get on with his life, ya know. I mean, since he views me as a kind of sister."

"*Ach*, ya should've told me," Verena said.

"It hasn't been easy to think 'bout, let alone share," Susie said. "You understand, *jah*?"

Verena pushed her foot against the floor and got the swing moving again. "Oh, believe me, I do. Relationships can be rough goin'."

"Obie knew at the time that I'd gone out with Del. He saw me with him at the farm auction back in March."

"Well then, I'd say the fact Obie wrote is a *gut* sign."

Susie pondered that. "I was so happy to hear from him."

Verena bobbed her head and smiled. "Will ya write back?"

"What do ya think?" Susie laughed softly.

Just then, Cousin Marnie poked her head out the front door. "Are yous conspiring again?" She was grinning.

"When was the last time we did that?" Verena said, adjusting her blue bandanna over her hair bun.

"You've forgotten?" Marnie pretended to be shocked.

"Let's see . . . was it a few years ago, when we told the teacher that you'd be a fine scholar to consider bein' a teacher's helper?" Verena asked. "Or maybe even a teacher yourself?"

Marnie crept outside barefoot and took a seat on one of the natural wicker chairs. "*Jah*, an' you can see how that turned out." She chuckled.

"Well, you can't say we didn't try," Susie said. "You'd be a *wunnerbaar-gut* teacher."

Marnie ducked her head. "The school board had other ideas," she said, "which is okay with me."

They sat quietly, watching the color fade from the sky. After a moment or two, Verena mentioned how she and Marnie used to catch baby caterpillars and let them crawl on each other's arms. "Those were the carefree days of childhood," she said, "before the drama of courting age came along." She sighed.

"So glum! Should I be worried, sister?" Marnie asked.

Verena regarded her. "About Jerome?"

Marnie nodded. "He's very good-lookin'."

Verena glanced at Susie, then at Marnie. "Well, not every relationship ends in heart-ache."

"I sure hope not," Marnie said.

Susie realized that Mamma and Britta would be having Bible reading and prayer soon, and her cousins here would be, too, with their family. "Well, I should be headin' home," she said, rising from the swing. "It's been real nice seein' yous again."

Verena rose, too, and went with her out to the pony and cart. She reached to give Susie a hug. "Careful going home."

Susie smiled and untied the pony from the hitching post. *"Kumme* over an' see us sometime," she said, waving.

Once home, Susie entered the front room, where Mamma held the Good Book in her lap. "I didn't want to miss our time together," she said, sitting next to Britta on the small settee.

"Glad you're home," Mamma said, then began to read slowly, but with expression, from Psalm 103. "'Bless the Lord, O my soul: and all that is within me, bless his holy name. Bless the Lord, O my soul, and forget not all his benefits. . . .'"

Susie listened, as always moved by the beauty and rhythm of King David's words.

When Mamma read verse twelve, about one's transgressions being removed as far as the east was from the west, Susie felt grateful.

Before kneeling for prayer, Mamma brought up the importance of forgiving each other at the close of the day, before bedtime. "When we open our hearts to each other and to God through forgiveness, our own mistakes are forgiven. It isn't easy—it can be very difficult, in fact—but you'll never regret forgiving someone."

Dear Mamma often shared her thoughts on the verses she read. She was devoted to her faith and believed, like Dat, that she must give an account before God of the way she brought up her family.

Lying in bed, hours later, Susie thought again of Obie's letter tucked away in her small wooden chest, next to the white pinecone he'd given her. *Would he be surprised to know I kept that little Christmas present?* she wondered.

And she prayed that, if it was His will, God would change her heart away from Obie and toward Del.

16

On the morning of Britta's birthday, she knelt beside her bed before dressing and prayed for wisdom about how to ask Mamma the questions she'd long held privately in her heart. *She's the dearest mother, O Lord,* prayed Britta. *I really don't want to cause her pain. . . .*

Later, while helping Susie make buttermilk waffles and sausage patties, Britta couldn't decide if she should wait to talk to Mamma before or after Cousins Verena and Marnie came over for their planned picnic and swim. But with Hazel dropping by later, there wasn't a lot of time.

Around midmorning, Aendi Emmalyn stopped in to wish Britta a happy birthday with a tin of fresh chocolate chip cookies and a pretty card. Later, Aendi Lettie, Mamma's eldest sister, and her daughter Naomi Flaud dropped by with a card and new book from the two of them.

Then and there, Britta decided she'd have to put off seeking out Mamma with her questions, not wanting to spoil the day for so many loved ones.

Britta rose early again the next morning, an off-Sunday from Preaching, to read from *Rules of a Godly Life*, then hurried to get ready and out to milk the goats, just like every other day of the week. Britta loved caring for the lively, playful animals, which they had purchased some years ago when Mamma had switched from cow's milk to goat's, hoping it might help with her allergies.

When that chore was done, Britta noticed Mamma sitting on the back porch, two of the cats curled up near her bare feet. Seeing that Susie wasn't anywhere nearby, Britta carried the bucket of goat's milk into the kitchen. There, she washed her hands thoroughly and poured the delicious milk into clean bottles before placing them in the fridge. Then she rushed back outdoors to talk to Mamma.

"If ya have a moment, I was hopin' I could

ask ya something," she said as she sat down in the chair next to Mamma.

"It's so peaceful out, ain't?" Mamma said, smiling at her. "What's on your mind, dear?"

Britta hoped she was doing the right thing. "I don't want ya to think poorly of me," she began. "But now that I'm a teenager, I thought it might be okay to ask you some things."

Mamma folded her hands in her lap, a little wrinkle forming between her eyebrows as she frowned slightly, as if puzzled. "All right."

Britta took a deep breath and forged ahead. "First of all, how did I get my name? I mean, I can tell Britta's not Amish, since nobody else has my name."

Mamma visibly stiffened. "Well, that was the name you were given by your *Englischer* mother."

Britta's heart beat faster. "So I wasn't born Amish, then?"

Mamma shook her head.

Britta nodded, relieved to have this confirmed. "But didn't *you* want to name me?" She shifted a little in her chair. "I mean, since you're Plain."

Mamma smiled now. "Well, I was only your foster Mamma at first, so I never gave it a second thought, really. I was just so happy to have you in my arms."

Britta pondered that; then another question bubbled up. "I must've been pretty small when you got me," she said.

"Just a wee infant." Mamma held out her hands to show how small.

"How old was I?"

"Ten days new."

Britta considered other questions but felt she should stop asking. She couldn't really tell by the way Mamma sat so straight in her rocking chair, not moving, if she welcomed more questions. It didn't seem like Mamma to be so still, as if she was on edge, and Britta felt worse than when she'd decided to forge ahead like this. "Sorry if I'm askin' too much."

Mamma turned to look at her again. "I understand your curiosity, dear. Honest, I do." She gave her a smile.

Britta simply said, "*Denki.*"

Mamma must have heard the uncertainty in her voice, because she added, "You should also know that your birth mother was unable to bear the responsibility of takin' care of a child." Mamma sighed. "I've always planned to tell ya the story of your adoption once you're eighteen."

Five more years is a long wait, Britta thought miserably. Mamma's few answers had made her feel even more unsettled about her past.

"Please try and be patient, Britta," Mamma

said. "And . . . remember how glad I am that you're my girl."

"*Jah*," she murmured, rising to walk over to the screen door, where she waited in case Mamma had more to say. But when the rocking chair began to move forward and back again, Britta opened the door and stepped inside.

Susie felt tired after supper but didn't let on when Britta asked her to go for a walk. "Okay," she said, matching her sister's brisk pace when they headed down the driveway. "You choose the direction."

"How 'bout we walk toward the bishop's farm on Hickory Lane? I like seein' those towering willows out front."

Susie nodded, wondering what was up. "Mamma says nothin' looks more peaceful than a willow tree . . . like ours round the pond."

Britta seemed to consider that. "I wanted to tell ya that Mamma shared some things with me this mornin' 'bout my first mother. That is, after I asked her some questions." Britta's gait slowed considerably. "I can't be sure, but it might've been awkward. She seemed uncomfortable."

"Well, she was her cheery self today when

Polly and family came to visit, though," Susie said, recalling how Mamma had cooed at Nellie Ann and played with little Joey.

Britta's cheeks puffed out as she forced air between her lips. "It was *wunnerbaar* to see Polly an' family again, *jah*. I think it got Mamma's mind off what I'd asked her earlier. 'Least I sure hope so."

Now Susie had to know. "What exactly did ya ask?"

Britta told her the questions and Mamma's answers, and then was quiet.

"Does it help to know?" asked Susie.

"Not really, 'tween you and me."

"Well, I remember layin' eyes on a sweet little baby who wore the softest yellow dress I'd ever seen—one with ruffles, too," Susie said, her *Kapp* strings blowing in the breeze. "Mamma and I instantly fell in love with ya."

Britta nodded. "You've told me that before, and it surprises me that you remember it so clearly."

"Clear as anything. It was wonderful when I came home from school and there you were, though I knew you were a foster baby, like the few others Mamma and Dat had cared for—infants and even several toddlers earlier, before you came along," Susie told her, recalling the initial surprise but also the incredibly warm feelings she'd had upon first seeing Britta. "Mamma sat with me on the settee and let me hold you, sayin' how she'd wished for another child to care for and believed God had answered her prayers." Susie paused. "It might have seemed odd to some people, ya know, for a widow to take in another baby."

Britta was quiet.

Susie reached for her hand. "I'll never forget how you snuggled into my arms, Schweschder. Like we were meant to be sisters. I grew very attached to you and wasn't ready to lose you after the foster care came to an end."

Britta smiled pensively, like there was more on her mind. "When Mamma told ya my name, what did ya think?"

"It was such a perty name for a perty baby. And I s'pose I should have guessed you were born to an *Englischer*—you were dressed that way, that first day—but I never learned for sure. Guess it didn't matter to me. I was just so glad to have ya to love."

Britta was swinging her arms now as she walked. "Well, I still wish *Mamma* would've been the one to name me, 'least after she adopted me." Then for a long time she was silent, as if she'd run out of things to say.

Susie stayed quiet, too, hesitant to break the silence and Britta's obvious reflection.

When they came to where the road curved

away to the home of Aaron Kauffman and his family, Britta stared at the large property, with its several *Dawdi Heiser.* Then she said softly, "I never told ya what Aaron said to me when we were in first grade." Britta shook her head sadly, then turned so she and Susie could head back the other way. "That ornery boy spouted off that I didn't belong here and never would."

"Oh, Britta . . . that must have been awful to hear. What a thing to say!"

"I never forgot it," Britta said, her voice breaking. "It keeps goin' round and round in my memory."

Susie continued to hold her hand while they walked, the sound of crickets in the thickets nearby as lightning bugs flickered over the meadow. "Remember, you'll *always* be my sister, and Mamma's daughter, too."

Britta glanced at her. "I know, and I'm grateful."

"Aaron wasn't thinkin' when he talked like that," Susie added.

"Honestly, I wonder how many others think that 'bout me." Britta sniffled, but she clung to Susie's hand.

"No one that I know," Susie said adamantly.

Just then, a boy flew past them on an Amish scooter, right down the middle of the dusty road. Susie looked and thought it might be the same impudent boy Britta had just mentioned. But Britta seemed too absorbed in her thoughts to have noticed whoever it was, which was probably a good thing.

As they walked toward home, Susie realized that, from this end of the road, Hickory Lane seemed to stretch out far into the distance before it faded almost out of sight, skirted by cornfields and alfalfa on either side. Behind them, in the opposite direction, an early Fourth-of-July firecracker went off, followed by two more distant explosions.

"Do *you* know anything more 'bout my adoption?" Britta asked unexpectedly.

"Only that it took a while before Mamma could officially adopt ya. Sometimes it's like that." She paused. "And I remember prayin' that we'd get to keep you."

"Would Allen or Polly know more, do ya think?" Britta pressed.

"I've never heard either of them talk about it."

Britta let go of Susie's hand and began swinging her arms once again. "Well, someone's gotta know somethin'," she murmured.

"Why not ask Mamma again?"

"She wants to wait till I'm older."

Susie wondered why that was, as well as why not having answers burdened Britta so.

"S'pose I oughta be submissive and quit askin' so many questions."

Susie glanced at her. "Could ya pray 'bout it?"

Her sister sighed. "I have . . . many times."

Susie slowed her pace. "This seems awful hard for ya, sister. I'm real sorry."

Britta nodded her head slowly. "I've kept it inside for all these years." She wiped her eyes. "Not sure I can wait five more to know where I came from."

Susie swatted at a shrill pitch near her ear. Then came the tiny prick on her cheek. *Mosquitoes!* she thought. "What's it matter where ya came from?"

Britta laughed a little. "That's kinda what Hazel said."

"Isn't where you are now more important?" Susie asked, then added more softly, "Ella Mae once told me that patience is a virtue the Lord rewards in His time."

"Must be where Mamma got that idea."

"Well, that, and from the Good Book," Susie reminded her, thankful Britta felt comfortable talking to her so freely now.

CHAPTER 17

The hot, sticky days of summer slogged along, and with the heat came an abundant harvest of vegetables and berries. The mosquitoes were thicker than in recent summers, and one could hear the chirping of grasshoppers from sunrise to sunset.

Susie and Britta took turns working in their garden and at their roadside farm stand, selling the surplus once the canning and preserving were done. When neither of them could be out there assisting customers, they left the cardboard honor box with its slot for payment.

Meanwhile, Mamma tended the little shop, where it was a bit cooler, thanks to a large gas-powered fan Henry had hauled over.

While the days were long, Susie took time to answer Obie's newsy letters when they came. She also went out with Del every couple weeks or so, which was about all either of them could manage during this busiest season of the year.

As September approached, Susie continued to be touched that Obie wrote to her so faithfully, offering an inside glimpse at his life in Sugar Valley. He even described some of the youth work frolics there, as well as the enormous corn maze at a nearby farm—though he made it clear he didn't have a lot of time to engage in such activities. In October, he also wrote of driving two big work horses to pull a hay wagon one night, instead of participating with the group of *die Youngie* out for the hayride. Susie wondered why.

Yet there was one subject Obie never touched on: Del's intentions. And she wondered if Obie would ever broach the topic. *He must assume we're getting serious by now*, she decided.

The harvest season came around again, and Susie used Dat's old wheelbarrow to transport large pumpkins and gourds from their garden to the farm stand out front. Britta had grown many chrysanthemum starters in pots in the daylight basement, then later brought them outdoors to grow larger in order to sell, too.

Twice in a single week, Del Petersheim dropped by to purchase a pumpkin and, the second time, a basketful of gourds for his mother. He invited Susie to go out with him and his friends Mervin and Cindy Jane— once to play Ping-Pong and, on another occasion, Dutch Blitz at the Gordonville home of Cindy Jane's aunt. Susie was happy to accept, but the more time she spent with Del, the lonelier she felt around him. He was kind enough, but he didn't understand her as well as Obie, and he didn't share the kinds of things Obie would have known she liked to hear. Yet she recognized it was unfair to compare him to Obie.

Do I just need to give our friendship time to grow? she mused. *How much longer should we continue to see each other?*

In late November, as they rode home from yet another double date, Susie thanked Del politely for his attention to her and the fun outings they'd shared, saying she was going to step back from dating for a while. Fortunately, Del seemed to take it in stride, not asking any questions and telling her how much he'd appreciated getting to know her before relaying that Mervin and Cindy Jane were very close to being engaged.

Susie was glad for the kindhearted couple, but she couldn't help wondering if she would ever meet someone who loved her enough to court . . . and eventually marry.

The snow fell so heavily the first Wednesday in December that it pattered against the windowpanes as Susie sat in the front room by the black coal-burning stove to read Obie's latest letter. She enjoyed his account of interacting with the repeat customers who'd become his friends, but the news he was coming home for Christmas caught her completely off guard. *His family will be happy,* she thought, feeling quite pleased herself.

Reading on, she was delighted to learn that he wanted to see her while he was home. She recalled the many Christmases they'd gone ice-skating on the pond by the willow grove, and the Christmas evening he had come to play Dutch Blitz with them and been stranded overnight when the snow became so deep and the winds so fierce that the roads drifted over. Mamma had folded several large quilts and blankets to make a comfortable pallet for him in the front room near the coal stove. The next morning at breakfast, Obie had kept them all in stitches with his stories and jovial personality.

Susie realized now she was daydreaming and looked at Mamma, sitting nearby. "Obie's comin' home for Christmas," she said with a glance at the letter.

Mamma chortled. "*Ach*, Susie, no wonder your face is glowin'."

Flustered, Susie backtracked a bit. "It's just nice that he plans to visit, isn't it?"

Mamma set her mending aside and gave her a thoughtful look. "Are ya happy Obie's coming or mostly surprised?"

Susie didn't have to think twice. "Both."

"Well, bein' happy's a very *gut* thing," Mamma said, her voice ever so tender now.

Susie pondered that and wondered how she'd feel seeing her friend again after all this time.

The following Sunday, another storm blew in—a ground blizzard, where snow slithered down the road like long white snakes. The mile and a half to Preaching service with the horse and buggy was hard going. Thankfully, after braving the weather to go out and milk the goats early that morning, Britta had urged Susie and Mamma to bundle up extra warm. She'd even heated some bricks to place at Mamma's feet in the carriage, to help her stay warm enough.

With the weather worsening, they left church before the fellowship meal. Once she'd helped Susie unhitch the carriage, Britta plodded out to the stable again to feed and water the horses, the pony, and goats. While there, she glanced at the telephone on the wall, wishing she could just dial up Hazel, whose family had a phone in one corner of their big barn. Something had crossed her mind about her adoption, and she longed to talk with Hazel privately about it. But, of course, with Hazel not knowing ahead of time about the call, it was unlikely anyone would even answer.

Besides that, the wind was so severe and the snow so heavy, she ought to get her chores done and head back to the house right quick. Dismissing her urge to call Hazel, Britta began to scoop up the feed and pour it into the horses' trough, working quickly.

When she was finished, Britta opened the stable door to snow falling so fast it was hard to see where to walk—she could make out only the dark tree trunks. *The snow hides some things and defines others*, she thought as she leaned into the harsh wind and cold.

Once the Monday washing was hung in the basement and Jonathan Ebersol had come to plow the driveway open, Susie and Mamma donned their snow boots and headed on foot to help Liz wash and cut up the chickens that Jonathan's widower brother, Joel, had just butchered two farms away. In exchange for their help, Joel had generously offered to share with Mamma.

After they finished and returned home again, Susie carried the wrapped chicken to the propane-powered freezer in the basement, then spent several hours stitching one of the largest family trees she'd ever agreed to make. Her goal was to complete it well before the school program the Saturday before Christmas. This year, Britta had been chosen to play the part of Mary, and there was even talk that Bishop Beiler's two-month-old great-grandson would represent the Christ Child. Susie could hardly wait, telling herself that her excitement had nothing to do with seeing Obie again.

The temperature had been falling the morning of the schoolhouse Christmas program, and Susie wondered if Mamma should even attempt to go out in the cold. Britta was stringing up Christmas cards over the doorway between the kitchen and the front room, as well as over two of the kitchen windows. Susie had added a couple Christmasy touches in her room, too, decorating her dresser with Obie's pinecone and holly sprig—placed so as not to be readily visible from the hallway.

Mamma suggested Britta bring down the colorful quilted table runner from the upstairs blanket chest, since the red and green would make the kitchen look festive.

Eagerly, Britta ran up to Mamma's room to get it, and when she returned, she remarked how unique the runner was. "I've never seen one like this anywhere else," she said. "Ain't hand sewn, either."

"A gift from a neighbor years ago," Mamma replied.

"*Englischer?*" Susie asked, surprised.

Mamma nodded.

Britta placed the pretty runner on the kitchen table, then stepped back to admire it. "You know, I think maybe Susie or I could make somethin' like this to sell," she said. "Using our treadle machine."

Mamma looked at them, smiling. Then she said, "I daresay Susie doesn't have a speck of extra time, but maybe you could, Britta."

Britta nodded. "I'll draw up a pattern

during Christmas break. If it turns out all right, I'll put it in my hope chest, then make more for customers, if ya think they'll sell."

Mamma smiled. "I'd be happy to display them in my shop."

Britta's face shone at the prospect.

Susie placed two candles on the table and centered them on the Christmas runner. "Have ya memorized your lines for the play?"

Britta laughed. "Actually, I've been practicing while I milk the goats every day," she said. "Really, though, I don't have much to remember. But I do want to please Tessie. Teacher's been helpin' us with our parts for quite a while now."

"You'll do fine, dear," Mamma encouraged her.

Susie agreed. "Mamma's right, and I'll be there to cheer you on."

Britta looked concerned and turned to their mother. "Aren't you goin', too, Mamma?"

"Wouldn't miss it." Mamma glanced out the window, which was beginning to frost over.

"Are ya sure?" Susie asked, worried. "It's awful cold."

"Well, we could call Rachelle Good to pick us up and bring us home." Mamma's eyes brightened. "What do ya say, girls?"

Susie wanted to suggest that she stay

home where it was toasty warm, with no risk of getting chilled. But Mamma's eyes were full of love for Britta, and Susie couldn't bear to discourage her from going.

A large wreath with a red bow graced the schoolhouse door as families entered. Inside, the large single classroom was bedecked with paper chains of red and green draped over the windows, as well as manger scenes drawn on the chalkboard behind the teacher's desk. Paper snowflakes and other artwork by the children decorated the windows.

The schoolhouse was filling up quickly, and the air of excitement was nearly tangible as Susie sat with Mamma along the north wall, where chairs had been set up in rows. The opposite side of the room also accommodated the same amount of seating, and Susie could see Josh and Becky Miller with two of their little children and assumed their older ones were in the program. Verena and Marnie were present, too, as were Bishop Beiler's twin grandsons, Michael and Jonas, and many others.

A number of Susie's school-age cousins, all wearing different colored dresses and matching capes and long aprons, stood along the front left, behind Tessie, who wore a bright green dress and cape apron as she welcomed everyone to this year's Christmas program.

Standing there among the other scholars, Britta looked bashful and uncertain. Susie's heart went out to her, and she hoped her sister would remember her lines.

Partway through the second half, Susie pushed back tears when Britta was seated beside the manger and leaned forward gently to touch the infant, whose tiny hands were moving. If Susie wasn't mistaken, the baby was cooing at Britta. Witnessing this precious exchange, Susie was moved by her sister's very natural portrayal of Mary. *What a wonderful mother she'll be someday. . . .*

Later, as the program was coming to a close, Susie shifted in her chair and happened to glance over at the other side of the room. And there was Obie, looking right at her!

She caught her breath at how very handsome he looked in his Sunday attire—and at his endearing smile as he held her gaze.

Goodness, she thought, trying not to blush and refocusing her attention on the front of the classroom.

As the young scholars lit candles, everyone began to softly sing "Silent Night" in German. Susie could hear Mamma's voice beside her. The glow on her dear face added to the reverent atmosphere, and the words of the old carol were a lovely reminder of that long-ago holy night.

Later, while families stood in line to give gifts of fruit, handmade items, and cards to the young brunette teacher, Susie noticed Hazel with Obie and was touched she'd come for Britta's sake.

Mamma remained seated as Susie walked to the back of the line with a wrapped package of Britta's *wunnerbaar-gut* popcorn balls and a jar of special peanut butter spread. Soon, Britta made her way over to stand with her. "Did ya see Hazel?" Susie asked.

"She's here?" Britta looked around.

Discreetly, Susie pointed to the back of Hazel's and Obie's heads, several families ahead of them.

"I was so busy bein' Mary, I didn't notice her." Britta's eyes shone. "Wait here." And she made her way up to her friend.

While Britta and Hazel greeted each other, Obie glanced back, and seeing Susie, he headed her way. "I hoped I might see ya here," he said, his eyes sparkling as he reached into the pocket of his black coat and handed an envelope to her. "Wait till ya get home to open it."

"Okay. *Denki*." She smiled, her heart ever so happy. "How've ya been?"

"Bein' home again is nice," he said, grinning. "Mamm is spoiling me with her cooking."

Susie smiled. "I'm sure she is. When did ya get in?"

"Last night." He glanced toward the front. "Looks like the line's movin'. I'll talk to ya later," he said, giving her a nod before he headed up to return to his spot beside Hazel.

Susie's face warmed at their brief encounter, and she slipped what appeared to be a Christmas card into her shoulder purse, ever so curious.

18

Susie, Britta, and Mamma stepped out of the schoolhouse and made their way down the walkway just as their driver pulled up. Appreciating the warmth as they settled in, Susie was grateful Mamma had suggested this means of transportation. Mamma sat up front with Rachelle Good at the wheel, and Susie and Britta slid in right behind them in the middle bench seat.

Britta leaned close. "Hazel said a bunch of the youth are goin' caroling on Christmas Eve. But I wonder if I'm old enough."

"Oh, you can go, if ya want to," Susie assured her. "Will Hazel?"

"I think so." Britta glanced at her. "Would you wanna go, too?"

Susie wasn't willing to leave Mamma alone if Britta was going. "I'll just have to see."

Britta nodded. "Remember how we went

caroling one year with Henry and Polly around their neighborhood?"

"*Jah*, and it was such a perty night," Susie said. "All snowy and bright."

"Sounds like the start of a poem," Britta said, smiling.

"I'm anything but a poet," Susie said and laughed softly, happy to have spent the afternoon this way with Mamma and Britta.

By evening, more heavy, wet snow had fallen. And by the time Susie had a chance to finally sit down and open Obie's beautiful Christmas card, the trees and bushes were bowed low to the ground with the tremendous weight of the snow. She went to stand at the window in her long robe, staring out at the countryside, silvery under a three-quarter moon.

Obie asked if I'm going sledding on Saturday, she thought, smiling at what he'd written. He'd said he hoped to see her there, but he had also been clear he was asking simply as a friend.

"He must not know I'm not seein' Del anymore," she murmured as she placed the colorful card beside the pinecone on her dresser. Then, pulling down the window shades, she headed to bed to read the Good Book.

Later, while nestled beneath the warm

blankets and quilts, she tried to convince herself that Obie was just abiding by what they'd established during their months of letter writing. *He still only wants friendship*, she told herself, though she couldn't help being a little confused by the way he'd smiled at her so endearingly during the Christmas program.

The next day was an off-Sunday from Preaching, and following a haystack supper with a variety of tasty toppings for the rice and ground beef, Susie told Mamma and Britta about the latest news while they lingered at the table. According to an *Englischer* neighbor, many homes all over the county, as well as corncribs and other outbuildings, had suffered roof damage from the snow over the weekend. Power lines were also down in Bird-in-Hand, the village of Intercourse, and surrounding areas.

"I didn't see much damage here when I went out to feed and water the livestock," Britta spoke up.

"Thank the dear Lord," Mamma said quietly as she sat at the kitchen table. "We haven't had such a big snow in years."

Susie rose to look out the back-door window, surveying the stable and the carriage shed. "So many branches are down."

"We'll get them cleaned up in no time," Britta said with a glance at Mamma, as though concerned she'd be worried.

"Oh *jah*, Henry'll be over first thing tomorrow." Mamma seemed unfazed. "He always comes after a storm, ya know."

"He and Polly sure do keep an eye out for us," Susie agreed.

The sun penetrated through the mangled mess of willow branches the next morning, illuminating the broken boughs that had splintered and scattered all over the ground. Soon, shrubs and trees began to cast off their white burden as the melting began, with clumps of snow dropping unexpectedly from time to time.

Just as Mamma had guessed, Henry arrived via passenger van with his chainsaw and went to work on the downed limbs even before breakfast. Britta seemed eager to help him, so Susie was content to offer companionship to Mamma indoors, cooking breakfast for all of them.

The noise from the chainsaw made it hard for Britta to talk to her brother-in-law, clad in a black knit hat and woolen scarf. Even though he and Polly still lived in the area, she'd never been close to him or Polly—not like she had been with Allen and Sarah.

Nevertheless, Britta managed to get a question in to Henry, though at first the words froze in her throat before she could let them loose. She wasn't sure if it was the bitter cold or that she was timid about asking.

"I've been wonderin' something."

Henry looked at her right quick, his thick blond bangs visible beneath his knit hat. "*Jah?*"

"Would ya happen to know anything 'bout my adoption . . . or my first mother?"

Henry straightened and studied her. "What do ya wanna know?"

Britta waved, trying to make light of it, but so far, she really hadn't gleaned anything more than what Mamma had already told her. "No one ever talks about it. I mean, doesn't that seem odd to you?"

Henry drew in a breath and let it out slowly. "Well, I don't know much, 'cept you turned out to be the answer to your Mamm's yearnin' for another child," he said, leaning down to gather an armful of branches.

"After Eli died?"

He looked thoughtful. "Polly said she'd been wanting a baby even before that, really— prayed that one of the foster babies she looked after might come up for adoption. And you were the one that came along . . . the one God gave her."

Britta considered this. "Know anything else?"

Henry shook his head. "Even if I did, it'd be your Mamm's place to tell ya." He dropped the branches into a dumpster. "Have ya asked her?"

Britta nodded. "She wants me to be older when she tells me."

"Ah, so ya must be patient, then."

"It's awful hard."

"Just keep yourself busy, and the time'll pass." Henry smiled at her. "You can trust your Mamma to know what's best." He started up the chainsaw again and walked over near the gazebo, where a sugar maple branch was bent and dangling.

Britta, shivering and still needing to eat breakfast before school, walked stiffly toward the house, disappointed.

Susie was delighted when Aendi Emmalyn arrived after breakfast Christmas Eve morning with a pecan pie in her quilted carrier. It was as if Mamma had told her how much Susie wanted to go sledding while Britta was babysitting for the Ebersols'. Surely Mamma knew Susie would have opted to stay home with her otherwise. But, realizing she was free to go, Susie hurried upstairs and pulled on warm leggings beneath her dress and a long apron, and then two heavy pairs of socks, too.

"Have yourself a nice time," Mamma said when Susie returned to the kitchen to put on her snow boots.

Susie gave her a mischievous look. "Just curious, Mamma. How'd ya know I wanted to go sledding?"

Mamma's face turned pink. "A little bird . . ."

Who could've known? Susie wondered, quickly zipping up her boots.

Emmalyn was grinning now. "Kate Yoder mentioned the other day that the youth were havin' a sledding get-together." She raised her eyebrows and continued. "And since Obie's home to visit, well . . . I figured you might wanna go, and your Mamma might just need someone to have some pie and coffee with before we head to market."

Susie opened her mouth to explain that Obie was only a friend, but she reckoned it wouldn't make any difference, not the way Mamma and Emmalyn were smiling at her.

All these December snows will make for good sledding, Susie thought. And by the time she arrived at the slope, quite a few of the youth had already gone down with snow saucers and a couple of toboggans, too, packing the sled run shiny slick in the sunshine.

Cousins Verena and Marnie were walking up to the crest of the hill, where Susie stood, all three wearing dark-colored bandannas and woolen neck scarves. Marnie towed their older brother's big sled behind them.

Verena waved to Susie, trudging through the snow to greet her. "Obie's here, did ya know?" Her breath crystallized in midair.

Susie nodded, glad she hadn't called to her loudly.

"I'm glad you came," Verena said, grabbing her arm to go down the hill with her. "Marnie wants to ride down with Jerome," she said conspiratorially once they got on the sled.

Susie chuckled. "Okay, you've got yourself a sledding partner."

They pushed off, gaining momentum as they went, and Susie recalled how much fun she'd always had with Eli as a child, when they came here to sled with her parents. *Mamma was so healthy and energetic then,* she thought. *And Dat so fun-loving.*

By the time they glided to a stop, Susie and Verena had sailed over at least two hundred feet, and the youth were hooting and clapping high on the hill behind them.

"Now for the fun of walkin' back up," Verena said, laughing.

"Here, I'll pull the sled." Susie reached over to take the rope.

They made steady progress up the steep grade, huffing and panting as they went.

"Do ya think Obie will ask ya to sled with him?" Verena cupped her mittened hand over her eyes as a shield from the sun's blinding reflection off the snow.

"I doubt it."

"But you'd like to, wouldn't ya?"

"It doesn't matter what I want, not when he's returning to Sugar Valley."

Verena frowned. "Love can change things, ya know."

"Goodness, Verena—we're just *gut* friends. And there's more to it."

"Like what?" Verena grabbed the sled rope as they reached the midway point. "It's not like you're seein' Del anymore, ain't?"

"Obie's made a commitment to work for his Onkel. He can't just take that back." Susie stopped to catch her breath and saw Obie waving at her. "Obie's watchin' us," she said quietly.

"Watchin' *you*," Verena said with a bit of a smirk.

Obie stood back from the others, his sled upright as he leaned against it. He was smiling now.

"See? He's waitin' for ya," Verena said, walking ahead with her sled tagging behind.

Susie waved at Obie and started toward him just as Laura Ann caught up to her.

"You and Verena were almost airborne, you were goin' so fast," Laura Ann said, motioning to the sled run.

"It *was* fast—and such fun," Susie said. "Have you gone down yet?"

"*Jah*, on the big toboggan with Jerome, Marnie, and Tessie."

"Tessie Yoder's here?" Susie asked, glancing around for the teacher.

"Just rushed over to talk to Obie, in fact," Laura Ann said, lowering her voice.

Susie could see Tessie with Obie now as the two laughed at something, and to her surprise, she felt a little envious.

Susie enjoyed sledding with Verena and Laura Ann, holding on for dear life, the run was that slick and speedy. Ice crystals hung in the air, and the sun kept peeking out of wispy clouds, its light twinkling like diamonds sprinkled on the snow.

As the three girls climbed back up the incline after the exhilarating ride, Susie tried to just enjoy herself instead of dwelling on seeing Tessie with Obie earlier. After all, they were distant cousins and might simply have been discussing family Christmas plans.

Who knows? she thought, shaking her head. *And why should it matter to me?*

She could see Obie hop onto the toboggan with three other fellows, and with a running start from the last person to jump on, down they went. In unison, they raised their arms high and howled with glee all the way to the bottom.

The parent hosts had built a bonfire on the other side of the rise, so Susie went along with Verena and Laura Ann to warm up. "Ain't the coldest day for sledding, thankfully," Verena said, rubbing her mittened hands together.

"Close enough," Laura Ann said, managing to look cozy in the folds of her thick scarf.

Susie leaned near the fire and listened as the girls bantered and then began to talk of the coming new year. She wondered what it might hold for her and Obie's friendship. Would he continue to write letters to her?

"You all right?" Verena asked Susie, her cheeks rosy red.

"Why?" Susie smiled.

"I *know* ya, cousin." Verena pressed her lips together.

Laura Ann must have detected that Verena wanted to talk privately with Susie, since she walked around to the opposite side of the bonfire, where she mingled with some other girl cousins.

Verena pressed. "It's Obie, ain't so?"

Susie looked away.

"I thought so." Verena was still for a moment, then said more quietly, "It must be hard to care 'bout someone while denying it at the same time."

Susie was surprised both at the words and that her cousin had been so frank. "You really think I'm doin' that?"

"Well, that's somethin' you should figure out yourself." Verena gave her a quick hug. "Remember, I care 'bout ya, cousin." She excused herself and walked around the bonfire to the other side to rejoin Laura Ann, leaving Susie there to contemplate.

It was almost as if Verena had seen Obie coming this way.

"Havin' a *gut* time?" he asked as he came to stand next to her.

She nodded. "Great sleddin', *jah*?"

"The snowpack's perfect." He slapped his gloved hands together and leaned in closer to the fire. "I was hopin' we'd get a chance to talk longer than at the Christmas program."

She smiled tentatively.

"It's been a while," he added casually.

More than six months, she thought, staring at the bonfire, thankful for the warmth.

"And, to be honest, it seems strange bein' back."

She didn't say anything, hoping he'd keep filling the pauses.

"Don't get me wrong—my family's *wunnerbaar* and so supportive of me workin' so far away," Obie said. "I've missed them, but as you know, I've made friends in Sugar Valley."

"Is it starting to feel more like home, then?" She hated to ask.

"In some ways." He glanced at her. "But not in every way."

She didn't dare smile, unsure what he meant, but her heart was listening.

"I'll be headin' back Wednesday," he said. "Onkel Leon has plenty-a work for me to do."

So soon! she thought.

Obie waved at several fellows walking toward the fire, including his brother Jerome. "But it's *gut* to be able to say *hallicher Grischtdaag* in person, Susie."

She nodded, smiling. "*Denki* for the perty card," she said. "And a merry Christmas to you, too."

He stood there, not saying more, but his shoulder brushed against hers, and she suddenly felt tongue-tied.

Following a light supper, Kate picked Britta up in the Yoder family buggy to go caroling with Hazel. Susie was glad for her sister; Britta deserved some fun with the younger youth, especially with Hazel.

Meanwhile, Susie stoked the coal stove in the front room and hummed "O Come, All

Ye Faithful" as she returned to the kitchen to redd up.

"How's Aendi Emmalyn?" Susie asked Mamma while scouring one of the pots. "Did yous have a nice visit this mornin' before market?"

Mamma laughed a little from where she sat at the table writing Christmas cards to hand out tomorrow after Preaching service. "Emmalyn seems glad she doesn't have to cook for Christmas, what with the common meal tomorrow."

"Honestly, I am, too," Susie said. "It'll be easier."

"Emmalyn's immediate family is providing Christmas dinner on Monday," Mamma said. "Like Polly and Henry are doin' for us."

"Polly's bringing roast beef and all the fixings, *jah*?"

Mamma nodded.

"I figured Polly'd want to cook, but I'm happy to make a cake or whatever ya need to round things out," Susie offered.

"Or you could simply *relax* a bit this year, dear."

"Actually, it's harder *not* to keep busy." Susie smiled. "You, on the other hand, can sit and rock Nellie Ann. That'd help Polly out."

Mamma looked wistful. "It'll be our first Christmas without Allen and Sarah and their children," she said, eyes glistening.

Susie rinsed her hands and dried them, then went over to sit with Mamma. "We'll have a nice time with Polly and her family. And we can always call Allen and Sarah, if it's not too cold for ya out in the stable," she said, trying to brighten her mother's spirits.

Sitting there, reminiscing about former Christmases, Susie was glad she'd stayed home tonight since Mamma seemed a little blue.

Dat would want me here tonight with Mamma, if he knew. His heart was always soft toward her, thought Susie.

An hour or so later, Susie heard a knock at the front door. Unusual as it was, Mamma wondered aloud if this might be an "unexpected surprise."

Susie opened the door, and there, standing in short rows across the porch, was a bundled-up group of a dozen or so Amish teens, including, in the front, a smiling Britta and Hazel. Immediately, their voices began to ring out in song, and Mamma slipped quietly to the window to watch and listen as Susie stood at the front door.

The jubilant melody of "Joy to the World"

filled the porch, and Susie and Mamma sang along in English with the verses and the chorus.

"When they're done caroling," Mamma said, "invite them in for cookies."

Susie agreed, thankful she and Britta had made extra cookies and chocolate nut bars for tomorrow and the days following, when Mamma's siblings and families would be dropping in for the holidays. The house would be crowded with all the youth, but having them come by and sing so cheerfully was truly the nicest surprise for Mamma.

As the carolers continued, Susie's thoughts wended their way to Obie, and she wondered what he was doing tonight. She remembered how he'd pressed his Christmas card into her hand at the school program, and she wished she'd had one to give him.

There's still time, she thought, deciding to make one later tonight and hand carry it to him before he left for Sugar Valley.

CHAPTER 20

Christmas Sunday brought an abundance of cheer to Britta, who always looked forward to going to Preaching, particularly on a special Lord's Day such as this. Here lately, she had been thinking ahead to one day being baptized and joining church.

What kind of church would I be joining if I hadn't lived in Hickory Hollow? she wondered, not sure why she was pondering all of this. *Where would I be living right now if my mother hadn't given me up?*

Back home, while she milked the goats that afternoon, she hummed a few of the carols she'd sung last evening with Hazel and the others. The cat trio wandered over, and two of them curled up near the legs of her wooden stool. "It's a happy Christmas Day, don't you think?" she said softly, looking down at the purring felines. Even Tabasco warmed up to her more quickly than usual.

When she finished the milking, the stable phone rang, and it was Hazel calling.

"How'd you know I'd even answer?" Britta asked, surprised.

"You've mentioned the four-thirty milking before—thought I'd take a chance," Hazel said. "Plus, I wanted to talk to you: Guess who just came by to see Obie."

"Susie, maybe?" Britta smiled that Hazel would call about this.

"*Jah*, but she wasn't here for long. Even so, they did see each other on Christmas," Hazel said, a lilt in her voice. "It's a *gut* sign, don't ya think?"

"So *that's* where she went." Britta glanced over her shoulder to make sure she was still alone in the stable. "Glad to hear it."

They talked a while longer, but Britta could scarcely keep her mind off her sister's errand—one she certainly hadn't mentioned. And when Britta hung up the phone, she could hardly keep from grinning. It was practically a gift just knowing Susie had seen Obie again.

Not even a half hour later, Britta heard Susie returning in the family buggy. Eager to talk to her but also not wanting to let on that she knew where Susie had gone, Britta stood by the back door of the house, waiting while her sister unhitched Atta-Girl and then led the mare to the stable.

This being Christmas night, she wanted to spend time with Susie, since Mamma had already gone to her room to unwind from the busy day and be ready for visitors in the morning. Britta felt surprisingly alone and hoped Susie might oblige her.

"Your cheeks sure are red," Britta said, offering to pour Susie some hot cocoa when she came into the kitchen.

"I'll get warmed up right quick." Susie made a beeline to the stove in the corner. There, she stood with her back to it. "Hazel says hullo, by the way."

Britta smiled. "You didn't go to see *her*, though, did ya?"

Shaking her head, Susie laughed. "I took a Christmas card over to Obie."

"Handmade?" Britta pulled up Mamma's rocking chair closer to the heat, enjoying this.

"Of course." She described the pretty candle and the wreath around it that she'd drawn. "It was nothin' like the card he gave me, but it was the best I could do."

"I'm sure Obie was glad to receive anything from you."

"Ain't so sure 'bout that," Susie surprised her by saying.

Britta frowned, hoping she might reveal more.

She looked down at her hands. "He didn't have much time to visit. And I'm not sure we'll get another chance, since his boss wants him back at work Thursday morning. So Obie's makin' the trip back in a few days."

"But his boss is his uncle, ain't so?"

Susie looked more miserable than Britta had ever seen her. "*Jah*," she said. "Evidently Obie's quite fond of his work . . . and of Sugar Valley, too."

Britta wanted to say how sorry she was but sat there rocking, glad her sister had trusted her with this understandable sadness.

The following day, Polly and Henry and their children arrived midmorning for Second Christmas, bringing small wrapped presents for Mamma, Susie, and Britta, as well as oodles of food.

Little Joey was dressed in his black church outfit with its white long-sleeved shirt and narrow black suspenders. The toddler jabbered constantly as he followed Britta all around, even wanting to sit next to her at the table on his black booster seat.

"Look how he likes you! If you can get a ride to Landisville, Britta, you can babysit any time you're available," Polly remarked.

Mamma spoke up from her usual spot at the table. "I'm sure our *wunnerbaar* driver, Rachelle Good, would be happy to take her."

Henry, the only man present, sat at the head of the table in what had been Dat's chair. "That's a long way to come to babysit," he said. "But we'd be glad to pay the driver."

Britta looked over at her mother. "It's up to Mamma."

Right away, Mamma nodded. "All right with me."

Britta was excited at the possibility. Being with sister Polly and family helped to take some of the lingering sting from missing Allen and Sarah.

"Let's ask the blessing," Henry suggested, folding his callused hands and bowing his blond head.

Joey and his older brother, seven-year-old Junior, did the same.

While Britta prayed silently, thankful for this food, she also thanked God for her dear family on this special day after Christmas.

When the prayer ended, Henry cleared his throat and raised his head.

Without delay, Mamma began to pass the platters—roast beef, creamy mashed potatoes and gravy, stuffing, green beans, butter noodles, coleslaw, homemade rolls, and bread pudding.

A feast, Britta thought, hoping she'd have room for a taste of everything on her plate. *With three little kids, how'd Polly have time to make all this?*

When dinner was finished, and Susie's applesauce cake and coconut cream pie were served along with Polly's chocolate pie and soft molasses cookies, Mamma rose and gave eleven-month-old Nellie Ann tiny bites of one of the cookies. Nellie Ann waved her arms happily, then gave Mamma's cheek a pat with her dimpled hand.

Meanwhile, Susie sat next to Junior, who was as fidgety as any child Britta had ever known, and not only at the table—quite different from Joey, still seated next to Britta. This made her wonder what *she* had been like at their ages.

After desserts, Henry opened Dat's old German *Biewel* and read the Christmas story from the gospel of Luke. Even tiny Nellie Ann seemed to listen to the beautiful account of the Christ Child's birth and the angels' visitation to the shepherds that holy night.

Later, when Polly slipped away to the front room to nurse Nellie Ann, Britta quietly followed and sat down on a nearby chair.

"Do you remember when I was a baby?" she asked, feeling more comfortable talking to Polly than she had to Henry the day he'd cleared the broken branches.

Polly smiled. "Oh *jah*. For one thing, ya scarcely ever cried," she said. "You were very sweet . . . still are."

"Mamma's said that, too—that I wasn't a fussy baby." Britta sighed. "I wish there was a picture of me when I was little."

"You know photographs are frowned on," Polly said, looking surprised. She adjusted the lightweight blanket covering Nellie Ann's face while she nursed. "Henry said you were asking him 'bout your adoption, too."

Britta nodded. "I didn't think he'd tell ya."

"Oh, we share everything—no secrets 'tween us." Polly gave her a kind look. "You'll know all 'bout that someday when you're married."

Smiling, Britta thought about one of the good-looking teen boys she'd caught glancing at her on Christmas Eve while caroling—Roy Lantz, a year older at fourteen.

"What did ya want to know?" Polly asked.

Britta wondered what Mamma would think if she walked in and heard them talking like this, but she took the risk. "Well, to start with, who was my first mother?" she asked, lowering her voice to a near whisper. "And why didn't she keep me?"

"I don't know that." Polly shook her head. "Not sure anyone does."

"Not a soul?"

Polly was quiet for a moment. "I'm not sure ya know this, but Mamma didn't think she'd be adding to our family permanently after Dat died. She was so grateful to be able to adopt you after carin' for ya for a couple of years as a foster Mamma," Polly explained, a thoughtful expression on her face. "'Course if *I* was adopted, I 'spect I might be curious like you."

This made Britta smile. "Do ya think it's natural to be this curious?"

"It's hard to know what I'd think or feel if I were in your shoes, really." Polly looked toward the window, then back at Britta. "I do hope ya know how dearly loved you are here . . . in this family."

Britta nodded and wondered how she'd feel once she was of age and hearing Mamma tell her all she knew.

Just then, Henry came in to stoke the fire. "We're gonna play some games in the kitchen," he announced. "Susie's itchin' to take us on in dominoes."

"Okay, I'll put Nellie Ann down for her nap," Polly said.

Evidently their little talk was over, but Britta was comforted to know that Polly would probably be interested in *her* family roots, too, if she were adopted.

CHAPTER 21

Everyone played several games of dominoes, then sat around and sang carols—Britta's favorite part of the festivities. Later, they opened the few simple presents, things like an insulated lunch pack for Henry and a book of home remedies for Polly. Junior and Joey each received bedtime storybooks, and Henry and Polly gave Britta and Susie bath and body wash, and to Mamma, a bottle of lightly scented lilac hand lotion.

Around midafternoon, Susie and Mamma brought the leftover cake and pie to the table to have with coffee or hot cocoa.

"Best be warmin' yourselves before going out," Mamma said as she placed clean forks and spoons in the middle of the table.

By the time Henry and Polly were ready to leave, the sun was beginning to set, and Britta had a little catch in her throat, realizing the day was coming to a close. She wished they would stay around for a late supper, even though they'd all had their fill. It was odd, really, she thought, how having more family around to fill up the house with their familiar voices and presence made her so contented.

Most of all, she was glad for the special moments with her older sister, few though they were, and Britta hoped Polly might visit again soon. And that Polly would line her up to babysit, just maybe.

That next day Susie took the family carriage out on the snow-packed roads with Britta to deliver a cherry pie and some snickerdoodle cookies to Aendi Emmalyn, who lived in a nice-sized *Dawdi Haus* next to her son's place. They were on their way home when they noticed Obie and Jerome parked off the side of the road in their father's enclosed carriage.

"*Was is letz do?*" Britta wondered aloud.

"Looks like they broke down." Susie eyed the carriage and slowed onto the shoulder, then stopped. "Maybe we can help."

Before they even got out, Obie came up

to the driver's side, and Susie opened the buggy door. "Susie! You're a godsend," he said, looking serious. "Could ya give us a lift home?"

"Sure," Susie said, and while Jerome tied their mare to the back of the buggy to lead her home, she quickly got out of the carriage to fold down the front seat so Obie could get in the back. Once Jerome squeezed into the buggy next to his brother and Susie had put the front seat back up, she and Britta climbed back in.

"Dat an' I'll come back later with tools to fix the wheel," Obie explained as Susie picked up the driving lines.

"Thank goodness it ain't blizzarding yet." Susie glanced over her shoulder at them.

"Snow's comin' later tonight," Obie mentioned. "Hopefully won't get too much, since I need to get back to Sugar Valley tomorrow."

"*Jah*, I remember you sayin' that," Susie replied, suddenly wishing Obie and she were the only ones riding together. There was so much she wanted to say to him, but letter writing had become their main way of communicating, and she felt too reticent.

"Say, I meant to ask ya the other day, but besides Britta here, how are your siblings?" Obie tapped Britta's shoulder and chuckled.

"Everyone's fine," Susie replied. "Allen

and Sarah are busy with their brood, of course, and Polly and Henry spent Christmas with us, like usual."

"Does Allen ever talk of comin' back to visit?" Obie asked.

"Not recently, but we would love to see them. Sure seems like we're missin' out on their lives, 'specially the children's. Not sure I'll even recognize them when I see 'em next."

They continued sharing news about each other's families, and Susie recalled the many times they'd played games and gone ice-skating on the pond. Memories all bundled up with the joy that had colored everything those years, at least when Obie was around.

There was the Christmas he had helped Susie string popcorn to decorate over the windows. Mamma had cheerfully let them have their fun; even she was in a better mood with Obie around.

Another year, Mamma let Obie and Susie clean out the big bowl with their fingers when she'd made chocolate pudding. Obie had ended up with a chocolatey nose and lips and afterward had looked around, asking if there just might be another bowl to clean out, too.

"Do you remember makin' taffy one Christmas?" Obie asked unexpectedly. "It was peppermint, I think."

"You're right!" She laughed. "That was, what, back when we were eleven, maybe?"

Britta glanced at Susie, clearly enjoying the banter.

"We should make some again," Obie said.

"Mamma surely has the recipe." Susie wondered why he'd mentioned it and found it interesting that they both were reminiscing. "Remember when we built that strange-looking snowman?"

"The Christmas after Eli died," Obie said. "We were so young."

Susie nodded, wishing he hadn't mentioned Eli. "I was eight, and you were nine."

Jerome spoke up just then. "Why wasn't *I* ever invited over for all this Christmas fun?" He tried to sound dramatic but ended up laughing.

"Oh, you were busy with other things," Obie replied.

"And *I* wasn't even born yet," Britta said. "Not the Christmas ya built the snowman."

"But once you were around, Obie made over you—you used to squeeze his finger ever so tight when you were a baby," Susie told her.

"That's the first I ever heard of it." Britta beamed.

"You had a mighty grip," Obie said, pausing. "And ya made your sister smile again."

"Mamma too," Susie added, enjoying the

back-and-forth chumminess, feeling like she and Obie were the old pals they had always been, yet unable to deny the tug of attraction she felt toward him. Even so, she braced her heart, knowing he'd be off again in no time.

Sugar Valley is his home now. Susie felt a wave of regret—she had missed her chance to share how she truly felt about his going that long-ago day when he'd asked her opinion about the move. *Why didn't I foresee how much I'd miss his friendship . . . and speak up when I had the chance?*

PART 2

22

In the dark, blustery days of January, Mamma came down with symptoms of pneumonia. Especially at night, she struggled with wrenching coughs, so hard and frequent that they caused her ribs to ache. Susie cared for her constantly, and Emmalyn and Lettie, Mattie, and the bishop's wife, Mary, took turns spending time with Mamma, as well, bringing homemade chicken soup and praying beside her. When nightfall came, Britta read the Bible aloud at her bedside, even when Mamma had finally fallen asleep.

Her breathing was so wheezy and shallow that Susie worried they might lose Mamma like they had Dat and Eli, and she prayed earnestly that God would spare her. Susie felt certain her mother needed to be seen by a doctor, but her appeals fell on deaf ears. *Only the dear Lord knows how to make it happen*, Susie thought.

Thankfully, over time, Mamma *did* manage to get back on her feet, but only till early spring allergies, far worse than other years, drained her of energy, causing another setback.

Since Britta had completed her studies at the schoolhouse the previous spring, she and Susie took turns being with Mamma indoors and working at the little shop. These days, Susie and Britta were responsible for making and selling all of its offerings, which included Britta's quilted table runners, as well as the usual popcorn balls, jams, peanut butter spread, goat cheeses, and of course, commissions for Susie's family trees. With that and all the domestic chores, there was very little time for leisure. Britta also continued to help with the Ebersol children whenever she could, and once a month, Polly took Britta back with her to Landisville for the weekend to help with her youngest ones. On those weekends, Susie realized how very much she missed Britta, especially at Saturday market. Mamma often remarked about it, too. Home just wasn't the same without her.

April crept up on them. Letters from Obie had become increasingly infrequent over the past year, so Susie was surprised to receive one saying he'd met someone. He briefly described the young woman whom he'd become acquainted with at the church district there.

I shouldn't keep writing to him, Susie thought, taking the carriage to go confide in Cousin Verena, who was now being courted by Isaac Lapp, Samuel and Rebecca Lapp's grandson.

"It looks like this is the end of my friendship with Obie," she told Verena as they talked quietly upstairs in her room, the door closed for privacy. "Honestly, I'm surprised it took this long for him to find someone." She sighed, feeling terribly sad.

Verena nodded her head slowly, like she was taking this all in.

"I'm going to let him know with one last letter. I'll bow out politely, like he said he'd do for me if I ever got serious with Del Petersheim."

"Oh, Susie . . . I'm so sorry." Verena reached for her hand.

"I guess I knew in my heart this was how things would be. I never had a chance, really."

Verena opened her arms and let Susie cry.

"I wish there was something I could do," she said, her voice cracking.

"But what?" Susie whispered, wiping her eyes as she pulled back. "The boy I've always loved thinks of me as his sister . . . and always has."

Verena reached for her again, and Susie realized they were weeping together.

Britta so wished she had been brave and asked again about her adoption during one of the times she'd read to Mamma while she was so sick with pneumonia. She guessed that, by now, both Mamma and Susie assumed she'd set aside her wonderings. In truth, she'd resigned herself to wait for answers when Mamma was ready to give them, but Mamma's ongoing health issues made her fearful her mother might not live to tell her about her family origins. This worried Britta terribly. Several times, she had wanted to plead with dear Mamma to reveal what she might know earlier, just in case. But, realizing how selfish that might seem, she hadn't gone ahead with it, and thankfully, her mother seemed to rally.

Now, though, the what-ifs crowded in again, and Britta found herself feeling anxious.

She kept herself occupied with working around the house and babysitting, especially enjoying time spent with Polly and the children. But she often realized she was holding her breath for Mamma's health to fully recover from what had been a real scare.

The first Friday in April found Susie still pondering Obie's news while scrubbing down the pantry shelves in preparation for the upcoming canning season. *Has he told his girlfriend about our friendship?*

Leaning down to rinse out her washrag in the bucket of warm water, she kept an ear tuned to upstairs, in case Mamma had another coughing fit or called for her.

Later that morning, Susie gently mixed chunks of canned tuna with some chopped hard-boiled eggs, minced celery, onion, and mayonnaise, placing the mixture on a bed of iceberg lettuce for the noon meal. Since Britta was over with the Ebersol children today, Susie headed upstairs and offered to serve Mamma in her room.

When she entered, Mamma was sitting in her chair, wheezing lightly. Concerned, Susie quickly settled on a different plan. "Would ya like to give Allen a call today? We haven't talked to him in a while."

"Well, I'm guessin' he's very busy out-doors this time of year."

She doesn't want him to know she's suffering again, thought Susie. Then, changing the subject, she said, "I was wonderin' if you'd like your meal brought up here. It's no trouble."

"*Ach*, I'll go down and sit at the table with ya," Mamma replied, getting up from her chair and pausing to cough.

"Are ya sure?" Susie asked, worried.

But Mamma waved it off, like usual, and followed her down the stairs and to the table. As Mamma folded her hands for the silent prayer, Susie inwardly thanked God for the food and asked for renewed health for Mamma, and for wisdom, too.

When Mamma cleared her throat and raised her head after the prayer, Susie was unsure how to broach the subject again. But bring it up she must. *If only Allen could hear Mamma's wheezing, that would get the conversation about going to the doctor started again. She's always listened to him.*

"Well, I'm sure Allen would be glad to hear from you, if ya change your mind. You could just leave a message for him to call back later, if no one answers," Susie added, hoping to convince her.

Mamma peered across the table at her. "You must really want this, ain't so?"

While she would never say it, Susie was very frustrated with her mother for refusing medical help, bad off as she was. "Let's just give Allen a call, okay?"

"My dear daughter," Mamma said, lifting her head, "there's a reason why the ministers urge us to use phones primarily for emergencies or to call for a driver."

"*Jah.*" *But this could turn into an emergency.* Her mother's illness worsened each week. "Still, I don't think it would hurt to call Allen and check up on him and the family. We've done it occasionally before."

Mamma's head turned, eyes probing. "I daresay this isn't so much about Allen. You're worried 'bout me, ain't?"

While that was true, Susie didn't want to own up to the real reason for the call: While Mamma might not budge on seeing a doctor when Susie suggested it, Allen would insist.

"Why don't I make some hot coffee for ya," Susie suggested.

"If ya don't mind, I'd like some herbal tea." Mamma patted her chest. "Feels a bit tight just now."

"Peppermint tea, like Ella Mae's?"

"That or chamomile."

Susie opened the cupboard and reached for the box of the chamomile. "This'll relax ya."

Mamma sighed and took a bite of her

tuna salad, and Susie sat down to eat as she waited for the teakettle to whistle, keeping an eye on her mother.

"Goodness, Susie. You and my sisters have been treating me like I'm near breakable." Mamma turned to sneeze into her hankie.

"Well, your allergies have gotten worse each spring. And the pneumonia was a real scare." Susie paused. "All of us just want to take care of you."

"*Ach*, don't fret over me." Mamma glanced out the window. "You know what the Good Book says 'bout that."

Susie wished again that her mother hadn't dug in her heels against seeing medical doctors—it had been that way for as long as she could remember, even after Polly's struggle with her thyroid years ago. Yet Polly's first visit to the highly recommended doctor in Landisville had changed her life for the better, teaching all of them a valuable lesson—or so Susie had thought.

Why wasn't that enough for Mamma? Susie recalled how exhausted and weak Polly had been at the time, her hair thinning as rapidly as she'd gained weight. That is, until the doctor had prescribed thyroid medication. The difference between then and now was so apparent.

The teakettle whistled, and Susie dismissed her thoughts. "Help is on the way," she murmured softly.

As her mother often did when her asthma flared up, she leaned over the cup and inhaled the steam slowly, deeply, while the tea brewed. There had been times that Susie had even put a towel over Mamma's head to contain the steam.

"This is just what I needed," Mamma murmured, glancing at her. *"Denki."*

A temporary remedy at best, Susie thought, wishing for a bishop-approved way to keep the nasty allergens outdoors or to filter them out of the house. *Just something . . . anything to help Mamma breathe easy again.*

Due to Mamma's lingering poor health, Susie, Mamma, and Britta skipped going to Saturday market the next day. Susie looked in on her upstairs frequently and felt at a loss to know what to do. Observing how fitfully her mother was sleeping, she thought, *Maybe I should just slip away to the stable and place a call to Allen and Sarah without Mamma knowing.*

Tiptoeing out of the room, Susie decided she must alert her brother without delay. He needed to know how bad Mamma's asthma had become.

A soft light trickled through the stable windows as Susie hurried to the wall phone beyond the horse stalls. Quickly, she dialed the number for her brother's barn phone.

On the third ring, Sarah answered. "Oh, Susie! It's *wunnerbaar* to hear your voice! I was about to call you and leave a message."

"Hope everyone's all right there."

"Oh *jah*, we're fine." Sarah went on to say she'd been meaning to catch up on things back home. Then she asked, "How's your Mamma? Haven't heard a peep from her in a while."

Susie was relieved she'd asked. "Honestly, she's not doin' so well, but *she* would say not to worry . . . that she has some *gut* days mixed in with the bad."

"I'm sorry to hear she's ailin' again."

"She drinks a fair amount of tea, but that only does so much, as ya know," Susie said. "Mamma tries other natural remedies, too, especially that syrup she likes, but I think she needs a doctor."

"*Ach*, such a challenge," Sarah said. "I suppose she won't agree to that?"

"*Nee* . . . not Mamma." Sighing, Susie added, "Even going for a consultation might be helpful—if I could get her to agree." She went on to ask if Allen might call and leave a voice message for Mamma specifically. "Just keep me out of it, okay?"

Sarah chuckled into the phone. "Your mother is one to do things her way, but I understand not wanting to spend the money to see a doctor. Our Maggie's had to go quite a number of times lately, so I do know that."

"*Jah*, but it could turn into an emergency . . . 'specially at night, and then what would we do?" Susie hoped she didn't sound pushy, knowing that, like Mamma, Allen and Sarah usually preferred alternative healing methods. "She's just so stubborn."

"That determination might be why she's made it through this long, what with your Dat gone and all," said Sarah, then added, "But I'll be sure to mention your concerns to Allen."

"Thank you, Sarah."

"How's Britta?" Sarah asked.

"Oh, she's a hard worker—enjoys helpin' in the shop and sewing and cleaning house. She also likes helping Polly with the children, though I think she missed being able to attend school this year. She does see her friend Hazel and other girls their age through their small buddy group."

"Britta's real perty. It won't be long before the fellas take notice, if they haven't already."

"That she is."

"You and your Mamma have your work cut out for ya when she's old enough to court," Sarah replied, a smile in her voice. "Well, tell Britta to give us a call sometime. We enjoy talking to her, too."

Susie agreed to let her know, then asked, "How're my nephews and nieces?"

Sarah was quick to tell her about the children, particularly their eldest, Al Junior. "He's practically jumpin' up and down about a job offer to build toolsheds with an Amishman from our church district here."

"Sounds like a *gut* fit for Al."

"He's mighty happy to make money from someone besides his father," Sarah said, laughing a little.

Susie listened as Sarah continued down the line of the younger children—Jake, Dora, Tilly, Yonnie, and, of course, little Maggie.

When they'd hung up, Susie felt a wave of guilt for going behind Mamma's back with this call. But with her well-being on the line, what choice did she have?

Then she remembered that Sarah had said she was getting ready to phone them anyway. *You did the right thing, contacting them.* With all of her heart, Susie hoped Allen would soon phone and leave a message for Mamma like Sarah had mentioned.

When the hoped-for call and voice mail for Mamma came that evening, Susie was mighty thankful. The only problem was that

Mamma said after listening to it that she suspected Susie of putting her brother up to it.

Susie reassured Mamma how deeply she cared about her. "I did what you would've done if you were in my shoes," she said as they sat together in the front room near the coal stove. "Ain't so?"

Mamma didn't react to that. Instead, she said, "Allen invited me for a visit come June."

Surprised, Susie asked, "Did he say anything else?" A trip hadn't exactly been what she'd had in mind.

"Not much. He sounded worried on the message he left—said he hoped I'd try some healthy remedies he knows about while I'm there."

No talk of a doctor. Why not? Susie realized that nothing had been accomplished.

Mamma continued. "Allen did mention that a change of scenery might be *gut* for me."

Susie nodded, her mind churning.

"He also said the visit could be an experiment to see how I do there."

This news bothered Susie. Didn't Allen think she was taking good care of Mamma? *Have I opened a can of worms?*

For a while, Mamma simply sat and looked

out the window. "For some time now, I've been wishing I could visit them . . . see my grandchildren again." She sighed. "Seems ever so long since they left, and it's too hard for all of them to come back here to visit. 'Specially with their farm."

During less stressful times, Susie herself had wondered what Allen and Sarah's life was like in Missouri. "Are ya thinkin' of going, then?"

"I'll pray 'bout it. Might talk it over with Ella Mae, too."

"Maybe Polly and Henry can help ya decide," Susie suggested, wondering how many weeks Allen was thinking.

"Oh, Polly would just want me to get a doctor's prescription for one of those drugstore inhalers she's been talking 'bout." Mamma grimaced.

"What if it helped?"

Mamma was already waving her hand in protest. "If the Good Lord wanted us to use such things, He would've made it clear."

"Well, you use folk medicine. . . ."

"Far better," Mamma retorted.

Susie didn't want to continue arguing, so she held her tongue. *I'll just keep praying*, she thought, still disappointed that Allen's voice mail hadn't encouraged Mamma to seek medical help.

It wasn't till two days later that Susie finally replied to Obie's letter, explaining that it would be her last, since he was now dating someone seriously. *I'm happy for you, Obie.*

She signed off, then went out and placed the letter in the mailbox, trying not to let the emotion overtake her.

I'll miss hearing from him, she thought, resigned to this as she headed back to check on the clothes drying on the line. *But it's only right for Obie to focus his attention on his girlfriend.*

Later that day, while waiting for Britta to return home from babysitting for the Ebersols, Susie and her mother chopped cabbage for slaw at the kitchen counter.

"I've prayed 'bout Allen's invitation," Mamma announced.

In spite of her misgivings, Susie had come to the conclusion that Allen needed to see Mamma's struggles firsthand. *Maybe then he'll urge medical help.*

"I think I should go."

Susie was relieved. "Do ya feel strong enough to make the trip?"

"How long a ride is it?"

"I'm not sure, but Allen can tell ya. It'll certainly take most of a day, though."

"I'll ask when I call him back," Mamma replied.

Susie set down her knife. "Have ya said anything to Britta about possibly going?"

"*Nee*, since I haven't decided."

"Well, Allen must think it's okay for you to go. Healthwise, I mean."

Mamma brushed off her chopping board. "Actually, you know me better than Allen these days," she said. "What do *you* think?"

Susie hadn't expected this. "Honestly, if I could get away, I'd go with ya. I hate to see you go alone, but I'm sure it'll do ya good to see all of them."

Mamma didn't dispute that. "You'd like to see Allen and family, I don't wonder."

"*Jah*, and Britta would, too." Susie frowned. "But we can't afford for all of us to go, and I wouldn't want to ask Allen to foot the bill. And there's the livestock to care for, too, and your little shop."

"Maybe someday," Mamma replied.

"Maybe," Susie said, feeling uneasy.

24

Late April brought the anniversary of Eli's passing. This year, Susie went to the accident site in galoshes and a raincoat, carrying her black umbrella, as the sky had opened up and poured buckets of rain all that day.

The usual bouquet of flowers with its blue ribbon was nowhere in sight, and it struck Susie that Eli's death, and Dat's, too, might eventually fade in people's memories. *Yet our family will never forget*, she thought, wondering if Mamma would be well enough to visit the cemetery once the ground dried out.

Susie took her still-frail mother over to visit Ella Mae. She waited in the carriage, cross-stitching, to give Mamma and her friend some time alone. After an hour or more of working her smooth stitches, Susie saw Ella Mae's screen door swing open, and Mamma stepped out. Setting aside her stitching, Susie got out of the carriage to make her way up the walkway, her attention on Ella Mae's little white porch, which was decked out with its familiar potted red geraniums, already bright and flourishing.

Susie walked up the steps and offered her arm, but Mamma stood there waiting for Ella Mae to step outside, too.

"It's delightful to see ya, dearie," Ella Mae said to Susie as she came out, a twinkle in her eyes.

Susie smiled, glad to see her. "I hope you and Mamma had a pleasant chat."

"Oh, we did." Ella Mae turned to grin at Mamma. "We certainly did."

"*Jah*," Mamma said. "I've told Ella Mae about Allen's invitation, and I'm thinkin' it'd be wise to stay put here for the summer."

Susie glanced at Ella Mae, who must have had something to do with this decision.

"I'll go to Missouri when I'm stronger," Mamma continued, and Ella Mae's head bobbed.

"September's actually a better time to travel." Ella Mae's small voice sounded encouraging and sweet.

Feeling torn about this news, Susie said, "Well, Britta will be glad if you're here for her fifteenth birthday." At that, she noticed the two women exchange quick looks, and it made her wonder. Offering her arm again to Mamma, this time they walked down the few stairs together, Mamma leaning hard on her.

"*Denki* for the visit, Ella Mae," Susie called over her shoulder.

"Take plenty of herbal syrup, Aquilla," said Ella Mae. "And let your girls help ya however they can."

Will that be enough to get Mamma through the summer? Susie worried.

The heat and humidity of early July made being outdoors plain miserable for Britta. Even so, she had been looking forward to attending a small gathering over at Hazel's neighbors' farm, home to the Lantz family and newly widowed Frona Glick. She was excited that Hazel and Cousin Marnie would be there, as well.

Susie, however, had quit attending any gatherings, including the Singings, when Mamma had fallen so ill last winter.

As Susie drove her over in the buggy that Monday evening, Britta remarked, "I wish you could come, too, Susie. I feel strange bein' the one to represent our family when I'm the youngest."

"Oh, I don't mind stayin' with Mamma. Besides, you're as shy as a fawn, so it'll be nice for ya to do something without your big sister hovering, 'specially so near your birthday."

"I've never felt that way." Britta paused and looked at her with compassion. "I've heard Mamma and Polly encouraging you to date here lately, but how are ya supposed to make that happen if ya don't go to Singings and whatnot?"

"Well, no sense worrying 'bout me. You just have a nice time bringing cheer to Frona tonight," Susie replied. "Do ya have someone to bring ya home?"

"Oh, I'll find someone," Britta said, knowing from experience that Susie wouldn't leave Mamma alone. She truly hoped Mamma wouldn't be sickly from now on. Or worse, succumb to her frail condition.

Insects fluttered and tapped against the carriage windshield while Britta tried to relax in the front seat next to Susie. Remnants of pink-tinged clouds were still visible in the west as the sun made its steady descent. Not far away, the Lantzes' farmhouse came into view.

Brambles continued her rhythmic trot, and Britta tried to imagine what it might be like a year from this July, once she was finally sixteen and attending her first-ever youth Singing. What would it be like to walk into the haymow and sit with the girls at the long table Susie had so often described, joining her own voice with the others in song? Hazel would be there to welcome her, Britta was certain. Turning sixteen would also mean being permitted to meet potential boyfriends, which could someday lead to courting.

And closer to hearing Mamma tell me about my roots, she thought.

Contemplating this, Britta thought again of Susie, always at home with Mamma. Would Mamma's health keep Susie from ever having a serious beau and a family of her own someday? Susie hadn't gone out with anyone since Del Petersheim, and the letters from Sugar Valley had ceased a few months ago.

My poor sister has no prospects for marriage.

Outside the Lantzes' spacious farmhouse, Britta spotted Hazel and Cousin Marnie waiting for her. Both were dressed in subdued colors—dark brown and gray.

"I'm so glad you came," Marnie said with a smile.

"Got your singin' voice ready?" Hazel asked.

"I'll do my best," Britta replied, seeing widow Frona Glick already seated, all in black.

The three took their seats with a few other women on one side of the front room, much like at a Preaching service. The men and boys sat on the opposite side. Only about thirty were there.

Someone blew a pitch pipe for the first song, "Jesus, Lover of My Soul," and the men began to sing the first verse with fervor.

The music was so inspiring, Britta got goose pimples on her arms and could hardly wait for the chorus. The song raised her spirits, even though she wasn't feeling blue, really—more tentative than anything.

The next song was "Love Will Bring Us All Together," and Roy Lantz's father instructed them to take turns yet again, with the men singing first, followed by the women.

At that moment, she saw Roy himself looking her way. *My goodness, he's even smiling at me!* She must have turned several shades of purple, yet she steeled her nerves . . . and smiled back.

Glancing away, Britta considered the fact that she was too young to court, and here she was already smiling back at a fellow. It certainly seemed like good-looking Roy Lantz was watching her, right in the middle of this beautiful and spirited song.

After a dozen or more songs, the group concluded their special singing and mingled as family members took turns talking to Roy's grandmother, who shook each person's hand and thanked them for coming. Eventually, Hazel said good-bye to Britta and Marnie to head home on foot.

Britta, however, stayed around to talk to Cousin Marnie, glad to have this opportunity, since she rarely saw her when Susie and Verena weren't along.

"Is Susie busy tonight?" Marnie said, slightly frowning.

Britta nodded her head. "At home with Mamma."

"Poor Aendi Aquilla . . . I wish somethin' could be done to help her."

"*Jah*, it's so hard to see her struggle."

"Has she gone to the Amish doctor?"

"Mamma won't go to him or any sort of medical doctor, either."

"What about an herbalist?" Marnie suggested. "My Mamma sees one now and then over in Ronks. I could give ya her number, if it'd help."

"That's kind of you." Britta wanted to talk more privately with Marnie. "Will ya walk with me out to the porch?" she asked.

They headed through the kitchen and the back screen porch, where rows of coats on wooden pegs hung in a line. Then they stepped outside, the sky alight with stars.

"What's on your mind?"

Britta felt a little bashful. "Have you ever heard anything 'bout my birth mother?"

Marnie shook her head. "Verena said you asked her about this once a long time ago. I didn't realize you were still interested."

"Well, I'm just tryin' to piece things together." *In case Mamma can't,* she thought solemnly.

"Surely your Mamma knows about it."

"I hate to bother her, considerin' her health," Britta said, and it was true . . . for the most part.

"Would ya want me to poke around, see what I can find out?"

"Better not. Just keep the fact I asked 'tween us, all right?" Britta felt nervous at the thought of Marnie doing any sniffing around. *What if Mamma found out?*

Right then, Roy opened the screen door and walked out with two of his cousins.

Once the fellas left to head toward the barn, Marnie said, her voice hushed, "Maybe ya didn't notice, but Roy kept lookin' over at ya tonight."

Britta felt her face warm. She'd noticed, all right, just as she'd noticed Roy at other times. Secretly she wondered if he might ask her out once she was old enough. *Another whole year.* It felt so far away.

Marnie continued, "Ya probably know he's already sixteen, but as far as I know, Roy hasn't asked a single girl out since he started goin' to Singings a few months ago."

Britta found this interesting. "Wonder why he hasn't."

Marnie laughed softly, covering her mouth with her hand. "Why do ya think?"

"Uh, let's not get the cart before the horse," Britta said, suddenly embarrassed.

"Well, ya never know—things can happen quickly sometimes." Marnie went on to mention how she and Jerome had become good friends right away. "For a long while, he just took me home after Singings and other activities, not really pushing for a date or anything more. We're still *gut* friends, of course, but here lately, he's been holdin' my hand. So things are changing."

"I s'pose it *would* be nice to date your friend." Britta thought of Susie and Obie, and it made her sad to think how they'd drifted apart.

"Mamma says it's the best way," Marnie said. "'Cause later in life, after your children are married and gone, you still have your *wunnerbaar-gut* friend to grow old with."

Britta caught herself nodding in agreement. "Poor Mamma, losin' her husband before she could enjoy that time with him after Susie and I are grown and gone."

Marnie smiled kindly. "Do ya believe Susie will ever marry?" she whispered.

"I hope so."

"Do ya think she feels responsible for your Mamma, since Allen and Sarah moved away? And maybe because of what happened to Eli . . . and Onkel Caleb, too?"

Britta pondered this, unwilling to share about Susie's and her conversation on the buggy ride over.

"*Ach*, don't tell her I said that," Marnie added suddenly.

"Then we best not talk behind her back." Britta said it with a smile, meaning it.

25

Cousin Marnie said good-bye to Britta the minute Jerome Yoder showed up in his courting carriage. It was then that Britta realized she'd waited too long to get a ride home, although talking with Marnie had been very nice.

Britta made her way down the long walkway, aware of how mild the evening was now as a soft breeze cooled her brow.

Walking back from the barn was Roy, who pushed his hands into his trouser pockets. His gaze glided up, and she knew he'd spotted her.

Her stomach clenched, her mouth as dry as yarn.

"Hullo, Britta," he said. "Did ya enjoy all the songs?"

She bobbed her head shyly. "I hope it cheered up your Mammi Glick."

"No question 'bout that." Roy took a step closer. "Say, you're not walkin' home alone, are ya?"

"*Jah*."

"Well then, let me take ya right quick," Roy said. "Dat's carriage is already hitched up."

Surprised yet pleased, she wasn't sure what to say, but she found herself falling into step with Roy as they walked toward the parked family buggy. Self-conscious, she recalled Marnie's comments about Roy not dating anyone yet, months into his *Rumschpringe*.

"Careful getting in." Roy offered his hand.

"*Denki*." She was thankful the night kept him from seeing the blush that heated her face at his touch. As she got settled into the buggy with its dashboard of switches for the side and back lights, he walked around to the driver's side. "Really, I could've walked," she said when he reached for the driving lines.

He glanced at her. "I don't mind."

She immediately felt shy, though she managed to ask, "What songs did ya like best tonight?"

As he steered the horse and carriage out of the driveway and into the turnaround, then toward the road, Roy named off several, including "Shall We Gather at the River."

Britta hoped he'd do all the talking, though she assumed that might not be what *he* was hoping for. And she thought again of his kindness in driving her tonight.

"Do you have a favorite, Britta?" he asked, shaking her out of her musings.

"'What a Friend We Have in Jesus.'"

"Mammi Glick likes that one, too. In fact, she sings it whenever she feels the saddest. Since Dawdi died . . . well, she's sung that one a lot. Says it's a source of comfort." Roy went on to share that his grandmother was a strong believer. "She likes to tell 'bout bein' a young schoolteacher, right out of eighth grade, and feelin' mighty timid. But with God's help, she grew into her role as a teacher. *'Like anything else,'* she says, *'ya step into it by faith and learn as ya go.'*"

"Sounds like a wise woman, for sure," Britta replied. She was glad Roy was so laid-back and kind; she enjoyed spending even this short amount of time with him. Pondering that, she realized with a start, *This is my very first ride alone with a fella!*

Susie decided to wait up for Britta, just as Mamma had often stayed up for her. She hoped her sister had gotten over her nerves once she was with Hazel and Cousin Marnie, both of whom were more outgoing.

A few minutes later, Susie heard a buggy come down the road and come to a stop in front of the house. *Marnie must've brought her home*, Susie thought, slipping on her cotton robe.

It wasn't long before she heard Britta's quick footsteps on the stairs, and Susie hoped she'd want to talk.

Stepping into the hallway, she saw Britta, all smiles. "By the looks of you, I'm guessin' you enjoyed tonight."

Britta nodded and quickly followed Susie into her room. "It was so special, really. Maybe a bit like what heaven will be like." She went on to tell about the various people who'd come to cheer up Frona. "And you'll never guess who brought me home."

"Not Marnie?"

Britta's eyes shone. "Roy Lantz . . . but don't tell Mamma," she added softly. "He didn't want me to walk home by myself."

"Well, everyone knows Roy's a fine young man. Devout too. He's already taking baptismal classes to join church this September."

Britta smiled and glanced down for a moment. "He's so nice, Susie." Pausing, she looked at the kerosene lamp on Susie's bedside table. "'Tween you and me, I think he likes me. Marnie said so, too, but 'course, even if he wants to, I won't be able to date for another whole year." She sighed. "Seems like all I do is wait."

"You'll have plenty to keep ya busy between now and then," Susie said, going to the dresser and getting her brush. "Just trust the Lord to give ya the patience till that time comes. . . . He'll never lead you astray."

Britta nodded. "I'll do my best. *Gut Nacht,* Schweschder," she added, a little more shyly now. "I enjoyed our talk."

"So did I. And I'm glad you had such a pleasant evening." Susie watched her sister head across the hall to her own room, curious about Roy's apparent interest.

Mamma already had eggs sizzling in her cast-iron skillet when Susie hurried into the kitchen the next morning. "You're an early bird," Susie said, opening the apron drawer, pulling out a white half apron, and tying it around her waist.

"I heard yous up talkin' last night," Mamma said, seeming livelier today. "Did your sister enjoy bein' at the Lantzes'? I hope she was an encouragement to their family during this hard time."

"Maybe Britta will tell you 'bout it. She'll be down soon." Susie glanced over her shoulder.

Mamma nodded. "Eggs an' bacon'll be ready shortly."

A few minutes later, Britta came into the kitchen, wearing a yellow dress and matching cape and apron.

Like a ray of sunshine, Susie thought, noting how cheerful her sister seemed and recalling their sisterly talk last night.

"Was it a nice turnout for Frona?" Mamma asked as she dished up the eggs and bacon onto each of their plates.

Britta said it was and went to make the toast. She poured some coffee for herself and Susie while waiting for the toast and remarked about some of the same things she'd told Susie last night, but left out Roy's name or how she got home.

Wednesday morning, Susie stared at the slant of sunlight falling across the counter in their little shop, thankful for this moment to reflect on Britta's noticeably more joyful countenance since Monday evening. If she wasn't mistaken, her little sister had the start of a crush on Roy Lantz, and it just might be the answer to Susie's prayers for Britta's "running-around" time, starting next year. *Rumschpringe* was for pairing up and meeting fellows in the church district, but for some, it was also a time to dip a toe into the outside world. Given Britta's interest in her adoption, Susie had worried this time could also lead Britta to go in search of her biological family, potentially leading her away from the Amish church and the People. *Her birth mother was English, after all. . . .*

Susie considered her family's losses. For her and Mamma, Britta's going outside the Plain community to search for her family roots could be a sort of loss. Not on the same level of sorrow as Dat's or Eli's passing, of course. Still, it troubled Susie whenever her sister started asking questions about her past.

Saturday evening, after a busy day at market, Susie was sweeping the back porch when Verena came by on her scooter and parked it at the end of the walkway. Glad to see her, Susie waved and went to meet her.

"Poor cousin! Aren't you all sweaty," Susie said, motioning Verena to go with her to the shade of the porch. "I'll get you a cold drink," she offered and hurried inside.

When she returned, Verena was seated on one of the porch chairs and fanning herself with the tail of her long black apron. She smiled, accepted the iced tea, and took several long drinks before continuing the fanning. "*Gut* thing I didn't come over earlier," she said as she wiped her face with a hankie. "Awful hot today."

Susie agreed. "It was nice to be in air conditioning with Mamma at market most of the day."

"Didn't Britta go?" asked Verena, glancing around for her.

"She's in Landisville again, helpin' Polly with the children this weekend."

"An extra pair of hands is a big help."

"And little Joey thinks Britta's the best thing since graham crackers." Susie laughed and noticed her cousin's face still glowed, though perhaps not so much from being overheated during her scooter ride. "You seem mighty happy this evening."

"Ain't I always?" Verena wiped her brow with a hankie.

"*Jah*, but there's something different . . . something more. Am I right?"

"Could be that I'm in love." Verena dipped her head, then she looked back at Susie. "And . . . engaged to marry Isaac Lapp on Thanksgiving Day."

"This is *wunnerbaar-gut* news!"

"Isn't it?" Verena went on to extol the merits of her fiancé, adding, "He plans to rent a house from his father once we're wed." Then, stopping, she reached for Susie's hand. "I'd like ya to be one of my side sitters at our wedding."

"Oh, cousin," Susie said, tears welling up. "I'd love to."

"Marnie will be the other bridesmaid, of course."

Now both girls were fighting back tears.

"It'll be the dearest day," Verena murmured, eyes gleaming.

Susie nodded. "I couldn't be happier for you!" And while she truly meant it, she couldn't help but feel a little wistful.

Verena smiled. "Wanted you to be the first to know after my parents and Marnie," she said, going on to add that, unknown to her, Isaac had talked privately with her father about his proposal weeks ago. "Then last Sunday evening, while we were out walking at sunset, he asked me to marry him."

"So romantic, ain't?"

Verena agreed. "The nicest setting for a proposal, really. I'll never forget it."

Isaac has made her forget any past heartache, Susie thought. "It's obvious the Lord had someone very special in mind for you," she said, truly pleased for her cousin.

Even though Mamma seemed all in from market, it was her idea to make homemade vanilla ice cream. So Susie insisted Mamma rest indoors while she and Verena took turns with the hand crank out on the back porch.

Later, when Susie dished up ice cream for

each of them, she spooned up some straw-berry jam to top it off and invited her mother to join them on the porch. Mamma came outside to join them, cooling her glistening face with a pretty hand fan she'd gotten at a farm sale years ago.

"Are ya lookin' forward to your trip to Missouri?" Cousin Verena remarked.

Mamma nodded. "I really am."

"When will ya go?"

"September. The farther away I get from springtime allergies, the better," Mamma told Verena.

"The grandkids out there are so excited." Susie glanced at her mother. "Of course, Allen and Sarah are pretty happy, too."

"That's a big trip," Verena said, eyes wide, as if concerned.

"The Lord will be right there with me," Mamma replied, still fanning herself.

Susie smiled and prayed all would be well.

Once Verena said her good-byes, Susie finished sweeping the porch as twilight fell. She even went inside to gather up the rag rugs in the sitting room and carried them out to hang on the clothesline, where she beat the dust out of them with a broom, even though she'd done this two days ago. Once the rugs were brought back in and placed in their usual spots, Mamma asked why she was still cleaning so late in the day.

"Just tryin' to keep the dust down for ya."

"Oh," her mother said, looking a bit *ferhoodled*. "Do ya think I'm allergic to that, too?" She continued to study her. "Or is something botherin' ya, dear?"

Susie refused to meet Mamma's eyes. "You know me. I like a spotless house."

Mamma's head tilted as if there was a whole lot more she might like to say.

Quickly, Susie offered her some fresh fruit or warm tea, but Mamma politely declined both. And once Susie finished sweeping, she excused herself to go upstairs to her room, lest she reveal the emotion she'd been holding back ever since Verena's visit.

"The dearest day," Verena had said of her wedding day, and the words continued to echo in Susie's mind as she brushed her long hair, one hundred strokes on each side before bedtime. She had to wonder how she'd feel serving as her younger cousin's wedding attendant.

But no, she knew, oh, how she knew.

The season for love has passed me by, she thought, staring at herself in the dresser mirror, refusing to cry about Obie.

CHAPTER 27

A hint of autumn pervaded the early September air the afternoon before Mamma was scheduled to leave for Missouri. Susie had been working with Britta near the carriage shed, using large sponges to wash down the gray enclosed buggy, both sisters talking quietly about how they would miss Mamma for the upcoming two weeks.

"'Tween you an' me," Susie said, glancing back at the house, where Mamma was doing some last-minute packing, "I'm glad she waited till now to go. For one thing, she's stronger than she was last spring."

"I think so, too," Britta agreed as she soaped the headlights. "It'll be a special time for her. Allen and Sarah will see to it."

"*Jah*," Susie said, a lump in her throat when she thought of the long fifteen-hour journey ahead for Mamma. "I'll be praying for that, and for traveling mercies."

While the three of them awaited the twelve-passenger van's arrival early the next morning, Mamma kissed Susie and Britta on their cheeks and thanked them for "keepin' the home fires burning."

"Of course, Mamma. We love ya and are glad to do it," Susie said as they stood in the kitchen together.

"I love yous, too . . . very much." Mamma's eyes gleamed with tears.

Britta's chin quivered. "You'll write to us, *jah*?"

Mamma coughed several times and patted her black shoulder bag. "My stationery and best pen are right here, along with some stamps. And Allen will leave a phone message for ya once I arrive late tonight."

Susie was heartened by that and picked up Mamma's suitcase for her, trusting that Allen would indeed take good care of their mother, like he'd mentioned when he'd first presented the idea.

Outside, Mamma repeated her good-byes as the van arrived, and Susie and Britta stood at the end of the driveway waving as the Mennonite driver took the bag and helped their mother inside.

Lord, be with Mamma, Susie prayed while she and Britta walked slowly toward the house afterward. She didn't voice her concern to her sister, but she felt it with everything in her.

For the rest of that morning, Susie poured her energy into the start of fall cleaning. The enormous chore began with washing all the windows inside and out, using the extension ladder. Susie and Britta worked together, each of them pointing to streaks or spots missed on either side of the window before moving on to the next.

When the windows were spotless, Susie and Britta scrubbed down the walls and floors. Susie only stopped working at mealtime. Britta was eager to cook, insisting Susie not skip eating just because Mamma wasn't around. But their mother's health and well-being weighed on Susie's mind, especially the little cough she'd had that morning, and she glanced frequently at the wall clock.

After evening prayers, Susie worked on her current family tree, recalling how Eli would often linger in the front room with her parents, sometimes asking questions about

Dat's evening Scripture reading. *My brother's heart was preparing for heaven. . . .*

Eventually, Susie headed upstairs to bed. Long after midnight, she awoke from deep slumber and couldn't find a comfortable position and had a difficult time returning to sleep. She thought of going to the stable to check for Allen's voice mail—surely Mamma had arrived by now. But she made herself stay put, thinking she should try to sleep and simply listen to the phone message in the morning.

But the idea rolled around in her head till she finally dragged herself out of bed, fumbled for her bathrobe, and found the flashlight on her bedside table. Yawning, she made her way out into the dark night and to the stable.

Inside, she shone the light on the old wall phone and listened to the short message from Allen saying that Mamma had arrived. "I'm afraid she sounds a little rough—has a bit of a rasp in her voice and is running a low fever. Hopefully she'll be doing better after some rest, but I'll be in touch to let ya know."

Susie groaned and hung up the phone, then trudged back toward the house. *I shouldn't've let her go. . . .*

The sky was pitch-black, and frogs croaked

eerily in the nearby pond. She turned off the flashlight and stared into the darkness, feeling even more responsible for Britta and the upkeep of the house and livestock.

I must trust God to care for Mamma, she thought, suddenly aware of the night's penetrating chill.

Britta was out in the stable the following afternoon, freshening the bedding straw for their horses and the pony, when the wall phone rang. Startled, she rushed to answer it. "Hullo?"

"Britta, it's Allen."

She tensed at the flat sound of his voice. "Is Mamma all right?" She looked out the window, toward the back of the house, wondering if Susie should have answered instead.

"That's why I called," Allen replied. "Her fever spiked this mornin', and she's developed a cough." He went on to say that they'd taken Mamma to a walk-in clinic. "She didn't wanna go, but Sarah and I talked her into it. The doctor there said she has a pretty bad pneumonia, and because of her asthma, he wanted us to take her to the nearby hospital."

Britta felt a wave of shock at the news. "The hospital? It's that serious?" She felt sick about this. "*Ach,* poor Mamma."

"She's getting *gut* care—don't worry. An' be sure to tell Susie, won't ya?"

She promised to, and Allen said he'd be in touch in a few days, unless, of course, something changed.

For the worse, he means. Hanging up the phone, Britta felt limp. *Mamma must be awful sick. . . .*

Heart pounding, she hurried back to the house to tell Susie, praying all the way for the dear Lord to have mercy on their precious mother.

For the next two days, Susie felt like she was holding her breath for an update on Mamma, sending Britta regularly out to the stable phone to check for a message during the daylight hours. It was hard to feel motivated to do anything, but with the fall vegetables coming on fast now, they had to continue the normal business of canning and working at their roadside stand and Mamma's little shop.

Susie also encouraged Britta to go ahead with her original plan to play volleyball in a few days at Hazel's with a group of other girls. "If Allen calls, I'll let ya know as soon as you return."

Britta frowned, clearly reluctant. "I'm too worried 'bout Mamma to enjoy myself."

"Neither of us can do anything here 'cept pray," Susie said, urging her to try to have some fun.

Allen's next phone call came while both Susie and Britta were in the stable, shoveling out the stalls. Susie literally ran to answer.

"*Gut* news." Allen's voice sounded so good in Susie's ear. "Mamm's steadily improving. And the doctor says she'll be discharged day after tomorrow."

"*Ach*, such a relief!"

"I would've called sooner but decided to wait till we knew more."

Susie wanted to ask what caused the sudden illness, but she couldn't bear to hear that the trip might have been too much for Mamma. "Tell her Britta and I are thinking 'bout her and praying, too."

"I'll do that," Allen said. "How are yous getting along?"

"Doin' okay . . . but missin' Mamma."

"Understandable. She's going to write ya when she feels up to it."

Hearing this made Susie smile. "I'll look forward to it."

"Meanwhile, could you and Britta send her a note?" Allen asked. "Also, since she's been in the hospital for part of her visit, Sarah and I will be keepin' her with us a while longer. We don't want to rush her home without some time to mend."

"I'm not surprised." Susie certainly didn't see the sense of Mamma going out there all that way, just to hurry home.

"We'll look after her real *gut*," Allen assured her. "Don't worry."

Susie was thankful for that. "*Denki* for callin'."

"Okay. Tell Britta hullo, too."

"She's right here, listening to my side of the conversation. She's been helpin' muck out the stalls."

"Wish Henry lived closer; he could help yous with that," Allen said, as if he really meant to say that he wished *he* lived closer.

"It's not the most pleasant chore, but it's *gut* exercise." Susie laughed.

After hanging up the phone, Susie immediately told her sister the news of Mamma's expected release from the hospital the day after tomorrow.

A look of relief passed over Britta's face; then she grimaced. "I hate that she can't come home when she'd planned to."

"I know. But let's be glad Mamma received the help she needed at the hospital. She seems to be recoverin' so much more quickly than last January."

"Thank the Lord for that," Britta said.

Later, after supper and before Bible reading and prayer, both Susie and Britta sat down at the kitchen table to write letters to their mother.

Susie made a fresh batch of chocolate chip cookies after Britta left on her scooter for the girls' volleyball games at Hazel's that afternoon. While the cookies were cooling, Susie slipped off to her room and found the box beneath her bed where she'd kept all of Obie's many letters.

She removed the rubber band and lifted the flap on one of his early ones, written some weeks after the very first. Seeing his familiar handwriting, she paused, something rising in her heart.

Recalling his first mention about writing to her, she easily put herself back in the carriage next to him in her memory. Oh, how happy she'd felt, yet tense. Her first and only ride with her dear friend.

There had been another time, after a Singing, when he'd seemed especially reticent—after all the youth had paired up and left—and she'd thought for sure he would ask to take her riding. But he hadn't.

Maybe if I'd let him know I was interested

in him that way, she thought. *Might that have changed everything?*

But no, I let Obie go, she thought as she began to read the letter.

Later, sighing, she thumbed through the pile and slipped that letter back into its envelope. She sat there, holding the letters, thankful for this time alone, though embarrassed she'd kept them this long.

I really should get rid of these, she thought, staring at the letters she had so treasured. *Obie's not mine to love.*

Britta's worry over Mamma had subsided somewhat over the past few days, and she played some of her best volleyball. She was thrilled to see Hazel again, as well as quite a few of Hazel's and her respective girl cousins.

After they'd played hard, Hazel served cookies and lemonade amidst plenty of chatter and a bit of gossip. Britta, for her part, spent time talking with Cousin Miriam Mast, who was newly engaged and very happy to tell Britta all about it.

"Say, is Susie seein' anyone?" Miriam asked quietly as they walked over to the springhouse near where Britta had parked her white scooter. They sat on the steps leading down.

"Not that I know of." Britta felt uncomfortable discussing her sister like this.

"Susie's real private, ain't she?"

"Susie's business is her own," Britta replied. "And that's just fine." Then, since Miriam had been nosy, she decided to ask her a question. "I've been wondering . . ."

Miriam leaned closer, her blue eyes questioning.

"You're close to Susie's age. Have you ever heard 'bout when I arrived in Hickory Hollow?"

"Are ya talking about before you were adopted?"

Britta nodded her head, hoping Miriam might share at least a morsel of information.

"Well, years ago now I heard that, at some point, there was a caseworker who checked up on ya several times. Prob'ly normal for a foster child."

"Where'd ya hear this?" Britta asked.

"Oh, Mamma telling one of her sisters. Just small talk, ya know."

"When did the person stop checking on me?"

"Ya musta been two or maybe three. Old enough to walk and talk and play with the other little ones."

Britta felt self-conscious, if not uneasy.

"What if *you* were adopted? Wouldn't ya want to know how it came about?"

Miriam's face scrunched up. "I'm not sure I'd care much, to be honest."

"Really?" Britta found this hard to believe.

Shaking her head again, Miriam glanced toward the small pond in front of the springhouse below. "How would your Mamma feel if she knew you were talking 'bout this with me?"

"Well, you're not the only one I've asked." Britta told her that she'd tried some time ago to get as many pieces together as possible. "Guess I want to finally satisfy my curiosity."

"Curiosity . . . or is there more to it?"

"*Puh!* I've prob'ly said too much already." Britta got up and reached for her scooter. "Nice talkin' with you, but I best be getting home."

"Okay, we'll talk another time. Bye-bye," Miriam called to her.

I shouldn't've mentioned anything to her, Britta thought, hurrying along.

Bringing the scooter was a good idea, Britta thought as she pushed hard with her left foot, then coasted slightly downhill as she drew near Aendi Emmalyn's. As she often did, she noticed the spot where Eli had died, and it crossed her mind that the flowers showing up every year on that day might mean something. But what?

She supposed it was best not to bring it up to Susie, considering how much she was juggling what with Mamma gone. *I probably should've stayed home today*, she thought.

Several family buggies passed by, and then a car, and Britta was careful to hug the shoulder as she scootered along.

A ways up the road, a spring wagon was coming toward her, driven by none other than Roy Lantz. She almost waved to him—a natural reflex—but she didn't want to be forward.

Just then, Roy waved to *her* and even slowed his horse. "Hullo there, Britta!"

Smiling, she waved back, and butterflies fluttered in her stomach on the rest of the scooter ride home.

28

At last, a letter from Mamma arrived. Susie was interested to hear all about her hospital experience—Mamma admitted to being surprised that the doctors and nurses had been such a help to her. *I'm feeling so much better. Hardly a wheeze at all . . . and only an occasional cough now, too,* she had written.

Susie couldn't have been more grateful but wondered that the hoped-for letter had not hinted at how long it might be before Mamma returned home.

A number of days passed again with no word from Allen or Mamma as to when her trip might be. Every walk out to the stable,

Susie or Britta checked the phone messages, in case there was more news from Missouri. Sometimes, Susie caught herself pacing from the stable telephone to Atta-Girl's stall near the door and back again, staring hard at the phone. It was all she could do not to inquire in her next letter, yet she didn't want to be pushy if Mamma was comfortable and enjoying her time there. *Even so, it's been nearly two weeks since she left*, Susie thought sadly.

The autumn sun, reddish like the turning sugar maples on either side of the gazebo, dipped earlier in the western sky each night. And one afternoon, the phone rang while Susie was grooming Atta-Girl after returning from helping Aendi Emmalyn with some deep cleaning.

"Hullo?" Susie answered.

"Susie! It's Allen. How're you an' Britta doin'?" her brother asked.

"All right. How's Mamma?"

Allen paused. "That's why I'm callin'. Wanted to let ya know what we've been discussing."

Susie set the curry brush on the shelf nearby and took a seat on the stool they kept next to the phone.

"I've been talking with Mamm 'bout staying with us longer yet, but I want you to be in on it, too."

Susie was surprised. "I appreciate that, but what're ya thinking?"

"Well, Mamm seems to have more energy lately and less coughing. She thinks she'd like to see how she feels in a few more months before making the trip back."

Months?! Susie thought. "Well . . . that's certainly not what we were expectin', but Mamma's always known what she wants, so I'll let that be."

"Okay, then . . . if we're in agreement." Allen went on to ask if she could box up and mail Mamma's clothing. "Also, she'd like to have her file of important papers from the blanket chest in her room, if you could grab that, too."

"I'll do that."

"Sorry to put ya out, Susie."

"No trouble," she replied.

"All right, then. *Denki.*" He grew quiet.

"Call any time, Allen . . . and tell Mamma we love her."

"Will do. Good-bye, *Schweschder.*"

"Bye," Susie said, tears pricking her eyes. She hung up the phone, picked up the brush, and walked back to finish grooming the horse.

"Goodness, I wanted Mamma to get medical help, and she has," Susie murmured. *But if she stays with Allen and family even longer than a few months, where does that leave Britta and me? Can we manage here alone that long?*

A wave of dissatisfaction swelled over her at the thought of not seeing Mamma again for who knew how long. Trying to quell her disappointment, Susie finished up with Atta-Girl, then put away the curry brush and trudged back to the house.

In the kitchen, she deliberately took a seat at the table in the spot where Mamma had sat for all the years of her married life.

Is this my kitchen now? she wondered, pushing her shoulders back as she looked around. *Will Allen look after Mamma from now on?* Though she disliked admitting it, a part of her felt somewhat relieved over that.

Staring out the window, she could see Britta walking across the yard with Lucy in her arms, heading for the gazebo. *How will she take this news? Will she resent me being a stand-in mother?*

Susie recalled Allen's initial hesitancy on the phone. "It could be a very long fall without Mamma around," she murmured and then gave a heavy sigh, longing for someone to talk to about this, to share her worries and even her dismay. Truth be told, since Allen had moved away, she'd come to think of Mamma as *her* responsibility.

Unexpectedly, Susie thought of Obie, missing their friendship terribly. And just when she'd hoped to have swept her memory clean of him.

Impulsively, she ran upstairs and pulled the box from beneath her bed. Sitting there on the floor, she opened the lid and removed the many letters she hadn't been able to discard, after all. And, one by one, she began to reread them, her heart still tender toward what she'd had and lost, wishing she had realized it before it was too late.

"Mamma's not comin' home?" Britta said, her eyebrows raised after Susie shared the news.

"She's just stayin' longer than planned," Susie explained gently.

"But for months?!" Britta's voice cracked. "What about Christmas? Will she be home by then?"

"I hope so." Susie went to her and held out her arms. "But in the meantime, we'll be okay," she said, holding her near. She began to describe how they would take turns running the little shop and doing the other chores. "Like we've been doin'. We'll still have each other to lean on."

"Still, it won't be the same." Britta rose

and went to the counter, placing her empty tumbler there. Sniffling, she walked into the front room.

Susie stood there alone in the kitchen, observing her sister standing beside the windows. Should she go to her and offer more comfort, or let her have some time alone?

By the time supper was on the table, Britta seemed less upset and more brooding. Susie assumed she was mulling things over and would likely sit down and write a letter to Mamma later, one filled with questions. *Might be a good thing*, she thought, remembering that Allen wanted Mamma's clothing and file of important papers sent to him. But she would wait till later tonight and make herself available to Britta during the evening. They would continue having Bible reading and prayer together, just as they had always done when Mamma was here.

Maintaining the routine is best, Susie decided.

"Do ya need help picking out Mamma's clothes?" Britta asked as she buttered her slice of bread.

"Sure, that'd be great."

Britta nodded. "Let me know whatever else I can do."

"We'll go to the post office together to-morrow and mail them," Susie said.

Britta brightened a little. "I'll line up a ride for us with Rachelle Good in a little while."

"*Gut* idea," Susie said, thinking that the distraction would surely lift her sister's mood.

Looking now at Britta lovingly, Susie hoped that tending to her sister's needs might soothe this new tear in her own heart.

Together, they boxed up Mamma's clothing, choosing the newest dresses, capes, and aprons, as well as everything else they knew she would need, including her warm bathrobe and slippers, coat, gloves, and her black outer bonnet for Preaching service. *In case she's there into early winter . . .*

Susie also tucked in a pretty embroidered doily she'd made for Mamma several years ago featuring her favorite flower, a golden sunflower.

Later, Susie watched Britta hurry to the stable to make the call to their driver, then stepped away from the back door window. There had been moments, after getting Allen's recent call, when Susie wished she had insisted on keeping Mamma home. But hearing how well she was doing, Susie knew she felt that way for selfish reasons. *I should be happy*, she chided herself.

Weary of the day, Susie decided to put off searching for Mamma's file folder till Britta went to bed. Opening the fridge, she removed two apples and quartered them, then set them in a bowl on the table. She also took out some store-bought vanilla yogurt and placed a teaspoon in it, wanting to sit with Britta and have a little treat.

Glancing out the window again, she wondered what was keeping her sister. Had she run into a snag getting Rachelle Good to drive them tomorrow?

Susie reached for Dat's old German *Biewel* and opened it to the front page, where the names of all of his relatives were listed in Dat's neat handwriting. Britta's name, however, had been added by Mamma.

Resting her hand on this special page, Susie wondered what Dat would have thought about Mamma adopting a baby. Of course, had Dat lived, he and Mamma might have had more children together.

Deep in thought, she was startled when Britta rushed into the house. "Sorry I was so long."

"What kept ya?" Susie closed the old Bible and turned to look at her.

Britta said that after she'd called Rachelle, Roy Lantz had dropped by to see her and offered to help around the stable or whatever else was needed. Her face reddened. "He walked clear over here to tell me that, and there I was in the stable, just as he'd hoped, he said." She shook her head. "*Ach*, I'm so *ferhoodled*."

Susie smiled. "And very happy, *jah*?"

Britta sat down with her. "S'pose I am." She began to laugh, and soon the laughter turned to tears.

"What is it?" Susie reached for her hand. "You all right?"

"How can sadness over Mamma turn into happiness over Roy in the space of such a short time?"

Susie understood. And nodding, she said, "Sometimes the weather's stormy and fierce, and then it clears up and the sun shines again all in a single afternoon."

Britta reached for an apple slice and spooned up some yogurt to dab on it. "You remind me of Ella Mae just now, Susie."

"*Ach*, no one else is *that* wise."

"Well, Mamma is . . . and now you." Britta took a bite and looked kindly at her.

"I agree with ya 'bout Mamma," Susie said, spooning up some yogurt, too. She could have told Britta that if she were so wise, she never would have let Obie go. But that was neither here nor there.

Later that evening, after Britta went to her room, Susie made her way up the hallway to Mamma's bedroom to look for the file folder. She lit the lamp that hung over the small table near the double bed. True to form, Mamma had left the place in apple-pie order—bed neatly made, dresser top all redded up, closet door closed, window shades drawn, and the tan upholstered chair set just so facing the windows.

Susie seldom set foot in there without Mamma sitting by the window or resting in bed. It felt strange and reminded her how, after Dat died so unexpectedly, Mamma would sometimes call her in just to sit with her. *She missed him so much,* Susie remembered. *She said she'd love him till the day she died.*

Moving slowly to the foot of the bed, Susie raised the lid of the large oak chest made by Dat's own hands. Inside, there were pretty handmade afghans and, beneath those, a heavy quilt for winter use.

Susie knelt to peer under two woolen blankets and found the black file folder marked *Vital Papers* in Mamma's careful printing.

Setting the file on the floor, she smoothed out the blankets and quilts, lest they be rumpled when needed, and gently closed the lid.

Turning to pick up the file, she noticed several pages had slipped out, along with a photo and what looked like adoption papers. Her eyes fell on Britta's birth certificate. Suddenly curious, Susie carried the papers and the file folder to the tan chair and sat down.

Thinking Britta would love to see this, Susie felt sheepish about reading the name and location of the hospital, as well as the time of birth. Kathleen Britta Stratton was listed as the biological mother, but the line for the father's name was blank.

Susie's interest piqued, she held up the photo of the woman she could only assume was Britta's birth mother. It was a near image of Britta herself. *Wavy auburn hair and big brown eyes just like Britta's,* she thought. But there was a marked difference: This young woman's features were accented with makeup, and her hair was cut in a feathery sort of bob no longer than her earlobe.

Britta's mother was clearly an *Englischer,* just as Britta had told her. Even so, the reality rattled Susie.

She slipped the birth certificate and adoption papers back inside the file folder but held the photo, intrigued by it. *If I were adopted,*

*would I want to know what my birth mother
looks like?*

Recalling the times Britta had probed
with questions, she was tempted to go to her
with this file. *But it's not my place to show her,*
she told herself.

She heard Britta calling and placed the
photo in with the birth certificate, leaving
the file folder on the chair as she headed out
of the room and down the hallway.

"I wrote to Mamma," a teary-eyed Britta
said when Susie arrived in her room. "I
wanted her to know how much I need her
here." She fidgeted with the fabric of her long
white nightgown.

"Well, you're pretty much raised already.
Won't be long till you're looking ahead to marryin' and creating your own family, ain't?"

Britta's eyes caught hers, and she stared
at her for a moment. Susie knew that expression. It was as though she were thinking, *But
what about you, Susie?*

Susie wanted to quickly change the subject, but Britta went on, "I really don't want
Mamma to stay away for much longer. It was
hard enough when Allen and Sarah up and
left like they did. Now this . . . it's too much."

Susie went to sit on the bed, slipping her
arm around her, not speaking.

"Allen and Sarah won't persuade her to

live there forever, will they?" Britta asked, leaning her head on Susie's shoulder.

Susie clenched her jaw, trying not to give in to tears herself. "Don't fret, sister. Mamma will come home eventually."

Still, Britta wept, and as Susie stroked her long hair, she recalled the photo of Kathleen Stratton. Why had the fancy young woman given her baby up to be adopted?

She couldn't help wondering how Britta would feel, knowing that Mamma had kept a photo of the woman. It crossed Susie's mind again that Britta might want to see it before they mailed the file to Missouri.

She struggled back and forth with the idea. *Mamma trusts me,* she thought.

Yet she longed to quell Britta's deep sadness . . . somehow.

CHAPTER 29

It took a few days for the truth that Mamma wouldn't be home anytime soon to fully sink in. The realization pierced Susie. *I've looked after her since I was a youngster,* she thought. *Wasn't it good enough?*

The latter thought nagged her nearly every waking hour.

Between keeping the household running, her own work, and helping Britta oversee Mamma's little shop, Susie began to feel spent at the end of the day. Never before had she run out of energy like this and wanted to simply give up, or even let a circumstance get the best of her. *But I can't quit,* she thought. *If only for Britta's sake.*

The next morning, after the kitchen was cleaned up and Britta left to babysit for the Ebersols, Susie trudged out to the stable to groom Brambles before getting the family carriage out of the shed. Afterward, she hitched up and headed off to tend to her list of errands, including the weekly grocery shopping at the General Store.

On the way home, she found herself turning into David Beiler's long lane, even though she hadn't planned to visit Ella Mae. She parked around the back, facing the Wise Woman's small *Dawdi Haus*, and there she sat, all in, wondering what had made her come here.

Am I making a fool of myself?

At that moment, Mattie Beiler walked across the driveway toward the main house, the hem of her long dress swinging. Seeing Susie, she waved and smiled and looked as if she was saying something to her.

Susie opened the buggy door. "Sorry?"

"Mamm's home, if you're wonderin'." Mattie pointed to Ella Mae's little house before hurrying up the back steps of the tall farmhouse that was her and David's own.

"*Denki*," Susie called back, realizing she was committed now.

Still feeling a bit hesitant, she climbed out of the buggy, tied Brambles to the hitching post, and made her way to the door of the cozy dwelling, having no idea what she'd say.

Ella Mae answered the knock with a bright smile and wearing a peach dress, a bright hue worn mostly by younger women. "*Kumme* in, dearie. It's been a long time, ain't so?"

Susie nodded, uncertain just how long it had been since she'd last stopped by to spill out her heart. She breathed in the aroma of bread baking and an inviting hint of cinnamon. Sunlight flooded the kitchen, and Susie accepted the kind woman's invitation to sit at her pretty table to have a cup of peppermint tea.

"As I recall, you take honey in yours," Ella Mae said, moving the honey jar from the end of the table nearest the window to the center. "Some folk drink tea without a speck of sugar or honey, like your Aendi Lettie."

What a sharp memory! Susie thought, extra grateful for the thoughtful attention. "It's so nice of you to let me visit unplanned."

"Oh, I'm *always* ready for some pleasant conversation." Ella Mae sat down at the table and poured the freshly brewed tea into two floral cups, then set the matching teapot between the two amber-colored placemats, near a plate of delicious-looking pumpkin cookies. "Let's ask the blessing," she said and folded her knobby hands.

Susie bowed her head with Ella Mae, and during the silent grace, she inwardly asked God how she ought to share what was troubling her.

Susie took several sips of the warm golden tea and wondered if Mamma felt this peaceful in Ella Mae's presence.

"So now, how's your Mamma?" The woman peered over the small glasses perched on the end of her nose.

She told about the sudden Missouri hospital stay and then, thankfully, Mamma's remarkable recovery. She paused a moment, not saying more.

Ella Mae studied her. "What is it, dearie?"

She deliberated what to say, not wanting to sound envious of Allen.

Ella Mae's expression was caring as she said, "I 'spect somethin's got ya stewin'."

There was no way to hold back the truth from Ella Mae, and Susie nodded slowly. "Mamma's planning to settle in with Allen and Sarah for a while. Months even." She sighed. "I mailed a large box of clothing to her not long ago."

Now Ella Mae was the one sighing. "*Ach*, had no idea. She'll sure be missed round here."

Susie felt sad being the one to tell her. "I guess Mamma hasn't written to you yet."

"Oh, she'll write when she can." Ella Mae bobbed her little gray head, her white head covering secured with several bobby pins.

"*Jah*. The two of yous are so close. . . ."

"*Puh!* There are ways to stay in touch, even long distance," Ella Mae said, a sudden twinkle in her eyes. "One of those ways ain't so well regarded by the ministers, though."

Susie knew what she meant and smiled because Ella Mae was still as plucky as ever. "That's the very reason Mamma's not too keen on usin' our stable phone."

Ella Mae waved it off. "Letters are fine, but a body needs to hear a friend's voice from time to time, I daresay."

Susie agreed and sipped more of her tea. The gentle flavor did her heart nearly as much good as sitting there with spunky yet sympathetic Ella Mae.

Eventually, she began to feel more at ease, enough so to say what was on her mind. "I hope what I'm gonna tell ya won't be a shock."

Ella Mae looked at her with kind eyes. "I've lived this long, so not much surprises me anymore."

Sitting up straighter in her chair, she began. "I've been by Mamma's side ever since Dat died, tryin' to help her however I can . . . to watch over her."

Ella Mae nodded, a glint in her eyes.

"Honestly, I thought I was doin' my best for her." Susie's voice broke. "I truly did."

For a moment, Ella Mae was still. Then very quietly she said, "That's all the Lord requires, ain't so?"

Susie paused, hesitant to reveal more.

"I'm not one to judge, Susie." Ella Mae's voice was gentle.

Taking a breath, Susie went on. "Mamma's been so prone to getting sick. It just strikes me that Allen must think I'm not the best caretaker for her. 'Least here lately. Why else would he keep her out there?"

"You mean because he's takin' charge?" Ella Mae reached for her teacup and had another sip with a look over at her.

Susie nodded.

Ella Mae's cup clinked softly as she set it down on the matching saucer. "Well now, might there be another reason your Mamm's stayin' in Missouri?"

Susie shrugged, unsure what it could be.

Ella Mae smiled faintly. "If ya don't know just yet, it'll come to ya when it's s'posed to," she said, as if looking straight into Susie's heart.

What on earth does she mean?

"You've done a fine job takin' care of your Mamma, Susie," Ella Mae said. "But now ya have a chance to decide what *you* want." She paused. "Weeks before Allen and his family moved away, his wife shared with me that both she and Allen were quite confident leavin' Hickory Hollow because of your excellent care of your Mamma and Britta."

"Really?"

"*Jah*, in fact, there wasn't a doubt in Sarah's or Allen's minds that you'd continue to be a loving, caring daughter and sister."

Susie's spirits were so low, she could scarcely believe this, though coming from Ella Mae, she knew she ought to trust it.

The Wise Woman offered more tea, and Susie accepted. "Have as much as you like," Ella Mae said, getting up to open the oven door.

Susie wiped her eyes. "I'm glad I visited today."

Ella Mae leaned down to remove the loaf pan from the oven and set it on a wooden trivet to cool on the counter. "I'm glad, too."

They talked about other things for a while, and then when Susie was ready to leave, she thanked Ella Mae for the tea and cookies. "And the *gut* conversation," she added.

"You and Britta are welcome anytime," Ella Mae said with a smile. "I don't leave the *Haus* much anymore, so ya know where to find me."

"*Denki*," Susie said, opening the back door, thinking she wouldn't wait so long again before making another visit.

"Remember now that all things work together for *gut* to them that love God," Ella Mae said, that familiar sparkle in her eye.

Heading down the porch steps, Susie was grateful for the promise of that verse. "Have a *wunnerbaar-gut* day!"

"Be kind to yourself, Susie Mast," Ella Mae said, standing at the door. "Life's not just 'bout constant work, remember."

CHAPTER 30

Britta was thankful it didn't take long for Mamma to reply to her letter. *I hope she didn't think I was selfish, asking her to come home,* she thought, hurrying toward the house, envelope in hand, on this gray autumn day. The murky clouds were laden with rain, and at breakfast Susie had said thundershowers were in the forecast, according to the newspaper.

Presently, Susie was assisting customers in Mamma's shop, which had largely become Susie's to tend. Britta was happy to do the behind-the-scenes work of making goat cheese, popcorn balls, runners, and more recently, specialty breads to sell.

Heading into the house, she enjoyed the privacy of the kitchen, where three loaves of raisin bread were almost finished baking. She sat at the table to open the envelope and read, pulse beating hard as she worried how Mamma had taken her remarks.

Dear Britta,

Your letter was a welcome sight, for certain. Denki for taking time to write to me, dear daughter.

How are you and Susie managing there? I miss you both and think of you every day, trusting you are both well. Susie is a thoughtful big sister, and I know she's good company for you. And you for her. I'm very grateful for that!

I've been surprised at how much better I feel here lately. I'm using a nebulizer with medication daily, and Sarah and her girls are doting on me just as you and Susie always have.

I'm not sure if Allen told you this, but my doctor has just recently urged me not to travel, so I'll be here for some months yet. I'm not sure how long, but Allen and Sarah are in agreement that it will at least be for this winter.

"All winter," she murmured, heart sinking. She rose to get some cold water and went to stand at the window looking out toward the stable. *I feel awful sad, Lord. I need Thy peace. . . .*

She glanced at the wall clock and saw that it was time to test the loaves for doneness and remove the loaf pans from the oven, which she did. Setting them on the cooling racks, she then went to the utility room to don her black work boots and coat. She would give the goats and the driving horses their feed and water, and hopefully, that would help her calm down. Although, the way she felt about Mamma being gone so long and no end in sight, she was afraid anger might take her over.

She pulled on one boot, then the other. As far as she'd observed, Mamma and Susie weren't much given to anger. *Am I like this because I'm not blood kin?* she wondered. *Or is it because I'm not baptized yet?*

Of course, it was hard to understand how the act of making a kneeling vow to follow God and the Amish church for the rest of her life could change her from the inside out. Maybe it was too much to expect. Mamma sometimes talked about how a life of faith required a daily renewing of the mind. Britta knew she'd do well to remember that, but it was just so hard to put into practice. There had been times before now when she'd let an irritation turn to anger. One was that long-ago day when Aaron Kauffman had said she didn't belong with the People. Britta hadn't told anyone about the intense anger that had welled up in her at the time. She'd stared at the back of his head during spelling class, wondering if a single strike of a book could knock him out.

Mamma would be horrified if she knew, Britta thought. *Susie too.*

Rushing to open the stable door, she made her way inside, tempted to dial up Allen's number and talk to Mamma about all this. *My feelings especially.*

Instead, she pushed the big scoop into the feed bag, knowing she'd regret it if she called now, upset as she was. *I need to get a hold of myself.*

After she'd fed the livestock, she stayed in the stable to play with the cats. Daffodil in particular seemed to sense Britta's need to cuddle. Oh, she wished she could bring at least one of the cats into the house, even into her room at night!

"Would ya like to read Mamma's latest letter?" Britta said to Susie at supper, handing it to her.

Susie's eyes moved quickly over the stationery while Britta waited.

When her sister was finished, Britta said softly, "It's been a while since I felt this disappointed."

"You sound more irritated than disappointed," Susie said, folding the letter and handing it back to Britta.

"Well, to be honest, I think Mamma *prefers* to stay with Allen and Sarah."

Susie slowly shook her head. "*Ach*, I don't believe that's it. Mamma loves all of us, and that won't ever change, no matter who she's with."

Britta gave a little shrug.

"We want what's best for her, and if stayin' there longer is what the doctor and Allen think is best now, then so be it," Susie said, getting up for some goat's milk.

Britta chafed under her sister's words, yet she had no choice but to agree.

Late that evening, Britta was filled with remorse to the point that she knelt beside her bed and asked God to forgive her. And she prayed for something else, too—for help in finding her birth mother. *If it is Thy will*, she reluctantly added.

Rising, she outened the gas lamp, lifted the sheet and quilt, and slipped into bed, wondering for the hundredth time if anyone else in Hickory Hollow knew about her adoption and would be willing to share with her. *I've already asked everyone I can think of*, she thought, frustrated at the idea of having to wait until Mamma was ready.

With Mamma not returning home anytime soon, maybe there was someone outside the family who knew something. Even a small detail would help relieve her desire to *know*. So far, Britta hadn't told Susie of the reappearance of this continual yearning. After all, that night more than two years ago now, Susie had advised her in so many words to wait for Mamma's timing. *And I've tried. . . .*

Lying in bed, unable to sleep, Britta wondered, *Would any of the ministers remember my beginnings here? Bishop Beiler, maybe?*

Rolling over, she contemplated the questions that churned in her mind, feeling trapped in a box with its lid on too tight.

Getting up, she sat and leaned back on the headboard, wondering what all had been involved in her adoption process. She noodled on that for quite some time, and as she did, she thought of Mattie Beiler, who had been a midwife for many years but had long since retired.

Might Mattie know something?

Then, out of the clear blue, Ella Mae

crossed her mind. *What if Mamma told her how I came to be adopted? Dare I ask?*

Somehow, Susie managed to maintain her hectic pace into October, including starting to sew her bridesmaid dress for Cousin Verena's wedding next month and completing two custom-made family trees on a shorter-than-normal deadline. Word of her fine handiwork had spread all over Lancaster County in the past years, even beyond the Plain community. *Stitched with Love*, she now called her little business, after some folk at market had started referring to her framed family trees that way. Susie was humbled by the praise and thankful for the extra income.

Britta's hand-quilted table runners were also quite popular, as was the beloved peanut butter spread. In addition to the many tourists who came their way, a lot of their regular customers dropped by to pick up a month's worth at a time, saying Mamma's version just tasted better than their own.

When Susie was alone with her thoughts while she worked on her royal blue dress, she couldn't help wondering how Obie and his Sugar Valley sweetheart were getting along.

Initially, it had been somewhat freeing, not waiting for his next letter, and she supposed he had taken her final letter as the termination of their friendship. But now, she wished she could remember precisely what she'd written. Was it too abrupt?

At the time, she'd believed she was doing the right thing in setting him free, and herself, too. Yet she still treasured his old letters. This, too, troubled her.

If Obie's seriously dating, I really shouldn't hang on to them, she thought while setting in the first sleeve. *Maybe Britta could ask Hazel about her brother,* she mused, realizing that this very thought signaled that something was still unsettled in her.

31

Mid-October arrived with a bumper crop of pumpkins to harvest and sell at their farm stand. Thankfully, Roy Lantz came over to wheelbarrow them out to the road. *Such a big help*, Susie thought, smiling whenever she caught a glimpse of Britta with Roy. Young though they were, it was clear how fond the two were of each other.

Truth be told, there were times when Susie felt protective of Britta, who perked up whenever Roy dropped by to help. Surely someday, in not so many years, Britta would be leaving home to marry.

If Mamma doesn't return, where will that put me? Susie wondered while lying snug beneath the quilts one night. *Am I to be a Maidel?* She was struck by the reality that she might at some point end up caring for an aging relative and living in their *Dawdi Haus*. No matter what the future brought, she refused to be a burden to anyone.

When the mail arrived the next afternoon, Susie was relieved to see a letter from Mamma. Anxious to read it, she opened the envelope on the walk back to the house.

Mamma's words leaped out at Susie, especially two particular lines.

> *I hope you and Britta will come for Thanksgiving. Allen has offered to pay for the van driver.*

"Oh," Susie groaned. "If only I could." Evidently, Mamma had forgotten that she was one of Cousin Verena's bridesmaids.

She glanced toward the shop, where her sister was working. Seeing no cars or buggies parked outside, she read the rest of the letter, then hurried across the yard to show Britta.

"I wouldn't think of goin' without you," Britta said after reading it.

"Well, I can't disappoint Verena."

"*Nee*, and ya shouldn't." Britta handed

the letter back to her. "She's counting on you."

"I really wish you'd consider going on your own." Susie leaned on the counter, eyeing the remaining table runners.

Britta shook her head. "I wouldn't wanna leave ya alone for Thanksgiving."

Susie argued that she would be at Verena's wedding all day. "I'll stay after the feast and the afternoon Singing and help with cleanup, so I'll be plenty occupied. Please think about goin', won't ya?"

This time Britta didn't respond as emphatically.

"Mamma misses you, I'm very sure." Susie folded the letter and slipped it back into its envelope.

"Well, she misses you, too, Susie. She did invite *both* of us."

"Just think 'bout it, won't ya?" Susie gave her shoulder a squeeze. "Well, I should get back to work," she said, returning to the house. *Britta would certainly enjoy some time away, especially with Mamma at Allen's,* she thought, seeing Lucy the cat poke her black head out the stable door. *But I'd miss her.*

Over a supper of creamed chipped beef and mashed potatoes, Susie attempted to get to the bottom of Britta's dejected mood. "Haven't ya often wished you could visit Allen and family?" Susie probed.

"*Jah*, but I already said I'm not goin' without you." Britta took a sip from her tumbler of water.

"Well, it'd make Mamma ever so happy."

Britta was silent for a while, as if actually thinking it over. Then she said softly, "Maybe if I went, I'd have a chance to talk to Allen privately 'bout what he might know of my adoption."

This again, Susie thought. But could she blame her? In that moment, she was tempted to mention the birth certificate and photo she'd inadvertently found in Mamma's file. Britta seemed so down. "Well, I discovered some facts 'bout your origins," she heard herself saying.

Britta's head jerked up. "Wha-at?"

"I shouldn't have, but I looked at a couple papers 'bout your adoption from a file Mamma has."

Britta stared at her a moment. Then quietly, she asked, "Can *I* see the file?"

"*Ach*, I mailed it to Missouri at Mamma's request."

"Well then, can ya at least tell me what was in it?" Britta's big eyes pierced Susie's heart. "*Sei so gut*, Schweschder?"

"Sayin' please won't make me do the wrong thing."

Britta stirred her mashed potatoes into the creamy chipped beef. "Honestly, I've considered talkin' to the bishop 'bout this. Wasn't gonna tell ya."

Susie guessed she might feel the same way if she were in Britta's situation. "I s'pose you could ask Bishop Beiler, sure."

Britta's left fist clenched. "But you're right here, Susie. And you know somethin' more, don't ya?"

"Well, only where you were born and your birth mother's name . . . and what she looked like." There, Susie had really put her foot in a mess now, blurting out what she'd seen.

Britta's eyes filled with tears. "You . . . you saw her picture?"

Susie nodded. "I actually thought of showin' it to ya, but I didn't want to betray Mamma's trust. I feel guilty for seein' it myself."

Staring at her plate, Britta asked, "Will ya describe her to me?"

Susie did her best, mentioning the short auburn hair and brown eyes and makeup, and when she was finished, Britta wanted to know the woman's name. Susie shook her head. "That I'd better not share. I'm sorry, sister. Really, I am."

She sighed. "You don't want to go behind Mamma, so I won't press ya."

"*Des gut*." As it was, Susie felt like she'd stepped deep into a hole with no escape.

"What about my birth father—did ya read anything 'bout him?"

Susie hated to tell her. "Well . . . the line for his name was blank."

"So, she wasn't married?" Britta frowned, clearly even more upset.

"I don't know for sure. I didn't look through the rest of the file."

"Well, does that mean he doesn't even know 'bout me?" Britta asked and abruptly excused herself from the table, leaving half her plate untouched.

Susie groaned inwardly. *Ach, have I made things worse?*

Britta closed the door to her bedroom and hoped Susie wouldn't follow her upstairs. *I need to be alone*, she thought, drying her eyes and pondering what this meant—this revelation of things she'd wondered about from the time she understood she was adopted.

She went to stand at the window, looking toward Jonathan Ebersol's farm, half anticipating Susie's knock at the door. She watched two of the children scampering about, undoubtedly having finished their supper. *My children won't look anything like anyone in the Mast family*, she thought a bit sadly.

Then, thinking ahead to possibly telling Hazel about what she'd learned, she wondered now if Aaron might have been right about what he'd said so long ago.

Dismayed, Britta went to lie on the bed,

missing Mamma more than ever. And in that helpless moment, her heart softened toward going alone to Missouri for Thanksgiving, after all.

The next morning, after Britta finished her barn chores and had breakfast with Susie, she hitched up the pony to the cart, not bothering to tell Susie where she was going. *She might worry I'll spill the beans*, she thought, promising herself she would not. *What Susie shared with me stays between us . . . for now, anyway.*

She had never gone to visit the Wise Woman by herself, although she knew that Hazel and Susie enjoyed talking privately with her over sweet peppermint tea and cookies, just as Mamma and a host of other women did. Hazel's first visit had been after her brother left for Sugar Valley.

She still misses him something awful, thought Britta. To this day Hazel did not understand why Obie hadn't chosen to work locally. *Ella Mae helped Hazel through that rough patch, so maybe she can help me. . . .*

What surprised Britta most was Ella Mae's casual manner when the elderly woman came to the door and welcomed her in. It was almost as if she had been expecting her, but how could that be?

"You an' Susie have been in my prayers," Ella Mae said, dressed today in a dark green dress and black cape and apron. She led her into the cheery kitchen, where Britta was told to sit wherever she liked at the small table laid with placemats in fall colors and a small pumpkin centerpiece.

"You've been prayin' for us since Mamma left?" Britta asked, admiring the lovely setting and Ella Mae's special way of making her feel at home.

Ella Mae nodded. "An' for your Mamma, too."

"You two have been friends for a long time, ain't so?" Britta asked.

"For all of your Mamma's adult life." Ella Mae's eyes squinted nearly shut with her big smile. "We've shared life's ups an' downs, for certain."

Britta rubbed her forehead, thinking this might be her lead-in to reveal what was burning a hole in her heart. Hesitating, she inhaled deeply, then let it out. "I've been, uh, thinking 'bout that recently."

Ella Mae smiled. "Life's ups an' downs?"

"S'pose ya might say that."

"Well, I'm here to listen," Ella Mae said, pouring tea into their cups.

Britta sat quietly with her hands in her lap while the dear woman brought over a plate of buttered toast and a little glass bowl of strawberry jam. Britta's mouth watered at the sight, and when Ella Mae asked the silent blessing, Britta quickly bowed her head.

Afterward, she settled into enjoying the tasty treat, delighted she'd come.

It may have been the calming effect of the peppermint tea or the sweetness of the jam, but she began to feel so comfortable with Ella Mae that she asked, "Would ya happen to know how I became my Mamma's adopted daughter?"

Ella Mae smiled brightly. "Well now, I'll always remember the day you arrived. The young woman who birthed ya needed help . . . wasn't able to take care of ya for a while. Your Mamma offered to keep you till the woman could get on her feet."

Britta let this sink into her mind. "Was it because she wasn't married?"

Eyes fluttering, Ella Mae looked surprised. "You know somethin' 'bout her, then?"

Britta shared what she'd learned from Susie.

"Seems you've been seekin' some answers for yourself, dearie."

Pausing for a moment, Britta finally admitted, "I've wondered nearly my whole life 'bout my birth Mamma. Guess it started 'cause my name ain't one any Amish family would give their child . . . and it's honestly bothered me a whole lot."

"Well, it's sure a perty name."

At her thoughtfulness, Britta gave a little smile. "And when I first brought this up to Mamma—I was thirteen at the time—she said she planned to tell me about it when I was of age."

Ella Mae's kindhearted gaze seemed to indicate she agreed with that line of thinking. "Might be wise."

Britta didn't know how to respond, because she couldn't understand why her age mattered. It seemed that Ella Mae knew something she was holding back.

"You ain't goin' against your Mamma's wishes askin' me, are ya, Britta?"

"Well, I don't want to snoop around, but Mamma's time in the hospital really shook me up. And now she isn't around to talk to."

Ella Mae's eyebrows rose. "There's a proper moment for everything. Takin' things into your own hands can be risky."

Britta felt Ella Mae's eyes look deep into her soul—or so it felt. "I don't understand why the details of my adoption have to be kept secret." She glanced out the window near the table. "Honestly, it's drivin' me crazy."

Ella Mae took her time sipping her tea and dipping her toast into the spot of jam on her plate. Then she said, "Can ya trust our heavenly Father for *His* timing?"

Britta wasn't sure. "It's just that I've been waiting so long." She paused to drink some tea. "Besides, if Mamma should die before she told me, I'd never know what happened."

Bobbing her head, Ella Mae said, "Waiting patiently with a *gut* attitude can be mighty hard. But it can be the best thing."

"My yearnin' to know is swelling up like it might burst." Britta went on to tell her about Mamma's recent Thanksgiving invitation. "I haven't told Susie yet, but I want to travel to Missouri after all. And Susie can't go with me since she's in Cousin Verena's wedding."

"Maybe you could wait an' go with her *after* the wedding, then."

Britta hadn't thought of that. "Well, Susie seems determined to keep the same hours for the customers at Mamma's shop, and to fulfill her orders."

Ella Mae nodded thoughtfully. "That does sound like your sister. And if that's the case, well then, I daresay you're old enough to go on your own."

"Ya really think so?" Britta asked, not sure she felt up to traveling without her sister.

"Remember, there're always other Plain

folk in the passenger vans. Ya wouldn't really be alone if Susie stayed put here."

Britta pondered that as Ella Mae poured more tea for herself. "Nice an' hot. Would ya like more, too?"

"*Denki.*" Britta held up her cup on its saucer.

"I have a question for ya." Ella Mae filled it and set down the teapot. "Have ya thought of praying 'bout this, so ya don't run ahead of the Lord's plan?"

Britta sighed. "I had been, but not so much lately."

"Why's that, dear?"

"If I told ya that I'm too frustrated right now, would ya think I was sinning?"

"Only the Lord sees your heart." Ella Mae smiled the sweetest smile. "And He loves ya still."

The tender words touched her.

Ella Mae was looking at her with eyes of compassion. "Frustration's not the same as anger, now, is it?"

Britta couldn't help but smile. "S'pose it can turn into that, if I let it."

"An' is that why you're here . . . so it won't?"

Britta reached across the table for Ella Mae's wrinkled, bony hand and let the tears fall. "Now I know why Mamma's so fond of you," she whispered.

Ella Mae beamed. "Your Mamma's real special to me, too. And never forget how much she loves *you*, Britta."

Nodding, Britta released her hand and noticed tears shining on Ella Mae's furrowed cheeks.

Susie had decided not to ask Britta where she'd hurried off to. Undoubtedly, she needed time by herself again, which was understandable. Learning that her birth mother was most likely unmarried was a lot for dear Britta to take in.

Several kinfolk dropped by the shop to check in on them that morning—Aendis Emmalyn and Lettie, and Cousin Verena, too—for which Susie was grateful. She would be sure to tell Britta when she returned home. Even Mattie Beiler stopped in for a little chat, saying if they ever needed anything at all to holler, a kind offer that others had made, as well.

The womenfolk sincerely care, Susie thought, touched even though she didn't plan on needing help anytime soon.

Following the nightly Bible reading and prayer, Britta and Susie sat quietly in the front room. *Taking time to do this as a family is the*

best gift Dat and Mamma ever gave us, Susie thought. Her parents' invisible fingerprints were everywhere in their lives.

The stove was plenty warm, yet Britta had carried little Lucy into the house and had the black furry bundle all snug in her arms while she sat in Mamma's chair. Susie stared across the room at the large gas lamp to the right of the comfortable chair, observing Britta, who appeared deep in thought.

At last Britta broke the stillness. "I've been thinkin' that we could travel together to Missouri, leaving the day *after* Thanksgiving."

This surprised Susie, but she contemplated it for a moment, not in favor of Allen paying their way, nor the disruption such a trip would cause to the shop and livestock.

"Maybe Mamma would travel back with us." Britta petted Lucy as the cat slept.

"If ya go just for that reason, you might be disappointed," Susie replied.

"*Nee*, ain't the only reason." Britta scratched under the cat's ears. "It'd be *wunnerbaar-gut* just to spend time with Mamma again."

"We'd miss having Thanksgiving dinner with them, though."

Britta wrinkled her nose. "Maybe they would move it till after we got there."

Susie wondered how Sarah and the children would feel about that. "I wouldn't think of suggesting that," she told Britta.

"But if they want us to come, they'll be glad whenever we arrive, *jah*?"

Susie smiled.

"I'd like to write back to Mamma soon. It'll give her somethin' to look forward to."

"Give me a day or so to think 'bout it, all right?"

Britta nodded. "Okay."

"Remember, we would have to close the shop during one of the busiest weekends of the year," Susie cautioned, not too keen on missing out on the necessary money. "Maybe only you should go." She waited for Britta to argue against that yet again.

But Britta glanced down at the cat in her lap. "Hope ya don't mind Lucy bein' inside," she said, changing the subject. "She's a comfort to me."

Susie shook her head. "I don't mind."

"I'll pick off any cat hairs on the furniture."

"It's just us, for now." Susie paused. "But when Mamma *does* return, that'll be a different story."

"So we won't tell her, then."

"No reason to," Susie replied, hoping Britta would also keep quiet about the information she'd shared from Mamma's file folder. *Scant as it was.*

CHAPTER 33

Thanksgiving Day dawned with intermittent sunshine and clouds, or so Susie noticed from the kitchen window as she prepared breakfast for herself. It was the morning of Cousin Verena's wedding, and with all her heart, Susie hoped the clouds would subside.

Two hours later, as the first sermon began, the sky became brilliant with sunlight, which grew throughout the longer second sermon, too. *A gut* sign, Susie thought, trying to imagine what her cousin must be feeling right now as she became a wife and ultimately a mother, Lord willing.

The farmhouse was filled with Isaac's and Verena's families, as well as unrelated youth group friends and church members. Verena's face shone with joy as she sat in the congregation, and her royal blue dress and white cape and apron—identical to Susie's and Marnie's—made her eyes look all the bluer.

When it was time for Susie and Marnie to walk to the front of the large room to be Verena's side sitters, Susie felt somewhat overwhelmed. Two days ago, Britta had left by passenger van for Clark, Missouri, and Susie missed her being in attendance at the wedding and the activities to follow. As was customary after the feast, the youth would be paired up, and Susie would be coupled with Isaac's younger brother Irwin, also a wedding attendant. *He's just nineteen,* she thought, wondering whether Irwin might feel uncomfortable about that. *At least it'll only be for a few hours.*

Susie's thoughts sailed across the miles to Mamma and the family there, soon to gather around Sarah's table to count their blessings. Never having seen the house where Allen and his family lived, she could only imagine Britta working together alongside Sarah's older girls in the kitchen, letting Mamma relax. Allen and the boys would undoubtedly wash up outside at the farm's well pump, flicking water at each other as their breath hung in the air. Al Junior, starting his courting years now, might even be thinking of attending a Singing this weekend, maybe even had his eye on a pretty girl, although Sarah hadn't mentioned it. Some couples liked to keep things mum till they were engaged.

The thought of courting brought Susie's attention back to the wedding at hand just as Bishop Beiler asked Isaac the first solemn question. "As you stand here before the Lord God and this congregation, do you promise that, should Verena become weak or ill, you will do your utmost to care for her as a devoted Christian husband ought?"

Dressed in black except for his white dress shirt, Isaac firmly answered, "*Jah*," his expression serious.

Verena's eyes teared up when it was her turn to respond to the same question. This holy and eternal bond of wedlock created by the Lord God was taking place before Susie's eyes, and she was deeply moved, having never been this close to the bride and groom during the five-minute ceremony of vows.

I wish Mamma could've been present, Susie thought. *How many Hickory Hollow milestones will she miss?*

After the bishop's benediction and a kneeling prayer for the congregation, Isaac's brother Irwin politely approached Susie, remarking how pleased he was to be her partner today.

She felt sorry for him, expected to spend the afternoon and into the evening with a twenty-four-year-old bridesmaid when undoubtedly he would much prefer to be paired with someone nearer his own age. So, to let him off the hook early, Susie told him she planned to help wash dishes after the wedding dinner and then head home.

"Are ya sure?" Irwin said, looking as nice as his brother Isaac in his for-good clothing.

"Definitely." She smiled and they walked outside together, where they met Cousin Marnie with her beau, Jerome Yoder.

"Obie really likes Sugar Valley," Susie overheard him saying. "And we all expect him to get engaged soon, too. Makes sense that he'd wanna stay close to her family."

Marnie glanced suddenly at Susie and back at Jerome, who seemed to catch her meaning and quickly changed the subject.

After that, the rest of the day was a blur, although Susie tried her best not to allow Jerome's remark to bother her. But she still felt rattled later while she washed dishes with Verena's aunts.

All the same, she wished she hadn't learned this on Verena's wedding day.

Hours later, when the many dishes were washed, wiped, and put away, Susie disliked the thought of going home to an empty house. So, at the turnoff to her driveway, she instead directed the horse onward and headed up the road to Aendi Emmalyn's, where her aunt was hosting her married children and their families for Thanksgiving.

A better way to spend the rest of the day, Susie thought, grateful for her extended family.

Britta enjoyed having Thanksgiving dinner with Allen and his family, but she missed being with Susie and tried to imagine her socializing with the youth after the wedding, especially with Irwin, one of the male attendants, and Marnie and her beau, Jerome, who was the other. Britta hoped Cousin Verena's wedding had been a wonderful time for Susie. Her sister had been so determined to stay home and follow through with her promise to Verena.

She did the right thing, like she always does, Britta thought, knowing how close Susie and Verena had always been.

Britta helped dry dishes with twelve-year-old Dora while Sarah washed, and ten-year-old Tilly put them away in the corner cupboard. It was a joy to spend this day with her nieces, including six-year-old Maggie, who had the cutest giggle and treated her like a big sister more than an aunt.

Later, settling in to the spare room to talk with Mamma privately, Britta wondered if this afternoon might be a good time to share about her recent visit to Ella Mae's. Mamma had already been resting awhile in her large but sparsely furnished room. Since Mamma's arrival, Allen had built in a closet with shelves to keep everything organized. He had done this with all of the bedrooms, including the largest one, just up the stairs, which was his and Sarah's own.

Thankfully, Mamma's room was far removed from the kitchen, so she had a private retreat and didn't have to climb any stairs, either, should she become ill again. *Something that's not possible at home*, Britta thought. *And for that reason alone, Mamma is better off staying here.*

"Seems you're thinkin' hard on something," Mamma observed as she sat in the lone chair in the corner of her bedroom.

"Oh, just that this room's so quiet and separate from the other living spaces. And it's on the main floor, too. Makes things nice for ya."

"'Tis a blessing."

"I noticed Ella Mae's *Dawdi Haus* doesn't

have any stairs, either," Britta said, not think-ing.

Mamma's eyes widened. "Oh, have ya visited her lately?"

Britta nodded. "I was feelin' upset . . . well, frustrated. But she helped me under-stand it wasn't a sin to feel that way, unless I let it turn to anger—which I certainly didn't want."

Mamma folded her hands and listened. Then, looking more serious, she asked, "Did ya bring up your adoption to her, maybe?"

Britta grimaced. "S'pose I did."

Mamma gave her a reassuring smile. "Susie mentioned in a letter that you hadn't been yourself lately. And I know there've been times in the past when you've sought out dif-ferent folk, tryin' to find out what they might know." She paused, a thoughtful expression on her dear face. "But what if we talk some right now . . . how'd that be?"

Hope rose in Britta. "Oh, Mamma, I'd love that. But I don't want it to upset ya, seein' how you're feeling better than you have in a long time."

"There are still days when my asthma pulls me under the weather, but for the most part, I'm doin' all right. I do miss you and Susie and Polly terribly, though." She sighed. "It hasn't been the easiest thing to relocate like this, even for a while." Her eyes caught Britta's and held them. "I've been thinking 'bout your eagerness to know more about your birth mother, yet I'm struggling with it, too."

"Struggling?"

"*Jah*, there are some tetchy things about it, which is why, for all these years, I haven't been sure if I should even share everything. Honestly, I haven't wanted to . . . haven't thought it too wise." She was quiet for a moment, looking out the window. "Some things are best left unsaid."

Now Britta was more curious than ever, yet she wouldn't press, trying to trust Mamma's judgment.

"I wanted to protect ya, dear—wanted to tell you just enough to satisfy your curiosity. . . ."

"So that must be why ya want me to be older."

Mamma nodded. "Still, I don't want ya miserable, wonderin'." She glanced heavenward. "I've been praying and ponderin' how I should share the things I know, not withholding anything."

Britta worried suddenly. Was she actually ready for whatever Mamma had to say, given how stressed and on edge she seemed? "Are ya sure?" Britta surprised herself by asking.

"Well, you're here now. It's better to talk this over in person than by letter or phone later on." Her mother clutched the arms of her chair. "*Jah*, I daresay this might be the moment to tell how you came to be an Amish girl livin' in Hickory Hollow. . . ."

It was July 12, one year after Eli's death, and Aquilla's young daughter, Susie, was spending the morning with Liz Ebersol, next farm over, when a knock came at the front door. Since it was rare anyone approached that door, Aquilla hurried to open it, and there stood a beautiful auburn-haired woman with dark eyes. The lovely young woman, scarcely out of her teens, was cradling an infant and asked apologetically if Aquilla might have a few moments to spare.

Such a tiny baby, thought Aquilla, opening the screen door and glimpsing a tan car parked in the driveway. She asked the woman to have a seat on the soft settee and offered some iced meadow tea. Shaking her head, the woman said she couldn't stay long and glanced down at the sleeping babe in her arms.

Tentative, Aquilla took a seat across the room and wondered what was on the pretty *Englischer's* mind.

"I've come to confess," the woman said, looking away as tears sprang to her eyes.

"Something I should have done more than a year ago. You see, I committed a terrible crime against you and your family."

Perplexed, Aquilla sat there, unmoving.

She shook her head and rocked the baby slightly, then continued. "I was drunk out of my mind that day . . . made a wrong turn off Route 340. In the murkiness of the evening— and my own stupor—I swerved when I tried not to hit a young girl walking along the road . . . and hit what I mistakenly thought was an animal."

Her words penetrated Aquilla's heart.

"Not until I heard on the radio that an Amish boy had been killed by a hit-and-run driver on Cattail Road did I know . . . I had struck your son." The young woman reached into her coat pocket and pulled out a newspaper clipping, her hand trembling. "This is how I knew where to find you." Again, the woman's eyes filled with tears. "I'm here to plead for your forgiveness, even though I know I don't deserve it." She broke down weeping.

Aquilla's hands were so clammy that she clasped them together all the more tightly, as if hanging on to herself was the only thing keeping her from falling apart.

"I was so horrified, I checked myself into

a rehab in Philly, but I should have turned myself in to the authorities instead."

Shocked, Aquilla coughed, then managed to find her voice. "Never did I expect to come face-to-face with the person who . . ."

The baby began to stir, and the young woman reached down to touch the infant's face. "I was such a mess back then. I hadn't found the Lord yet . . . or, I should say, He hadn't found me." She went on to explain that, after months in rehab, where she met a man who said he loved her, she discovered she was pregnant. "By December, I was very much alone again, and so down on my luck. I decided to attend a Christmas Eve service not far from my studio apartment, and a compassionate middle-aged couple there took me under their wing and introduced me to Jesus. Up until my baby was born ten days ago, they've been encouraging me along in this new life I've embraced . . . 'discipling me,' as they say. They urged me to own up to my wrongdoing."

Aquilla's pulse was pounding in her head. Yet she knew what she must do. Getting up from her chair, she made her way over to the rocker, pulled it close to where the woman sat with her little one, and sat down. Softly, she said, "Our heavenly Father has already forgiven you . . . so I must do the same."

Tears began to course down the woman's face again. "Thank you," she whispered. "Sounds like I'll be going away to prison for quite a while."

Aquilla replied, "Yet God will be with ya, even there."

"I've heard of Bible studies for inmates," the woman said.

A momentary lull filled the room, and Aquilla looked down at the tiny pink face, still sound asleep. "Who will care for your little one while you serve your time?" she asked.

The woman shook her head, and then her shoulders shook. "No one in my family knows about my baby girl." She tucked the blanket gently around her sleeping child. "I guess Lancaster Social Services will give her a temporary home."

Aquilla struggled to keep her tears in check. "Would ya trust me to care for her instead?"

"Oh, Mrs. Mast, I couldn't—"

"*Ach*, call me Aquilla." She touched the young mother's arm, mentioning that she had done foster care and worked closely with social services in the past. "Your baby will receive all the love I have to give until you return. You have my word on that."

"I . . . I don't know what to say. This is the last thing I expected." The young woman traced her little one's cheek, then caressed the downy curls on her head. "She's all I have left in the world."

"Aw, but you have our dear Lord Jesus . . . and He's walkin' with ya, leading you with tender mercy and love." Aquilla paused for a moment. "In fact, I believe He's led you here to me this very day."

With a kiss on the baby's forehead and some words murmured softly in her ear, she lifted her child into Aquilla's arms. "How can I ever repay you for this kindness? It might be two years or more before I'm a free woman."

"Well then, I'll give your little girl a loving home till ya return for her. I promise to treat her like my very own."

"I believe it." The woman's face broke into a sweet smile, the first since she'd arrived. "I'm sorry, I never even told you my full name. I'm Kathleen Stratton, and my baby's name is Britta, same as my middle name."

Aquilla wondered about the woman's relatives and the young man who'd fathered little Britta, but the precious bundle in her arms moved ever so gently, and the thought of anyone's plan to search for this child quickly flitted out of her mind.

Kathleen must have sensed her concern, since she mentioned that the baby's father had already signed away his rights. "Britta's all mine." Here, Kathleen smiled a sad sort of smile and leaned forward to kiss the baby's tiny forehead once more, her gaze lingering on the darling infant.

After Kathleen's reluctant departure—leaving her newborn and a diaper bag with a stranger—Aquilla went to sit in her comfortable chair and looked down into the eyes of the baby waking in her arms. She placed her pointer finger in the miniature hand and felt the strength of the little one's grasp. "Your Mamma will be thinking 'bout ya every minute she's away . . . and then, one day, she'll come for ya, I'm sure of it." And as she talked softly in *Deitsch*, she realized that this dear one would learn to speak it, too . . . and just how would she understand her mother when she returned?

We'll cross that bridge later, Aquilla decided, her heartstrings tightening around the helpless babe gazing up at her.

CHAPTER 34

Britta couldn't move, she was so stunned. "My birth mother drove the car . . . that killed Eli?" she murmured.

Mamma rose to go to her and clasped her hand in both of hers. "This is the reason I hesitated to tell you the details." Her voice was gentle, and she coughed a little, like she was holding back tears.

I never should've asked, thought Britta as Mamma sat beside her on the bed.

Then Mamma raised Britta's hand to her lips and kissed it.

Feeling numb, Britta said, "Now I understand why you were struggling. I'm sorry I pressed ya so."

"There were many times I agonized over this moment. . . . It seemed that you wouldn't have peace unless I told you everything, dear girl."

Britta let that sink in, realizing she had stirred up that worry.

"And, truth be known, I wondered while I was in the hospital if I would even live to tell ya 'bout your birth mother."

"You were awful sick," Britta replied, looking at her with new eyes.

Mamma nodded. "I never would've agreed to medical treatment otherwise. But thankfully Allen and Sarah urged me to go."

"I'm so glad you're all right now, Mamma."

Mamma smiled. "The Lord God numbers our days. I can trust Him for what's best."

Britta had heard Mamma say this all her life, but hearing it again now made her all the more sympathetic toward her.

They talked further of Kathleen Stratton, and Britta marveled at Mamma's kindness toward the woman. "I'm so glad she came to me," Mamma said softly. "The Lord's plans are perfect . . . always for our *gut*, remember."

For Britta, one question still lingered. "So I guess Kathleen Stratton never returned for me, then."

"Oh, quite the contrary," Mamma said and began to tell her that story. . . .

On an early July day two years after Kathleen Stratton left her baby in Hickory Hollow, a letter arrived in Aquilla's mailbox, alerting her that Kathleen would be coming to pick up her little girl—she had completed her jail sentence.

Though fighting tremendous sadness, Aquilla had expected this moment. She gathered up all of little Britta's clothing, including the Amish attire the petite toddler had been wearing—dresses and aprons and little nightclothes Aquilla had lovingly hand sewn.

When Kathleen appeared at the door, she looked thinner, and her lovely hair had grown significantly. There was a joyfulness on her face, though, and her eyes lit up when she saw Britta sitting on the floor playing with her faceless doll, wearing her Sunday best—a pale pink dress, white organdy cape and apron, and a tiny heart-shaped white head covering. Aquilla hoped it was all right to present Britta in church clothes to her mother.

"She's grown so much!" Kathleen got down on the floor at eye level with Britta, clearly eager to hold her. "She looks so healthy, too." Kathleen held out her hands to her daughter, who shrank back, frowning and looking up at Aquilla. The young woman momentarily grimaced. "Ah . . . of course. She doesn't know who I am."

Despite her own sadness at Britta's impending departure, Aquilla's heart ached for Kathleen. "Given time, she'll bond with ya," she told the young woman, wondering if she sounded convincing enough.

Shy as she was, tiny Britta got up and went over to Aquilla, wanting her to lift her up, which Aquilla did.

Kathleen continued to sit on the floor cross-legged in her jeans and tennis shoes. "She looks so cute in that outfit. Is that how she usually dresses?"

"*Jah*, but just for church or special occasions, so she fits in with the People. Usually she wears little aprons that match the color of her dresses. It's all I know how to sew. Hope that's okay."

Kathleen didn't seem to know what to say.

"I'll go an' get her things." Aquilla excused herself, taking Britta with her to get her favorite blanket.

When she returned with a suitcase, she set it on the floor and put Britta down, wondering if she might warm up to Kathleen a little.

But Britta toddled back over to Aquilla's chair, carrying her blanket, and curled up in it, starting to cry. "Mamma," she whimpered. "Mamma . . ."

Still seated on the floor, Kathleen scooted over to her, trying to cajole her, but Britta cried all the more. Perhaps seeing how futile this was becoming, Kathleen left to go out to her car, where she sat for the longest time.

Aquilla looked out the window to check on her and saw her walking up the road now, wearing dark sunglasses under the bright cloudless sky.

The poor woman's troubled, and no wonder, she thought, holding Britta close in her arms, not knowing what to do.

A half hour later, Kathleen returned and knocked on the front door, the rims of her eyes red. "All this time, I've been imagining what my baby's been up to, looking forward to when I could hold her again and start making a life with her. I should have realized it wouldn't be that simple." She sighed and looked away, tears welling up. "You've obviously been a great mom to her."

"*Denki,*" Aquilla said. "She's a dear little one to care for."

Kathleen's chest rose and fell as emotion seemed to build in her. "And . . . hard as it is, I see now that it would be heartless to take her away. Britta belongs here with you," she said softly.

Astonished, Aquilla looked over at Britta, contentedly playing with her toys on the floor again. "I love her dearly," she said, "but she's *your* daughter. Are ya sure?"

Wiping tears away, Kathleen said, "Yes, and you can give Britta a more settled life. I truly believe God is prompting me to do this. It's something I've had in the back of my mind for a while now." She paused. "I just needed to know I wasn't making a mistake." She went on to say that she would hire an attorney to draw up the adoption papers and have them sent to Aquilla.

Amazed at the young woman's willingness to make this sacrifice for her little daughter, Aquilla couldn't speak for a moment. When she found her voice, she said, "I'll take *gut* care of her. I promise."

"I know you will." Kathleen nodded, a faint smile on her pretty face. "This is the hardest, yet the best thing I've done." She looked across the room with the saddest eyes. "I'd like to visit her next week, if that's all right."

Aquilla agreed. "And there's still time to change your mind. Maybe till the adoption is final, you'd like to see her?"

Kathleen brightened, her eyes still on Britta. "I would love that." Then, rising from the settee, she said, "Bye-bye, sweetheart. I'll see you again soon." She paused, as if struggling for composure. "I pray you grow up to live for Jesus . . . my little Amish girl."

Aquilla reached for the young woman and wrapped her arms around her, their tears falling on each other's shoulders.

Britta brushed tears away as she sat on the edge of the bed, listening intently as Mamma shared her long-ago memories. *Kathleen said I belong here.*

"Are you all right?" Mamma asked, her face registering concern.

She nodded. "It's hard to understand all of this. And what you did for Kathleen—and for me. I mean, she took Eli's life, yet you forgave her . . . and were willing to raise me!"

Mamma nodded her head slowly. "Truth be told, it was the beginning of a lasting healing in me."

Britta considered that, a swirl of emotions fluttering through her. "But I can hardly believe she let you bring me up as your own . . . that she believed God *wanted* that."

Mamma remained silent, her face flushed. "I've often wondered how I would've managed if she'd left with you that day."

Britta's heart felt heavy. "But Eli would be alive today if it weren't for her."

"Ya mustn't think that way—I certainly don't."

"What else can I think?"

Mamma paused to gather herself for a

moment. "I miss Eli every day—nothing can take away my love for him, or those *wunnerbaar* years we had together. But if there hadn't been an accident, Britta . . . I never would've known and loved *you.*"

Britta had always been sensitive to Mamma, but now her heart swelled with overflowing love. "I can't imagine being raised by anyone else."

Long into the night, Britta relived Mamma's shocking disclosure and her description of Kathleen's tearful decision to let her go. She wondered about her, curious if her birth mother ever thought about her or prayed for her, after that final parting.

Where is she now? Did she ever marry . . . start a new family?

Sleep was evasive, and despite prayers of gratitude—and contrary to Mamma's protests—the old doubts began to play again in Britta's mind. She felt she must somehow share in the guilt of what Kathleen had done not only to the Mast family, but to the entire Hickory Hollow community. And she was convinced now that young Aaron Kauffman was right.

No matter what Kathleen thought, I don't belong to the People.

As these thoughts played over in her mind, she realized that a revelation like this might complicate her possibilities for dating in the future. Most of all, she worried how it would affect her close relationship with Susie.

How will she feel if I tell her that my biological mother caused the death of her beloved brother?

CHAPTER 35

Four days after Thanksgiving, Susie bundled up and dashed out to the stable phone to check for messages. She was pleased to hear the recording of Britta's voice, all the way from Missouri.

She leaned her ear into the receiver. "I've had a nice time here but really wish you could've come, too. Mamma sends her love along with Allen, Sarah, and all the *Kinner.* Mamma seems a little stronger but still frail. Lord willin', I'll leave first thing tomorrow and hope to arrive home around ten o'clock."

Susie smiled, then hung up. She looked forward to their coming reunion as she rushed around to finish cleaning out the horse and pony stalls, and then the goat pen. She wished with all of her heart that Mamma were returning with Britta, but she couldn't wait to see her sister.

At that moment, she recalled Ella Mae's remark about why her mother might have chosen to stay in Missouri—*"If ya don't know just yet, it'll come to ya when it's s'posed to,"* Ella Mae had said during the visit in her cozy kitchen.

"What on earth did she mean?" Susie was still baffled.

As she worked in the stable, she brushed Ella Mae's comment aside. When she was very young, she'd sometimes helped Eli with this particular smelly chore, his daily task. Yet never once had he grumbled about it, always displaying a cheerful attitude. *So much like Dat*, she thought, wondering how Eli would feel about Mamma now living in Missouri. "One thing's sure, he wouldn't have resented Allen for it," she murmured as she swept the cement floor.

So why do I? She felt helpless to surrender caring for Mamma to anyone, even Allen.

Britta dozed off and on during the latter part of the seemingly endless journey toward home, but when she was awake, she relived the strange yet informative conversation with Mamma. Mamma had told her the day after

Thanksgiving that she would leave it up to Britta if she wanted to share her story with Susie or anyone else. "It's yours to tell . . . or not." The way she'd said it made Britta believe that Mamma would not be returning home for a very long time.

Britta had decided she wanted to tell close family, and she asked Mamma to tell Allen and Sarah, as well as write to Henry and Polly about it. "Everyone else should know, too," Britta told Mamma.

Mamma had agreed but suggested she talk to Susie herself. "Since you're such close sisters."

"I'll think about when that should be," Britta had replied, feeling heavy at the thought of doing so.

Mamma had also confided that, through the years, she had talked to Ella Mae Zook about Kathleen. So Ella Mae already knew.

Yet the Wise Woman has never held it against me. It was this fear that nagged at Britta as she rode toward home—that she might bear the blame in some way for the accident that had eventually linked her to her adoptive Amish family. If she let herself ponder it all too much, it made her terribly uneasy. *Did Kathleen give me up as a kind of substitute for Eli? A sort of guilt offering for her crime?*

It was difficult to get all the facts settled

in her mind, let alone in her heart. But Britta was very tired and yearned for home, to sleep in her own bed, under the roof where dear Mamma had brought her up as her own daughter. *She forgave Kathleen for Eli's death*, thought Britta, still astounded by it. *I always knew Mamma was good, but to show such compassion and acceptance . . . Could I have done that? She's loved me like her own flesh and blood!*

Britta leaned against the passenger van window, watching the lights of an industrial park whiz by as the vehicle moved along bustling Route 30 and then exited onto the off-ramp to Route 340. Mamma had also told her that she was quite sure who had been leaving the bouquet of flowers at the site of the accident on the anniversary of Eli's death. "I've seen it there every year since Kathleen got out of prison."

Pondering this once more, Britta tried to imagine Susie's reaction, dreading the difficult memories it would dredge up for her dear big sister. *When should I tell her, Lord?*

When Britta finally arrived home late that night, Susie immediately sensed something bothering her, or at least an air of distraction. Or was it melancholy? Perhaps she was only tired, and who wouldn't be after all those hours riding in the van? Even so, she knew her sister well enough to see something was off beam.

Susie offered to help her unpack upstairs, but Britta shook her head, as if ready to call it a day. Susie hugged her again and, feeling disappointed, made her way to her own room. *Maybe she'll want to talk more tomorrow,* she thought. Even so, Susie hoped all was well as she sat on her bed, perplexed.

But the next day, Britta seemed even more preoccupied at both breakfast and the noon meal, and she spent an unusually long time in the stable—far longer than necessary. For a while, Susie wondered if she might be calling to let Mamma know she'd arrived safely, but when she asked Britta about it later, Britta said she'd called Allen first thing that morning, after milking the goats.

"So early?" Susie asked.

"Well, Allen's up before dawn" was all Britta said.

"Did somethin' upset ya in Missouri?" Susie pressed, wanting to know.

Britta only shrugged, then politely declined dessert and headed to the utility room to don her coat and scarf. After she had left the house for the stable yet again, Susie rose and went to peer out the back window, observing the slump of Britta's shoulders as she slowly walked to the barn.

What could be wrong? Susie wondered as she returned to the table to cut a small slice of the custard pie she'd made as a special surprise for Britta, then poured some coffee for herself. *Has Mamma's health worsened?* But no, Britta's voice message had indicated their mother was doing better. So what could it be?

As Susie sat there and opened Dat's German *Biewel* to read from the Psalms, a powerful yearning came over her. She wished for the thousandth time that Dat and Eli were still alive, and that Mamma had never left for Missouri. Yet Dat had always said one could draw strength from Scripture, so while Susie read, she tried not to fret over Britta's detachment but to trust in her earthly father's promise . . . and in her heavenly Father's care.

Another day passed, and Britta continued to be pleasant enough, even going out of her way to be extra kind, but Susie could read between the lines that all was not well. Her sister was more silent than sullen, and while this worried Susie, she went about her work in the house and in the shop, praying for whatever was causing Britta to behave like this.

That day, a letter arrived in the mail from

Allen. It was thicker than usual, and she pulled her coat and scarf tight against the chilling wind as she took the mail to the house. Britta was taking a turn in the little shop, helping several customers who had braved the cold in their horse-drawn carriages.

Stepping into the kitchen, where she'd left a hearty ham and cabbage soup simmering on the stove, Susie noticed that her name was the only one on the envelope when, before, Allen had always included Britta.

Susie took a seat at the kitchen table in her coat, loosened her scarf, then opened the envelope, hoping Mamma was still doing okay.

A quick scan of the lines revealed the letter wasn't about Mamma at all. Rather, Allen was planning to rent out the family home within the next six months or so.

> *This might come as a shock to you, but I'm going to need the money to help offset the expense of having Mamma here. The farm hasn't done as well this year as I'd hoped, and I don't want to drain the community alms fund to pay for her medical expenses.*

"And Britta's almost grown, and we're livin' here rent-free." Susie whispered what he hadn't said, resentment beginning to rise.

She continued reading.

I appreciate all you and Britta have done to help keep your heads above water financially, but it's hard for me to maintain two households. With only the two of you living in the big farmhouse now, you should start to think about one of you possibly moving in with Polly and Henry for the time being, to assist with the children, and the other with Aendi Emmalyn, who could use some help about now, too.

Of course, you're also welcome here and could help Sarah with Mamm and the younger ones.

Susie could scarcely believe this. "He's offering us to move *out there*?" she murmured, distraught. Looking toward the window, she shook her head and groaned.

Why hadn't Allen suggested that both she and Britta move in with Polly or another relative here . . . together? But maybe he'd already talked with Polly and Henry about this, and they weren't in a position to take in two more.

Even so, Allen was the eldest son; what he decided on their behalf was how things would be. All the same, Susie felt sad thinking of Britta having to move away and no longer enjoying the good fellowship of the church youth here. And, more important, her growing friendship with Roy Lantz.

Terribly frustrated, Susie wondered if perhaps Britta had gotten wind of this while visiting Mamma, yet was afraid to say anything to her. Was that the reason for her distraction since returning home?

CHAPTER 36

By the time Britta closed the shop for the day and came inside, Susie had made a delicious supper of macaroni goulash, one of her sister's favorites.

After the silent prayer, as they took turns dishing up the plentiful food—enough for leftovers—Susie mentioned that she'd received an interesting letter from Allen, hoping to engage her sister, who seemed unusually withdrawn and serious yet again.

Britta's head popped up. "Oh?"

"He seems to be thinkin' ahead."

Suddenly, Britta looked worried. "What about?"

Susie hadn't brought this up to trick her into talking, but now that Britta seemed attentive, she said, "I believe he's been discussing some things with Mamma."

Now Britta looked startled.

"Do ya know anything 'bout this?" Susie blurted.

A cautious expression came over her sister's face. "What're ya talking 'bout, exactly?"

"I just wondered if this might be why you've been so quiet since your trip." There. Susie hoped she'd opened the door for some meaningful conversation.

Britta took another bite and chewed for the longest time. Susie felt on edge, waiting.

When Britta finally did speak, there was a softness to her voice. "Actually, I've been tryin' to decide for days when to tell ya something."

Now Susie was confused. If Britta already knew about Allen's hope of renting out the house, why hadn't he included her sister in the address or the letter's salutation?

Britta stared up at the day clock on the wall and squirmed on the wood bench across the table from Susie. She seemed uneasy. "Before I left Missouri, Mamma said *I* should be the one to talk to you 'bout this."

So did Mamma discuss this with Britta? Susie studied her sister. "Are ya worried, maybe, how all this could affect your friendship with Hazel? Or, maybe, Roy?"

Britta locked eyes with her, seemingly speechless at first. "Do you think it could?" She paused, eyes wide.

Susie could see that Britta was both baffled and hurt. "*Ach*, I didn't mean to—"

"*Nee*, maybe it's best that we *do* get this out in the open," Britta said, tears brimming. "I just didn't know how to bring it up." She took a deep breath. "Honestly, I needed time to think things through." She sighed again.

Confused, Susie reached for her coffee cup and took a sip.

Slowly, falteringly, Britta began to tell Susie that the driver who hit Eli had come to visit Mamma more than a year later to confess her crime. "Mamma never told either of us."

Susie gasped and realized that she and Britta had been mistakenly talking about two very different things. "The hit-and-run driver came here . . . to see Mamma?" Susie could hardly voice the words.

Britta nodded. "*Jah*, and Mamma not only forgave the woman when she confessed, but she offered to keep her newborn baby while she served her time in jail." Britta stopped for a moment to brush tears away. "And . . . that baby was *me*."

"Wha-at?" Susie's hand flew to her chest as she tried to comprehend what Britta had just said. "I don't understand."

"Remember the name you saw on the birth certificate—Kathleen Stratton?" Britta asked.

Susie was still struggling to make sense of all this. "I remember."

"Honestly, Mamma said she only decided to reveal this now since I've been so miserable," Britta said. "And I think it worried her when she became so sick."

"It made sense to tell ya while you were out there visiting," Susie managed to say, head still swimming.

"That's what Mamma said." Britta began to share that Kathleen had eventually returned for her but couldn't bring herself to take Britta away from the only mother she knew. "The bond 'tween Mamma and me was so strong by then. . . ."

Susie fought hard not to stare at her. "I don't know what to say. This just doesn't even seem possible."

"I know," Britta replied. "I lost nearly a night of sleep after Mamma told me."

There was an awkward pause between them as Susie tried to get it through her head that Britta's birth mother had been the one driving that terrible night. *She killed Eli!*

"You'll have to excuse me," Susie said, getting up suddenly.

Britta rose to her feet. "You okay?"

Susie put her hand on her forehead. "Stress headache, I guess." She paused. "I just need . . . uh . . . maybe an aspirin."

"Can I get ya one?"

Susie shook her head and rushed from the room.

Britta leaned her face into her hands, feeling abandoned at the very moment she needed solace and acceptance. *O Lord, help me*, she prayed. *Susie's devastated.*

She got up from the table, poured some hot water from the teakettle, and found a little box of peppermint tea in the cupboard, thinking there was a good reason why Ella Mae always had this tea simmering. She stared out the window and wondered if Susie was all right. Should she go upstairs and check on her?

Trying to be calm, Britta steeped the tea while Susie cried or prayed—or whatever she was doing upstairs. *Poor sister*, she thought, remembering how astonished she'd been when Mamma had told her.

After praying in her room for a time, Susie began to feel more peaceful. *What a burden this knowledge must be for Britta!*

Thinking back on their years together as a

family, she realized that Britta had been held
securely by the hand of God through every
aspect of her growing-up years. There was
no doubt in Susie's mind.

Eventually, she left her room and made
her way downstairs, where she saw Britta sitting alone at the table, having tea. Her heart
broke for her, and she made her way across
the room and sat down. "Britta . . . the accident wasn't your fault. I hope ya know that."

Britta nodded, eyes fixed on her.

Susie gave her a smile. "And what an unexpected blessing that Mamma got to keep
you. *We* got to keep ya, sister."

"After Mamma told me all this at Thanksgiving, I actually wondered some if I should
stay in Hickory Hollow." Britta set aside her
empty cup. "I've been worryin', and still am,
that Hazel might have doubts now about what
kind of person I am, or just how Amish I
really am. That is, *if* I decide to tell her."

Susie was concerned to hear Britta talk
like this. "But don't ya *want* to be frank with
your friend?"

"What if she rejects me?" Britta replied.
"And what if Roy does . . . if I tell him someday?"

Susie considered what was best to say; she
did not want to risk the wrong thing. "Seems
to me that bein' Amish is less about being

born into a community than 'bout purposefully choosing that community and pledgin' yourself to it." She paused a moment, trying to gather her wits. "And most important, to God and to the church."

Britta sat very still, as though considering what Susie had said.

Then Susie asked, "You *are* planning to be baptized, *jah*?"

Again, Britta paused before answering. "Well . . . I *had* been."

Susie's heart was in her throat now. "But how does knowin' all of this change something as significant as that?"

Britta leaned her head into her hands, obviously troubled.

Susie looked at her lovingly, having cared deeply for her ever since that day she first held her as a tiny infant, with Mamma sitting nearby. "Sister, have ya thought, just maybe, that God brought you to us for a reason?" she asked quietly. "That He planned for you to be raised Plain?"

Removing her hands from her face, Britta brightened slightly. "I can't help but wonder."

Susie was encouraged. "What if you could honor Him by starting baptismal classes next year?"

Britta's eyes grew wider. "Join church early, ya mean?"

"If that's what you intend to do eventually, why wait?" Susie asked, not wanting to pressure her even though it was her greatest desire to somehow keep Britta safely in the Amish church, living and working among the People.

Britta's face clouded again. "Oh, Susie," she said gloomily, "I honestly don't know how to tell Hazel, or even Roy . . . if we're still friends once I'm courting age, that is."

Susie reached her hand across the table for Britta's. "I believe Hazel will always be your friend. As for Roy, if he cares for ya, he'll listen with his heart."

Britta nodded slowly, her eyes glimmering.

"None of us chooses the family we're born into." Susie breathed a prayer before slowly continuing. "When all's said and done, our hearts have more to do with us bein' Amish, and I think both Hazel and Roy would agree with that."

Later, as they cleared the table and began to wash the dishes, Susie felt she should not tell Britta about Allen's plan to rent out the house just yet. *This is more than enough for one evening*, she thought, glancing at Britta wiping dishes with the hen-and-chicks tea towel Mamma had finished embroidering before she left for Missouri.

Susie rinsed the next plate with hot water

and stacked it on the dish rack. She and Britta had worked together so well all these years, even when little Britta would push a chair up to the counter to dry dishes.

Glancing at her now, Susie hated the idea that she and Britta might have to live apart till Britta was ready to marry. The thought made Susie feel almost ill.

CHAPTER

37

O ver the course of the next day, Susie
and Britta talked more about Kathleen Stratton and how amazing it
was that she'd willingly relinquished her baby
. . . and of Mamma's loving generosity toward her and little Britta. They discussed it
during breakfast and while redding up the
kitchen, and later, while shoveling snow and
working together in the stable. And all the
while, despite this tender time with Britta,
Susie tried not to feel disappointment that
this would be their first Christmas without
Mamma home—and their last Christmas in
this wonderful house.

When should I tell Britta of Allen's plans?

Susie offered to do Britta's barn chores that evening, frustrated with herself at still not having told her sister about Allen's intention to rent the house. *With Britta still processing Mamma's news, the timing hasn't been right.*

Britta was quick to say she didn't need help with barn chores and that Susie was working too hard as it was. "Like always," Britta added, giving her a sideways glance.

Susie ignored that and mulled over how to reply to Allen. She had hoped to simply give him a call while working in the stable, but she'd let Britta have her way instead. So Susie spent the evening finishing up the latest family tree, one a fancy customer had ordered with a border of pink and blue hearts.

Later, when she heard Britta clump indoors and remove her snow boots, Susie wished she could talk to Mamma about all of this. *Oh, to have her here right now!*

Saturday at market, the corridors were crammed with customers in search of unique options for gift giving. Not only were *Englischers* rushing about, but many Plain folk were Christmas shopping, too.

She spotted Kate Yoder walking toward

the specialty crackers and dip booth and immediately recalled a time when Obie had stopped by their market stand to ask if she'd go with him right quick to help him find some items for his mother. With only a couple of days left till Christmas, she'd teased him about cutting it so close.

"That's why I need your help," he'd said, grinning.

"You must think I'm a *gut* shopper."

"Well, aren't ya?"

"It depends."

"On what?" He glanced at her.

"Well," she said with a laugh, "on how much ya have to spend."

Obie had paused right there in the middle of the aisle and rubbed his chin rather dramatically. "Hmm . . . I'd give my Mamma the moon if I could, or anything else she might want."

"Okay, then," Susie replied, "what about a year's worth of that fancy relish she likes so much?"

Now Obie was laughing, and he nodded his head. "*Gut* idea, Susie. Let's go an' see 'bout that."

Susie couldn't believe it, wondering if he would actually purchase that many jars of the spicy relish his mother so enjoyed.

In the end, he bought up a full dozen—

one for each month of the year—and thanked Susie profusely, though comically. And to this day, she remembered how very happy she'd felt when he walked her back to Mamma's market stand, having taken her advice without a blink of an eye.

Despite the awkwardness of recent days, Susie enjoyed working alongside Britta. While typically subdued in public, her sister brightened when wrapping up one of her quilted table runners or a half dozen popcorn balls for a customer. The jams and jellies they'd brought along had run out, so Susie was very happy to take multiple orders for her cross-stitched family trees.

After the hectic noon hour, Roy's mother, tall, blond Elizabeth Lantz, and his two younger sisters, Lizzy and Jessie, came strolling up to the market table. Elizabeth sought out Britta and inquired about her table runners. "They'd make real nice Christmas gifts," she remarked, smiling warmly while her daughters glanced at each other as if sharing a secret. Susie noticed Britta's cheeks flush, although she seemed to be enjoying the attention. *She seems comfortable with Elizabeth*, thought Susie, wondering if she might become Britta's future mother-in-law.

"*Jah,* I'm accepting custom orders," Britta was telling Roy's mother.

Elizabeth looked quite pleased. "It's only a few weeks till Christmas. Are ya sure?"

"Just tell me which colors you'd want," Britta replied. "I'll find a way."

Susie detected an eagerness to please in her sister's demeanor. *Is she still worried what people will think of her if they know how she came to be in Hickory Hollow, maybe? Or is it because Elizabeth is Roy's Mamm?*

Lizzy and Jessie were chattering quietly between themselves, admiring the tiny stitches in Britta's table runners, oohing and aahing. Susie took notice of their sweet interaction and close companionship. In spite of their age gap, she and Britta had always had a similar relationship, and thinking about that, she suddenly felt determined not to take Allen's suggestions as to where she and Britta should live once the house was rented out.

Not separately, she thought with a sigh.

It was late that night when Susie crept down to the outer room to put on her coat and boots, then darted out to the stable through the snow with the big flashlight. She'd waited till Britta was asleep and even slipped into her sister's room to listen to her slow, steady breathing, just to be sure.

Now, as she dialed Allen's phone number, she planned to leave a voice mail, knowing there was little chance she would reach him at this hour. Even so, it was only right to tell her elder brother how essential it was for Britta to remain in Hickory Hollow to eventually be courted by Roy. *They should at least have a chance.* And, if at all possible, she and Britta should stay together.

The phone rang and rang, but just when she assumed it would go to messaging, Allen answered, "Hullo, Masts."

"Allen." She faltered at hearing his voice. "It's . . . Susie."

"*Ach,* so late there! Yous all right?"

"*Jah.*" She paused. "I just need to talk privately . . . 'bout your recent letter."

"What's on your mind?"

She sensed his tiredness. "Do ya have a few minutes? Don't wanna keep ya."

"Well, you've got me now—was just checkin' on one of the calves—so go ahead."

She began by saying that Britta and Roy Lantz had been friendly for some months now.

"Mamma mentioned somethin' a while back. Real *gut* young man, Roy is. *Gut* family, too."

Susie agreed. "Yes, and it's one reason I think Britta and I need to stay in Hickory Hollow."

"Oh . . . is that right?"

Susie held her breath, unable to speak now that she'd said what she felt she ought to.

"I'm sorry, Susie, but I can't wait to rent the house till Britta weds. As I mentioned in my letter, I don't want to run up a big bill with the community alms fund. Besides that, Mamm's takin' some mighty expensive medicine, and so is little Maggie here lately, too." Allen paused. "Between the two of them, the bills for the doctor visits have been sky-high."

Susie knew that her young niece also struggled with asthma and allergies.

"Well, what if Britta and I took jobs outside of Hickory Hollow to pay you rent?" Susie felt panicked. "We could bring in more money that way."

Allen was quiet for a moment. "I'd never expect that of you. It wouldn't be right."

"But we *need* to stay here, together." Her voice broke. "Please let me do my part, at least."

"I've put pen to paper and tried to make things stretch as best I can," he said apologetically. "*Nee*, I won't put yous through that."

"Allen, I'm willin' to do whatever it takes

. . . and if ya get the rent money, what's it matter who pays it?"

"It would be quite a lot," he said. "Listen, Susie, I'm sorry the timing isn't better. This pains me, too."

Not as much as it does me, she thought. *I don't want to lose Britta this way. I'll have no one. . . .*

"We're just dealin' with so much right now," she finally said, then added, "Maybe this isn't the right time to mention it, but Britta said Mamma was going to tell you 'bout her birth mother . . . and her connection to Eli."

Allen was silent a moment. "*Jah,* Sarah and I were shocked to think Mamm kept it quiet all these years—such a secret! But Britta is family no matter where she came from."

Even though he couldn't see her, Susie nodded, clutching the phone.

After she and Allen said good-bye, Susie hoped her brother would reconsider. *He needs to take his time deciding . . . not rush things.*

Sighing heavily, she hurried back through the cold to the dark house.

38

At Preaching the next morning, Susie couldn't help noticing Britta talking to Roy's teenage sisters, Lizzy and Jessie, before they lined up with the womenfolk outside the temporary house of worship. It was a sunny but blustery day, and snow sparkled on the field with jewel-like radiance.

Waiting quietly, Susie gazed toward the front of the line, where Mamma usually stood. As each week had passed, she missed her mother more. She realized anew how very close she and Mamma and Britta had always been. But based on Mamma's continued fragile state, in spite of some improvements, Susie had begun to doubt she would ever return home.

Would it make sense for me to move out there? Susie thought. Allen had actually offered that in his letter. That way, Britta could live with Aendi Emmalyn till she was old enough to marry. *Might be for the best,* Susie thought reluctantly as she stepped forward to the women's entrance.

That evening, Britta headed over to visit Hazel, thanks to Susie's offer of a buggy ride, since the wind remained gusty and cold.

When Britta arrived, Hazel ushered her inside and closed the door. "I made fudge yesterday, and there's some left for us tonight." Hazel grinned.

"Sounds yummy."

"We'll have hot cocoa to drink, too, unless ya want coffee. Double the sweets!" Hazel glanced toward the door. "It's mighty chilly out there."

Britta followed her into the kitchen, where some white paper and two sets of scissors lay on the wood table. "Looks like you're gonna make snowflakes."

"*Jah*, and angels, too." Hazel's eyes shone. "Know how?"

Britta nodded. "Mamma taught me when I was little."

Hazel moved to the stove, where a small

pan of milk was warming. "So, coffee or cocoa?"

"Whatever you're havin's fine."

"Well, I could live on chocolate, so . . ."

Britta laughed. "Then cocoa it is."

Hazel stirred the milk, glancing at her. "Say, did I tell ya that my Mamm plans to give each of her sisters one of your Christmas table runners?"

Britta was delighted. "She must've bought them at market when I wasn't around."

"Maybe you were getting lunch or a snack," Hazel replied, pouring the hot milk into two large mugs before adding her homemade cocoa mix. She topped it off with miniature marshmallows. "Do ya know where you and Susie will spend Christmas this year?"

Britta didn't want to dwell on the sad fact that Mamma would be so far away. "We'll be with Polly and her family in Landisville. I'll keep the two younger children occupied while Susie helps Polly get dinner ready." Britta went on to say how attached her four-year-old nephew was to her. "Over the years, Joey's become my little shadow," she said, smiling at the thought.

"I'm sure he has." Hazel nodded. "Children are really drawn to ya."

"And cats, too," Britta said with a laugh.

"Well, both must sense your gentleness."

Hazel motioned for them to sit at the table, where she removed the plastic lid from the fudge and offered some to Britta.

"This time of year, it's hard to quit nibblin'," Britta admitted, taking a piece.

They enjoyed the rich fudge and sipped their cocoa, talking about the different kinds of pies and cookies they planned to make. Hazel mentioned wanting to make a brownie mix and put it in jars with pretty bows on top as gifts for some of their *Englischer* neighbors.

"Great idea!"

"'Specially for women who work all day away from home, ya know."

Britta agreed, glad for this visit with Hazel, but later, as they were cutting out paper snowflakes and angels, she felt somewhat tense. *Should I tell her? Is now the time?* she wondered, remembering what Susie had said about Hazel always being a friend.

"You're awful quiet—are ya thinking 'bout something?" Hazel asked, glancing at her.

"*Ach*, sorry," Britta said quietly. "I've been wanting to talk to ya, since you're my closest friend."

"Everything okay?"

Britta couldn't back out now. "Well, while I was in Missouri, Mamma finally talked with me 'bout my adoption." She went on to share all that she'd learned. "I wanted you to know, hard as it is to tell ya."

Apparently dumbfounded at this revelation, Hazel frowned, and her eyes fluttered.

Britta's heart pounded. *Have I made a mistake?*

"How do you feel 'bout all this?" Hazel asked at last, her voice pinched.

"I felt just sick at first . . . and awful sad, too. I didn't know what to think or how to feel, really. Sometimes I still don't."

Hazel shook her head, as if trying to absorb this. "*Ach*, to think that the woman who birthed ya . . . well, it's shocking."

Britta drew a slow breath. "I was hesitant to share it, worried you might see me differently."

"Aw, Britta, I *know* you, and I know your adoptive family." Hazel stopped for a moment, then continued. "Your birth mother made a terrible mistake and caused a painful break in Caleb and Aquilla Mast's family tree. But she also did a selfless thing by letting Aquilla raise you as her daughter." She reached for Britta's hand. "I'm thankful for that."

Ever so relieved, Britta gave her a smile.

"This doesn't change anything 'bout our friendship. You're my best friend."

Britta squeezed her hand. "If ya don't mind, will ya keep this to yourself? At least for the time being."

"Sure, you can trust me."

"I've thought of talking to the bishop and his wife," Britta said. "I'd like to get his wisdom on what to tell or not tell folks. And, too, I have some questions to ask."

"Bishop Beiler will know how to handle it, if anyone does," Hazel said, encouraging her.

Britta truly hoped so.

Susie sat in the front room next to the stove, addressing Christmas cards. Always before, Mamma had mailed cards to the extended family on behalf of the three of them, while Susie and Britta would send a few to their closest cousins and friends. This year, though, with Mamma in Missouri, Susie wanted to send out more of her own, thinking Britta might want to do the same.

She got up to stretch and look out at the snow, wondering about Britta.

Staring at the front door, Susie remembered what her sister had said about Kathleen appearing there on the porch with baby Britta in her arms. She wondered if Mamma had kept this under her bonnet all these years because she realized how it would affect Britta and, possibly, her future.

Turning, Susie looked down to see a black cat hair on Mamma's favorite chair, evidence of Lucy. *Even as a little girl, Britta liked to sit in this chair and play with her faceless dolly,* she recalled.

Despite the heartbreak of Britta's tale, there was an unmistakable silver lining: Britta had come into Mamma's life at just the right time. *And I sure needed a little sister,* Susie thought, remembering how she'd secretly believed that God had sent Britta along as a gift after Eli's death.

Now if I can just tend to Britta's troubled heart and help see her through to joining church. She stacked the completed Christmas cards and set them to the side, imagining the wondrous day of her sister's future baptism. *O dear Lord, be our Compass and gentle Shepherd,* she prayed.

39

The minute Susie and Britta finished pinning the washing to the basement clotheslines the next morning, Britta dashed upstairs to the kitchen. By the time Susie trudged up there, Britta was already sitting at the table with her writing paper nearby.

Susie began to prepare the ingredients for a beef stew for the noon meal, wanting to make something warm and hearty when it was so bitter cold outside. Even though winter hadn't officially arrived by the calendar, it was making itself known.

Now and then, Susie glanced over at Britta, aware of how rapidly her hand was moving across the page. Although she was curious about whom she was writing to, Susie did not inquire.

When Britta finished and was folding the

stationery, Susie asked, "How're the table runners comin' along for Elizabeth Lantz?"

"I got up early this morning to cut out all the pieces," Britta replied, pushing the letter into an envelope.

"*Des gut,*" Susie said, continuing to chop celery and onions for the stew.

Britta leaned her elbows on the table and looked now at Susie. "I went out on a limb and told Hazel 'bout my birth mother last night."

"I wondered."

"She encouraged me to go ahead and talk to the bishop. So, after dinner today, I'm goin' over there before the snow starts up again."

Susie nodded, a little surprised. Even so, she replied, "You can always trust the bishop."

"Mamma's often said that, too." Britta began to address the envelope.

"He and Mary'll be glad to see ya, sister."

Britta rose and went to the utility room behind the kitchen. When she returned wearing her winter things, she said, "I want to get this letter in the mail to Mamma. I'll be right back."

"Okay," Susie said, wondering what Britta had written.

Britta felt as if she were walking on eggshells as she entered Bishop Beiler's farmhouse later that afternoon. Mary welcomed her into the cozy kitchen, where a number of the bishop's white long-sleeved shirts were drying near the stove. The familiar smell of baking bread pervaded the room, giving Britta a sense of comfort.

About that time, Bishop Beiler appeared in the back doorway and greeted her with a smile above his long white beard. *"Wie geht's, Britta?"* he said, removing his work coat and hat, coming in from the blacksmith shop, Britta assumed.

For an instant, she was taken aback at how casual he looked in his heavy black sweater over a blue shirt, open at the throat. "I hope I'm not interruptin'. . . ."

Bishop shook his head and moved a chair over near the stove for her. She was glad for the chance to warm up while waiting for Mary to join them. *They're kind to welcome me,* she thought as the bishop went to wash his hands at the sink.

Then, suddenly, the realization of why she'd come made her jittery, and she wanted to change her mind and go home.

Mary broke the stillness. "Would ya like some warm tea?"

Britta nodded and thanked her.

"Looks like more snow's comin'." Bishop Beiler glanced toward the windows near the table as he pulled up a chair for himself.

"Weren't many buggies on the road just now," Britta replied.

He nodded, his big eyes soft. "What brings ya today?"

She glanced at Mary at the stove, pouring hot water, and wished she would return to the circle of three chairs. Her presence was a comfort, and Britta needed the support. "*Ach*, this is the hardest thing I think I've ever done," she finally managed to eke out.

"Comin' here?" Mary asked over her shoulder.

Embarrassed at how it sounded, Britta nodded all the same. She'd never had any reason to seek out the man of God on her own like this.

"Just relax," Mary said. "I'll bring ya a sugar cookie, too, with your tea."

They must think I've come to confess sin, Britta thought, all the more nervous.

"I'll have one, too, dear, while your hand's in the cookie jar," Bishop said, his gaze shifting toward Britta. He gave her a thoughtful look over his spectacles.

"Well, ya best watch your sugar, John," Mary said, coming over with the tea, and a cookie for only Britta.

"Sad yet true." Bishop gave a chuckle.

Britta felt a little sorry for him and, because of it, decided as she sipped her tea to eat her cookie later. Suddenly, the kitchen felt too warm. *I must say what I came here to say.*

"Take your time with your tea," Mary said sweetly, as if sensing something was troubling her.

"I'm all right," Britta said, again thankful Mary was there. She took a breath and began slowly. "While I was in Missouri, Mamma told me some things that alarmed me but also confirmed my feelings . . . of not fitting in. Well, of not bein' worthy to be one of the People."

Bishop's eyes were fixed on her. He leaned forward and folded his callused hands, then pressed them against his full beard. "Go on."

Slowly, she revealed everything she knew about her birth mother, and how she had ultimately given up her baby girl for Aquilla to raise.

Mary sighed as a big tear rolled down her round face.

Britta continued, "For most of my life, I've wondered if I belonged here in Hickory Hollow. Could this perhaps be why?"

Clearly shaken, Bishop leaned back in his chair and ran his hand through his gray hair. "You were raised by a fine, godly Amishwoman who taught ya the things of the Lord." He paused and drew an audible breath. "Because of that, you know that *Gott*'s ways are just and true . . . and sovereign."

She agreed with a nod, weary from repeating this difficult account.

Bishop Beiler went on to say that, the way he saw it, she had been given the gift of a Plain life. "The beginning of a wondrous blessing, in fact."

His words made her stop and think.

"I love Mamma so much, and my whole Mast family. And I've enjoyed growin' up here, but learning that my birth mother killed Eli makes me feel unworthy." She stopped to catch her breath. "It was a terrible tragedy for my adoptive family. And knowin' now what I do, I feel I'm a reminder to them of it."

Mary's gaze skittered across to her husband.

"I understand why ya might think thataway," Bishop said, rubbing his wrinkled forehead. "But listen when I say that it's not how our Lord sees ya a'tall." He shook his head. "*Gott* knows your heart better than you do, Britta . . . and He sees your faithful obedience."

In that moment, she wanted to ask the bishop something but hesitated, instead taking another sip of tea, needing time to gather courage. At last, and still holding the cookie in her left hand, she said timidly, "I wonder if ya might be willing to tell the membership 'bout the woman who birthed me . . . that she was the driver who caused Eli's death. So I don't have to be worrying 'bout it coming out." Britta also told the bishop that her mother had left it up to her to decide whether or not to tell anyone. "Mamma's told my older siblings, and till now I've only shared this with Susie and one other person."

Mary's sweet face expressed gentle concern as the bishop said he would handle things for her. "And there'll be no condemnation of you, I'll see to that. What happened to Eli Mast wasn't your doing. I urge ya to commit any feelings of shame to *Gott*." He gave her a reassuring smile. "The People will be understanding toward ya."

Britta appreciated that. Like the bishop, Mamma and Susie had also been kind and merciful. But a thick wall around her heart kept her from surrendering the burden she carried. Very early this morning, she'd awakened with a renewed sense of what she had to do. And an urgency unlike any she'd ever felt.

"There's something else," Britta said. "What would ya think if I tried to find the woman?"

Mary's breath puffed out distinctly, and her shoulders slumped.

The bishop studied Britta, as if trying to give her his best guidance. "Well," he said, followed by a lengthy pause, "biblical faith rests in God's promises. Leavin' the Amish life even for a time to find this woman would be a test of that faith."

For a moment, Britta pondered the fact that she would soon be in her *Rumschpringe*, which meant she would be free to search for Kathleen as soon as her July birthday. "I'd still like to find her, though—mostly out of curiosity . . . to see her, to talk to her, to know what she's like." She paused. *And if I fit in with her.*

"Keep in mind that she might not want to be found, though. *Ach*, I'd hate to see ya hurt or disappointed." Mary reached over to pat the back of her hand. "And if you do find her, I hope you'll be careful how close ya get. She's an outsider, dear."

But also my flesh and blood, thought Britta.

Thick snowflakes began to fall as Susie watched Britta make the turn into the driveway. Before her sister could unhitch Brambles up near the stable, Susie went out to help, the snow coming faster now.

"I told the bishop and Mary 'bout Kathleen Stratton," Britta said as they worked together. "Everything Mamma shared with me."

Aware of the anxiety in Britta's voice, she asked, "Are ya all right?"

"It was hard." Britta tightened her scarf. "And Mary cried, which made it even harder. I think it *ferhoodled* them both . . . and no wonder."

"*Jah*," Susie said.

Britta glanced at her. "I also stuck my neck out and asked for the bishop's help in tellin' the People. I want it out in the open—don't want the grapevine to get a hold of it."

"*Gut* thinkin'." Susie assumed he'd do that at a members' meeting after the next Preaching service.

Britta paused, then continued. "I asked Bishop somethin' else." She shivered a little. "About searching for my birth mother."

Susie felt a wave of shock. "You want to?"

Britta nodded. "I do."

Susie thought of asking if she'd try to visit her, too, but she could see how difficult this was for Britta. "Does Mamma know?"

"It's what I wrote in the last letter I sent."

Susie cringed, afraid how it would affect Mamma to hear this. *Would she have told Britta about the past if she'd known Britta would search?*

Britta led the mare out of the shafts and toward the stable, while Susie moved the buggy over to the carriage shed, somewhat comforted that Britta had opened up to her about all of this. But now she was concerned how Kathleen, if found, might affect and influence her dear, uncertain sister.

40

Susie walked across the backyard to the house, contemplating all that Britta had revealed from her visit to the bishop. Inside, she headed to the basement to check on the hanging clothes, which were still damp. It would likely take the rest of the afternoon and possibly overnight for them to dry.

Standing there, she remembered the times she and Britta had helped Mamma hang the washing on these lines Dat had strung up so long ago. Mamma had used some of that time to help teach them the Beatitudes and how to say the Lord's Prayer. Britta had always been so eager to learn, like a little sponge soaking up the things Mamma shared about the "simple gifts"—love, joy, peace, patience, kindness, goodness, faithfulness, gentleness, and self-control—signs of the Holy Spirit in their lives.

Surely Britta won't abandon those essential teachings, or the things that have made us a family, Susie thought. *Or will a relationship with her birth mother put a wedge between us?*

Sitting on the bottom step, Susie stared at the wringer washer in the large area where they always sorted the laundry. This space where she and Britta sometimes played on wintry days while Mamma ran the clothes through the wringer and into the rinse tub. One time, her sister had pinched a clothespin on the end of her nose and chased Susie around till it was quite bruised. For more than a week afterward, it had turned nearly every color of the rainbow. *Britta has filled my days with life and fun.*

Susie trudged back up the stairs and spotted the mail truck moving along the road. Hurrying to slip on her coat, she headed out to get the mail.

Nice, she thought, seeing a letter from her sister Polly and another from Allen.

In the house, she hung up her coat and walked to the front room to sit near the stove to open Polly's letter. Like Mamma, Polly was faithful about writing nearly every week, sometimes more.

Susie was warmed to read Polly's thoughtful invitation for her and Britta to spend Christmas Eve afternoon and night with them—an addition to her original invitation to the family's big Christmas dinner. *No sense in making extra trips, and Henry's already arranged for Jonathan Ebersol to look after your animals.*

Polly also mentioned that Mamma had recently written about the events that surrounded Eli's death, particularly the identity of the driver. *I had no idea, Susie. Did you? Mamma's always loved Britta like her own. But I'm glad Britta knows the truth about it. Is she taking it okay?*

Susie shook her head and stared at the letter, uncertain of the answer.

Quickly, she opened Allen's letter and scanned through it, fervently hoping Allen had come up with a solution to at least keep Britta in Hickory Hollow. *That's even more important now, considering her desire to find Kathleen,* Susie thought, still unnerved by that prospect. *I can't let my sister be enticed away by an outsider, birth mother or not!*

Then, reading the letter, she was surprised that he was moving forward with his plan to rent out the house. She groaned inwardly. Yet, wanting to share the happy news of Polly's latest invitation, Susie made her way upstairs to tell Britta. "How would ya like to spend the night of Christmas Eve at Henry and Polly's?"

"That'd be fun." Britta glanced her way while dusting her dresser. "A *wunnerbaar* time to be with the children."

"I agree." Susie thought ahead to the season's youth activities as she stood in the doorway. "I 'spect some of the younger teens will be caroling the night before that, *jah*?"

Britta nodded. Then, turning, she asked, "What 'bout you, Susie? Don't you ever want to go out with *die Youngie* again? It's been so long, and ya don't have Mamma here to take care of anymore."

"Right now, *your* future comes first," she answered, a bit *ferhoodled.*

Britta sat on the edge of her bed, still holding the dustcloth. "That's kind of you, but I'm not even courtin' age yet. Shouldn't you still be goin' to youth activities and what-not?" Her eyes searched Susie's. "Don't ya hope to ever marry?"

She didn't want to tell Britta that she believed the time for courting and love had passed her by. "I'd be happy to be a wife and mother, of course. But none of that's within my grasp now."

Britta pursed her lips and seemed to be contemplating something. "I don't believe that's true, sister. Really I don't."

Although grateful for Britta's words, Susie didn't think her sister understood just what she was saying. Besides, Susie's heart was still fixed on one person, yet he'd never been hers to think about. "Aw, Britta. *Denki* for carin', but I'm fine. You're such a sweet sister," she added.

Britta stared at her hands in her lap. "I've been worried you'd treat me differently after I told you 'bout my birth mother."

Surprised, Susie frowned. "Nothing could make that happen, sister. Nothing."

"Not even that I want to try and contact Kathleen?" She looked at Susie with expectancy.

"I understand why you'd want to do that," Susie replied, feeling hesitant yet also grateful they could still talk like this. She realized then that it was finally time to tell Britta what she'd been keeping from her. "I appreciate your openness with me, and I need to do the same. You see, Allen wrote me a while back, but it was so upsetting I didn't know when to break it to ya—not when you'd just learned about your past from Mamma."

Britta's eyes blinked. "Goodness . . . what did he have to say?"

She quickly told her about Allen's need to rent this house . . . and for the two of them to move in with relatives.

Britta's dismay was written on her face. "I had no idea money was so tight. Do you think he'll go through with it?"

"I don't think there's any other option for Allen," Susie replied.

They went downstairs, where Susie and Britta sat in the front room together on the settee as the snow continued to fall steadily outside. Britta read their brother's most recent letter silently, her head leaning toward Susie's.

Partway down the first page, Susie saw again what Allen had written. *I plan to contact Aendi Emmalyn sometime after the new year about the possibility of you staying with her, starting early March. At least till something more permanent comes up. I respect your hope to stay together if possible.*

Britta frowned and looked at her. *"Ach,* so soon! What do *you* think?"

Susie swallowed her disappointment. "Well, it's better than havin' to move to Landisville like Allen had first suggested. This way, you could still see Hazel and participate in the activities with *die Youngie* if we stayed with Aendi Emmalyn."

Britta bowed her head. "I know you're right, but all this upsets me."

"And of course we'll have to work out somethin' for our little shop. Aendi Emmalyn doesn't have any spare space for that."

"She does have a little extra room for the two of us. But we'd be sharin' a bedroom there," Britta observed.

"Just so you are quiet next summer when ya come in from dates with Roy."

Britta blushed. "What'll we do 'bout the goats?" Then she gasped. "*Ach*, and the cats!"

"I wouldn't be surprised if Aendi Emmalyn's just as happy as we are to have the goats' milk. Hopefully her son will find a place for them." She grew thoughtful as she puzzled it out. "I'm not sure how she'd feel 'bout havin' the cats around, though."

"Well, I can't leave them behind." Britta's voice broke. "Oh, Susie, this is just awful."

Susie wouldn't let herself get down about this; she had to be the strong one.

"And what 'bout the horses and pony?" Britta asked, sniffling.

"Allen will likely sell at least the pony, and probably a horse, too," she admitted. "Hopefully, there'll be room for one of our road horses in Emmalyn's stable. We really only need one. We'll be able to be more independent that way and won't have to borrow her horse and buggy."

They sat there without speaking for a moment, the implications sinking in.

Britta leaned her head against Susie's shoulder. "This'll be our last Christmas in this house, and we won't even be here on Christmas Day," she said, sniffling.

"Well, would ya really want to be here with just me?" She slipped her arm around her sister.

Britta shook her head. "It'll be hard enough without Mamma."

"What if we exchanged a homemade gift for each other on Christmas Eve morning, before a nice hot breakfast? I'll cook whatever you want," Susie offered, then paused as another idea sprang up. "And you could have the cats come into the kitchen, if you'd like."

"Really?" Britta's face beamed as she straightened. "We'll see if they can make up their minds 'bout going out or coming in."

Susie laughed. "Typical kitty cats."

Britta hugged her.

When Britta stepped out later that afternoon to go to the stable, Susie walked to the window and looked out toward the beautiful frozen pond. She recalled staying overnight with Cousin Verena one late October. She had walked home the following day, and rounding the bend not far from Ebersols' farm, she had seen the white gazebo in the side yard highlighted by the flaming red sugar maples, and the pond glittering through the willows. Her heart had lifted at the familiar sight, and in that moment, she'd felt especially grateful for the privilege of growing up in such a grand house.

The awareness of all the happy years—and even the sad ones—linked to this special place played across her memory as she stood there alone in the front room. But she refused to be forlorn. In just sixteen days, it would be the Savior's birthday, and she would make the best of it, for Britta's sake.

While Britta milked the goats, she relived her visit to Bishop and Mary, and though she wanted to accept the words the man of God had spoken about being loved and cared for by the People, she was filled with doubts. After all, she was beginning to feel let down by Mamma, and now Allen.

How can I feel like I truly belong here when Mamma is out in Missouri, likely never to return? she thought sadly. *And when my brother's ousting me from the only home I've ever known?*

Aendi Lettie Hostettler stopped by the shop to visit with Susie the next morning, dressed for the cold weather in her black coat, thick gray scarf, and high-top black shoes. She smiled broadly as she invited Susie and Britta to visit at any time, particularly during the holidays. Susie thanked her warmly, and before Lettie left, she purchased a half dozen popcorn balls and five jars of peanut butter spread for Christmas gifts.

Soon after, Mattie Beiler arrived to ask if the girls needed help with anything, volunteering her husband, David, as she often did. Susie told her that she and Britta were handling things just fine for now and thanked her for offering.

Over the course of the morning, the steady stream of customers continued, mostly *Englischers*. Then, around eleven o'clock, the bishop's wife stepped into the shop, waving to Susie. "Oh, I thought Britta might be workin' today," Mary said, looking a little disappointed as she pulled her black scarf away from her face.

"I can run an' get her for ya," Susie offered, glancing toward the house.

Mary nodded, her chubby cheeks bright pink from the cold. Then she said, "On second thought, why don't you just pass this along to her."

"Sure," Susie agreed.

"I hope I'm not talkin' out of turn, but Britta told us what your Mamma shared with her . . . about her birth mother." She paused, apparently gathering her thoughts. "My husband has been goin' from family to family to let the Hickory Hollow church members know. The response has been very caring. As he expected, no one's holding a grudge toward Britta or the woman. Your sister shouldn't worry herself."

"It's kind of him to do that. Britta will appreciate it, I know."

"After prayin' for wisdom, he felt strongly 'bout doing it one-on-one like this." Mary stopped again, her expression changing. "Bless her heart, Britta was so shy talkin' to us. We want her to know how accepted she is amongst the People. And by the Lord."

Susie smiled. "Thank the bishop for Britta and me."

"I'll do that." Mary examined the remaining table runners. "Say, these are real perty. I'd like to purchase a few." She opened her purse and pulled out her wallet, mentioning how different Christmas must be for them this year without their mother home.

"Britta and I are makin' some nice plans with Polly and her family," Susie assured her.

"I'm glad to hear it." Mary waited as Susie folded and wrapped the runners in tissue paper, then added, right out of the blue, "'Tween you and me, I hope Britta changes her mind 'bout wanting to search, ya know."

"I understand. But she's quite determined."

Mary shook her head. "I'd hate to see her get caught up in the world, this close to being ready for baptism."

A twinge of pain flew through Susie. "Well, since we were wee ones, Mamma's prayed for all of her children to make that decision, so we'll continue to trust our heavenly Father to see Britta through."

"*Jah*, trusting's the best way." Mary reached for the large sack. "You're always so encouraging and cheerful, dear."

Susie's shoulders dipped as she watched her walk to the door.

If she only knew . . .

41

A week passed, and Susie kept noticing a large number of Christmas cards coming in the mail for Britta, some from folks who had never sent one before. Each day, when Susie passed Britta's room, she could see more cards on display on the dresser and on her bedside table.

"I've never received this many," Britta remarked to her. "Not even sure where I'll put them!"

"The People are so encouraging," Susie replied. "Remember what you said the bishop and Mary told ya?"

Britta nodded, like she was trying to make sense of it.

The next day, there was a letter from Mamma for Britta, which she scampered off to read upstairs. Susie's curiosity rose as she wondered if Mamma might be writing to discourage her from looking for Kathleen. The thought of Britta's interest in locating her birth mother still troubled Susie as she considered the possible pitfalls ahead, not least among them Kathleen's own possible reaction to Britta's sudden appearance.

And while she rustled up a light supper for the two of them, Susie asked for divine direction, especially for Britta, still so young to be making such a risky decision.

Maybe Mary should've talked directly to Britta when she stopped by the shop, Susie thought, hoping Mamma had written something to quell Britta's yearning.

When the grilled cheese sandwiches and homemade tomato soup were ready, she called Britta down for supper. After washing her hands, Britta joined her at the table, where they bowed their heads for the silent blessing. Afterward, Britta cut her grilled cheese sandwich into strips and began to dip them into the soup, something she had done since childhood.

"So Mamma had a surprise for me in her letter," Britta announced.

"A pleasant one?"

"Was it ever!" Britta said between dips. "She sent me Kathleen's mailing address."

Susie almost dropped her spoon. "What on earth?"

"I know." Britta was nodding. "And wait'll ya hear this—Mamma has been in touch with her all this time, writing a letter once a year since my adoption. She said it was her idea. But Kathleen has only written back a few times."

Mentally, Susie was trying to catch up. *Mamma* gave *her Kathleen's address?*

"I can't believe it," Britta was saying. "Looks like God has opened a door for me."

"Does Mamma have a guess as to why Kathleen hasn't written regularly?" Susie asked.

"Evidently she didn't want to interfere with my life or confuse me . . . ya know, with letters arriving here from a stranger."

Susie was speechless.

"Mamma continued writing, though, because she thought it was only right to keep Kathleen updated 'bout my life," Britta added. "And apparently Ella Mae knows Mamma's kept in touch with Kathleen."

Hearing this baffled Susie. "So are ya sayin' that Mamma doesn't mind if you contact Kathleen?"

"Here, you can read the letter."

Susie shook her head. "I was just curious if Mamma had any, uh, advice for you."

"She did. And don't worry—I'll be very careful."

Susie stirred her soup as the startling news churned in her head. She sent a quick prayer heavenward, then attempted to turn the conversation to upcoming holiday activities.

"*Ach*, I forgot to tell ya—Jerome invited Cousin Marnie for Christmas dinner with his family. I wouldn't be surprised if they're planning to wed next year," Britta said.

Susie reached for her water glass and took a drink. "I've always thought Jerome was a real nice fella. I'm very happy for Marnie."

Britta agreed. "And to think, they've been nearly best friends right from the start."

"They should be well matched as husband and wife, then," Susie replied, recalling a time when she might have had such a close relationship with Obie.

Five days before Christmas, Susie and Britta baked a variety of cookies for Aendi Lettie's upcoming annual cookie exchange. This being Friday, the shop was closed for business, so it was the ideal morning to make lots of goodies.

"It smells *wunnerbaar*," Britta said, sniffing the air. "Like when Mamma was here."

"Say, once we're finished," Susie said, "let's go down and sort through the boxes in the basement."

Britta agreed. "I wish Mamma could tell us what to do with certain things. There's so much stuff."

"Well, don't worry—I've been makin' a list to send her."

"That'll help." Britta kept spooning up cookie dough for the peanut blossoms.

"Have ya decided when you'll write to Kathleen?"

"Oh, I've already made a pretty Christmas card and mailed it. She should have it soon."

"So soon!" Susie said, surprised and disappointed.

While dozens of cookies cooled on wax paper, Susie and Britta headed to the basement. Susie wanted to get a head start on organizing the things they wouldn't have room for at Aendi Emmalyn's. Even though Allen had said he would not contact their aunt to finalize arrangements till after the new year, Susie still thought it was important to dispose of things and decide what to give away, with Mamma's permission.

Presently, Britta was rummaging through a large box, and when Susie glanced over at her, Britta was pulling out Dat's old black work boots. "Why'd Mamma keep these?"

"Those . . . no idea. I thought she'd given them to Allen." Susie remembered how tall and handsome their father had looked in them and how careful he had always been not to track in mud when he entered the outer room. She'd slipped her own small feet in those boots when she was little, and the memory was still keen in her mind.

Now Britta was pulling out a child-sized yellow safety vest. "Lookee here," she said, holding up the vest. "I used to wear one like this sometimes after dark when I was little."

Susie gulped but tried to hide her emotions. "That was Eli's vest," she admitted. "Mamma was a stickler 'bout us wearin' reflective vests when we walked back and forth to Aendi Emmalyn's at dusk."

Britta examined it. "Where's yours?"

"After I grew out of it, Mamma gave it to Polly for her future children."

"But she kept this one." Britta looked at Susie. "I wonder why."

Susie looked away, the lump in her throat growing. "Well, to tell ya the truth . . . that vest is part of the reason . . . Eli died," she said, faltering.

"I . . . I don't understand." Britta's voice was soft.

Breathing deeply, Susie began to relay what had happened that terrible evening. "I'd forgotten to bring my vest along for our walk home from Aendi's, so Eli insisted that I wear his." She choked down her tears. "If Eli had worn it, instead of me . . . he might still be alive today."

Britta looked horrified. "*Ach,* you can't know that, sister!"

"Don't ya understand? The driver—Kathleen—could've only seen *me,* because of the safety vest I had on. Not Eli." The lump in her throat returned. "He was walkin' closer to the road, and I'd lagged behind, stopping to pick up a bird feather. There was only one vest between us."

Britta fell silent, like she was trying to picture this. She sighed, staring at Susie. At last she said, "Eli was only lookin' out for you, like a *gut* Bruder." She reached for Susie's hand. "He surely wouldn't want ya thinkin' this way, Susie. Not all these years later."

It felt peculiar, the way their roles reversed in that moment.

"Maybe runnin' from the truth—workin' yourself to the bone like ya do—makes it impossible to stop long enough to face what really happened," Britta said now.

"What truth?"

"That you didn't cause Eli's death."

Susie fought to accept Britta's words, but they could not erase the guilt she'd long felt.

Britta's eyes watered as she reached to hug Susie, holding her tight.

A few moments later, several loud knocks came from upstairs, and a woman's voice called to them from the back door. Quickly, Susie and Britta lifted their apron hems to wipe their eyes.

Susie hurried up the basement steps and through the kitchen and utility room. She opened the back door and found Mattie Beiler standing there with her mother, Ella Mae, beside her. Mattie was holding a prettily wrapped fruit basket. Despite the difference in height, the women looked identical in their black coats and black bandannas, except that Ella Mae's neck scarf was bright red. Susie couldn't help recalling how Ella Mae liked to inch past the boundaries at times. *Though in the most gentle way.*

"*Willkumm.*" Susie stepped back from the door to let them in, hoping her eyes weren't puffy.

"We came to spread some Christmas cheer." Mattie moved inside. "I can't stay, but Mamma can, if that's all right."

"Of course," Susie replied promptly.

Ella Mae smiled. "Yous are mighty special to us," she said, and with how rarely Ella Mae left the house anymore, especially in this coldest season, Susie knew they were special indeed.

"We're very happy to see you both," Susie said as she took Ella Mae's coat and hung it up in the utility room.

Britta appeared in the doorway that led to the kitchen, her face tear streaked.

Mine must be, too, Susie thought. "*Kumme* and get yourselves warmed up," she said, leading Ella Mae slowly into the kitchen, with Mattie coming behind carrying the fruit basket. "Here, I'll make it easy for ya," she told Ella Mae, pulling out Mamma's chair for her.

Mattie placed the fruit basket on the counter, and Susie thanked them for the wonderful surprise. Then Mattie excused herself, saying she would return for Ella Mae in an hour or so.

"That'll be fine." Susie eyed the fruit basket. "I see some bags of nuts and chocolate in there."

Britta smiled at that, as all the while, Ella Mae seemed to study the girls.

"Let's open it," Susie suggested and pulled out some scissors from a nearby drawer to cut

the pretty cellophane wrapping. Inside were
bananas, two grapefruit, and several oranges
and apples, as well as the nuts and chocolates,
and peppermint sticks, too. "This is such fun
. . . and so kind of you."

"We wanted to do somethin' a little special for yous with your Mamma away," Ella
Mae was quick to say.

At that, Susie managed a little smile.

Carrying the nuts, chocolates, and peppermint sticks to the table, Susie returned to the
sink to fill the teakettle. "Would ya like some
tea?" she asked Ella Mae, delighted to treat
her this time.

The woman nodded. "Tea's always a *gut*
idea, ain't?"

As she set the gas burner to high, Susie
wondered if Ella Mae had any sense of what
she'd interrupted. She opened the cupboard
where Mamma always kept the boxes of tea
bags and removed the peppermint one. "This
kind? Or did ya bring a bag of dried mint
leaves in your purse?"

Ella Mae smiled. "S'pose your Mamma
told ya that."

"She said you liked to have some available, just in case."

Ella Mae tittered. "Well, since I don't go
out much, I quit that."

Britta took down three teacups and saucers

from the cupboard, not having said or shown her face much since Ella Mae's arrival.

But Ella Mae was looking toward the counter where Susie and Britta set out the cups and saucers, along with three spoons. "Say now, I hope I didn't walk in on somethin'," she said softly, giving them a searching yet kind look. "Are you girls missin' your Mamma?"

Britta glanced at Susie. "*Jah* . . . and missin' Eli."

Surprised at Britta's reply, Susie felt her breath catch in her throat.

Britta's gaze held Susie's; then she quickly explained that they had been sorting through boxes downstairs. "I stumbled across Eli's safety vest," Britta said. "But my sister can tell the rest."

Susie felt squeezed into a corner. "Well, it's just that I never realized Mamma kept that vest all these years—the one I wore the night Eli died on the road." Her voice broke. "She never mentioned to me that she'd saved it."

The teakettle began to whistle, a welcome distraction.

Britta and Ella Mae said nothing as Susie poured the boiling water into a white teapot, then placed three tea bags inside to steep. She took a container of raw honey over to the table and, not forgetting about Ella Mae's sweet tooth, gathered up a selection of cookies from the wax papers still on the counter—cranberry crunchies, sand tarts, snowballs, and peanut blossoms—and arranged them on a plate for the table.

"Time for our tea party." She carried the teapot over, complete with its quilted tea cozy. Then, sitting, she waited for Ella Mae to signal the beginning of the silent blessing, like she always did over tea.

The Wise Woman smiled sweetly at each of them before bowing her head.

Afterward, Susie poured the steeped peppermint tea into the three cups and passed the plate of cookies. She hoped to goodness the conversation would not return to the discovery of Eli's safety vest.

Thankfully, Ella Mae brought up something completely different, about life being like a cornfield maze with twists and turns and sometimes roadblocks in the way. "Each of us bumps into piled-up hay bales now an' then, so we hafta go back a different way, and then we find yet another barricade, and on an' on." She paused, her pale blue eyes ever so solemn. "But our heavenly Father looks on us with arms outstretched. He sees our struggles as we try 'n' move through the seemingly endless web of stops and starts to the glorious end. From the beginning to the end, His view is clear. And from His high vantage point, He alone knows how to get through. But He's also patient, so He waits for *us* to ask directions."

Susie had never thought of life quite like this.

Ella Mae continued, her eyes searching Susie's. "And, dearie, I hope ya know you're not at fault for wearin' your brother's vest that evening."

Blinking with surprise, Susie wondered how she could have known.

"Your Mamma worried you might blame yourself for Eli's death," Ella Mae said in the most tender tone.

"She did?" Susie murmured.

Nodding slowly, Ella Mae held her cup in her small, gnarled hand. "She realized that Eli must've wanted you to wear the only vest you children took along."

Susie swallowed hard. "*Jah*. Mamma was right 'bout that. And all this time, I thought I was the only one alive who knew." She had to stop and cough as emotion overtook her.

"Your Mamma mentioned that she'd tried to talk to you 'bout this several times, but you'd shied away, maybe from the sheer pain of it," Ella Mae said.

Susie nodded. "I've always thought my

poor Bruder would still be alive if I had just stood up to him and refused."

"My dear Susie, God is sovereign, and we needn't second-guess the accident or which of you should've worn the vest, or what else might have happened." Ella Mae paused to brush tears from her wrinkled cheek. "The Good Book says clearly that not even death can separate us from God's great love."

Britta reached under the table and squeezed Susie's hand. "I'm so glad ya came to see us today, Ella Mae," she said, leaning against Susie's arm.

Nodding her head, Susie had to agree, deeply moved by the woman's wisdom. "*Denki*, with all of my heart."

That afternoon, Britta helped Susie bake a German chocolate cake, both of them excited to surprise Ella Mae with it on their way to market tomorrow. The timing of Ella Mae's visit had been so providential that Britta didn't want to discuss it, preferring to let the Wise Woman's words sink deep into her heart.

Susie also seemed quiet and thoughtful as they worked together. The truth was that Britta had not told her sister everything about Kathleen Stratton. Remarkably, Kathleen lived less than ninety minutes from Hickory Hollow by van, on the southern edge of Allentown.

Will she be shocked to get my Christmas

card? Britta wondered while the cake was baking. *Will she write back?*

Later, while they were nibbling on the nuts and chocolates from the gift basket as the cake cooled, Susie excused herself to put on her snow boots, then headed outdoors. Britta stood at the back door window, watching her and wondering if she was going to the stable to call Allen, maybe, but she headed in the direction of the willow grove and the pond instead.

Is she as blue about moving as I am? Britta thought, wishing something might happen to change Allen's mind. But then again, she didn't want to be selfish if he needed money from the rent of this house to help care for Mamma and little Maggie.

Stepping away from the door, she plodded upstairs to her room, where she opened her bottom drawer and lifted out the quilted pieces for what would soon be Susie's surprise Christmas gift—a Bible cover. Something extra special this year, to help ease the sadness of Mamma's absence.

Thinking again of Susie, she went across the hall to her sister's room and stared out the window. She could see Susie walking near the pond, beneath the stark, bare branches of her beloved willows, carrying her ice skates. And soon she was sitting on a boulder and putting them on. "Ah, perfect," Britta whispered, thinking this might be just what her sister needed to unwind.

Is she planning a fresh start for herself in Missouri, if Aendi Emmalyn can't take us both in? she worried.

By Monday, Susie had finished the list of furnishings and other items to send to Mamma. *She'll know how to advise us.*

Closing the envelope, Susie was anxious to get it sent off to Missouri. *Maybe we'll need to have an auction,* she thought. She felt sad about the thought of saying good-bye to so many of their furnishings. At least she had this evening's cookie exchange with a few of her cousins to look forward to. Aendi Emmalyn was hosting, so Susie hoped to poke around to see if there was room for the goats and Brambles or Atta-Girl in the stable. She wondered exactly when Allen would contact their aunt about his plan—how long after the new year. As for the cats, Susie figured that if their doting aunt had any idea how much they meant to Britta, she would let them bed down in the stable straw.

Britta seemed quite happy to take Susie's letter out to the mailbox before heading on foot to babysit for the Ebersols a couple of hours that afternoon. And while she was gone, Susie worked on her top-secret Christmas present for Britta. *Only a few more hours of stitching till it's done.*

Emmalyn's kitchen and sitting room were more decorated for the cookie exchange than Susie had ever seen before, with red and green streamers and a single tall red candle surrounded by holly and tiny red berries centered on the kitchen table. Like other Amish families, Emmalyn had strung Christmas cards over the doorways and windows, as well.

A handful of Susie and Britta's close cousins were present, including Laura Ann, Verena, Marnie, and Miriam—most of them around Susie's age.

Susie was happy to trade her cranberry crunchies, sand tarts, snowballs, and peanut blossoms for different kinds of cookies from each guest. With all of the cheerful chatter at Emmalyn's, Susie couldn't help noticing that each young woman in attendance made a point of interacting with Britta. And though she wasn't privy to every conversation, Susie could see that her sister was enjoying herself. *They're going out of their way to show kindness,* she thought, thankful Bishop Beiler had taken time to talk with individual families about Britta's birth mother.

On the ride home, Susie listened as Britta talked about their cousins. "Each one let me know today how much they care," Britta told her. "Marnie even hugged me and said the only thing that mattered was that I'm her cousin and always would be."

Holding the reins, Susie glanced at her under the moonlight and nodded her head. "Marnie's right, ya know."

Britta smiled. "I've been shown so much love. Ya can't know how *gut* that makes me feel. 'Specially when I was so worried."

Susie's heart was warmed by this, and she hoped Britta might focus now on the People's loving attention and be satisfied with merely having sent Kathleen a Christmas card.

Early Christmas Eve morning, while still in their nightgowns and bathrobes, Susie and Britta exchanged their homemade gifts in Susie's room. Susie was delighted by the beautiful quilted cover for her Bible, and Britta read aloud the embroidered quote on the wall hanging Susie had made for her: "A sister is God's way of proving we never have to walk alone." Britta smiled as she studied the delicate handiwork. "This is the perfect gift from you, Susie. And I know right where I'll hang it."

"I can't wait to see where." She gave her a hug.

Christmas Eve afternoon, the sky was growing dim around the time Susie had scheduled Rachelle Good to take them to Landisville. Susie looked out at the snowy landscape in the fast-fading light as she and Britta waited in the utility room with the pineapple upside-down cake Susie had baked that morning, as well as a large box of cookies and their overnight bags.

"It's the prettiest Christmas snow I ever remember," Britta said, leaning closer to the window.

"If we had a full moon, the landscape would sparkle," Susie said. "A perfect night for ice-skating."

Britta glanced at her, a question on her face. "Do ya ever think 'bout Obie and all the times you two went skating on our pond?"

"Well, sometimes, but I try not to. He's seriously courting, don't forget."

"I know, but I miss him," Britta said, then apologized. "I still remember the day he came for your birthday and I interrupted you two talking."

Susie laughed a little. "*Jah.*" She paused. "But that day feels so long ago now, and there's no point in dwelling on the past." She was relieved to see the van pull into the driveway just then and made her way toward the outside door, the cake in its secure carrier.

Britta picked up both of their bags and the box of cookies as the van inched up to the walkway, which Susie had shoveled twice already that afternoon.

"Let's go!" Susie said, eager to see Polly and the family.

"We're gonna have a white Christmas!" Britta said, following behind.

They waved to Jonathan Ebersol, who was walking across their backyard to milk the goats and feed and water the horses and pony.

"*Denki!*" Susie called to him, and he waved back. "We'll return home tomorrow night, Lord willing."

Jonathan waved them on. "Have yourselves a *gut* time. *Hallicher Grischtdaag!*"

"Merry Christmas to you, too," Susie replied.

Rachelle greeted them warmly as they opened the van doors, and Susie urged Britta to sit up front in the passenger seat, knowing how fond she was of the driver. *Anything to encourage Britta's connections here in Hickory Hollow,* Susie thought, settling into the second seat behind them.

The smell of baked ham filled Henry and Polly's farmhouse as Susie stepped inside the back door and removed her snow things with Britta.

Polly came right away to greet them, a white work apron over her full black one. "Almost suppertime," she announced, giving each of them a quick hug.

In the kitchen, Henry stood dressed in his church clothes at the long counter, mashing a mound of potatoes by hand. "Yous are just in time," he said with a smile.

"I'll call the *Kinner.*" Polly removed her small apron and left it on the counter as she headed toward the front room.

"It's so *gut* to be here," Susie said, moving to the sink to wash her hands.

Henry nodded. "Wouldn't have it any other way."

Soon the children came into the kitchen with Polly. Towheaded Joey flew past his mother and straight to Britta. Little strawberry-blond Nellie Ann, now nearly three, rang a silver bell on a red ribbon and smiled up at Susie to show her. And nine-year-old

Junior came over and shook their hands. "Nice seein' yous again, Aendis."

"Look at you, Junior—you're getting so tall!" Susie marveled. "*Ach*, bein' with family is best." She turned to her older sister. "Anything I can carry to the table?"

"Oh, Henry and I'll do that," Polly said, encouraging them to take their seats.

Susie took her usual spot at the table while Britta washed her hands at the sink. Little Joey stood nearby, holding the hand towel and looking mighty pleased to be able to wait on his favorite Aendi.

By now, Polly was bringing over the glistening ham on a large platter, and Henry carried the enormous bowl of fluffy mashed potatoes, a pool of melted butter on top. There were also serving dishes filled with various vegetables, including cooked carrots and baby onions flecked with parsley, buttered lima beans, and chow chow, as well as a large gravy boat.

Once everyone was seated, including little Nellie Ann, who climbed into her booster seat and sat quietly, Henry folded his callused hands to ask the blessing. All of them bowed their heads in silent reverence and gratitude for the splendid meal on this cold and snowy day before Christmas.

Susie added her own silent thanks to God

for each person present and trusted that Britta might come to realize her adoptive family was the only one she really needed.

After Susie's moist and delicious pineapple upside-down cake was served for dessert, they lingered at the table, and Henry asked Junior to tell about the Christmas program at the nearby Amish school. At first, Junior seemed almost too shy to share that he'd been chosen by the teacher to represent Joseph for the annual nativity scene.

"What a meek and kind Joseph he was," Polly said, beaming at her firstborn.

Little Nellie Ann piped up to declare she'd like to be an angel in the school play someday. This brought a round of chuckles, and when things quieted down, Henry opened the Bible to the gospel of Luke to read the account of the angels' visitation to the shepherds on the night of Christ's birth. Afterward, he offered a second silent prayer.

When it came time to clear the table and put the leftovers away, Susie, Britta, and Polly all pitched in to help while Henry played with the children in the front room. Then came the job of washing dishes, with pleasant chatter from Polly, who seemed delighted to have her sisters' company on this special night.

A while later, carolers from the local Amish youth group came to the front door and sang three Christmas songs. Susie insisted they go and listen as Junior, Joey, and Nellie Ann stood at the storm door, looking out.

Nellie Ann began to jingle her little bell in rhythm, and Joey bobbed his head to the age-old melodies. A hay-filled wagon pulled by two large draft horses had brought *die Youngie*, and Susie remembered all the years of caroling with the Hickory Hollow youth, Obie beside her. Gently, she pushed the memory away.

Much later, when Polly told the children it was getting close to bedtime, Susie volunteered to read a story in the front room near the coal stove. Nellie Ann went to sit in Susie's lap, her silver bell with the red ribbon tied loosely around her tiny neck, while Britta sat close by with Joey next to her. Junior carried the large bedtime storybook in from the sitting room and handed it to Susie, who received it with joy, surrounded by so many precious little ones.

Britta experienced a wave of sadness as she watched Susie read to the children. *She loves them so*, she thought. At this point in life, unless her sister someday married a widower with children, it was unlikely she'd have a husband of her own. *And such a good wife and Mamma she'd be, too,* Britta thought, observing sweet Nellie Ann nestled in Susie's lap.

After they sang "The First Noel" together, the children said good night to Susie and Britta, then to Henry, before heading upstairs to bed. Polly went along with them while Henry stayed in the front room with the current issue of *Family Life* magazine on his lap. He fiddled with the pages as if there was something on his mind.

At last, he spoke, looking at Britta. "I s'pose ya know your Mamm wrote to Polly and me 'bout your birth mother."

Britta nodded. "I'd hoped Mamma would." *Why is he bringing this up?*

"Just recently, she wrote again . . . said she mailed ya the woman's address and gave you her married name, Williamson."

"*Jah,* she did," Britta replied, a bit tense now.

"Well, I hope an' pray ya keep your upbringing in focus, despite your curiosity, Britta," he said. "Hold firm to the Lord God and the Old Ways."

Annoyed, Britta didn't feel like discussing this at the moment. Not if it was going to spoil the peace of this most holy night of the year.

"I don't doubt you're curious," Henry continued. "Who wouldn't be interested, in your circumstance? But you also must know how much it'd mean to the Mamma who raised ya for you to remain Amish." His eyes met hers.

Britta was surprised her brother-in-law would talk so directly.

Susie gave her an encouraging smile, as though she hoped this wouldn't turn into an argument.

"So far, I've only sent her a Christmas card," Britta replied quietly.

Henry frowned and raked his hand through his golden hair. "I see."

Susie spoke up, undoubtedly to ward off any possible conflict. "*Ach*, it's Christmas Eve."

Henry must have caught her meaning and nodded. "All I'm sayin' is, you belong with us, sister. You always have." He opened the magazine once more and began to turn the pages.

Britta's shoulders relaxed, and she gave Susie a look and motioned with her head toward the stairs. It was time to call it a night.

On the way upstairs, Susie touched Britta's arm. "Henry cares about you, ya know," she said softly. "That was just his way of showin' it."

"Well, the way he said it seemed more bossy than anything."

Susie sighed but let it go. Her sister's Plain life was colliding with what might await her. *If she chooses to do more than send a card to her birth mother, none of us can change that or make it easy for her. But we can help guide her along with our love.*

The Christmas Day dinner of stuffed turkey, noodles and gravy, mashed potatoes, buttered cut corn, peas, and creamed cabbage made Susie feel almost too full, but the food was so tasty. Next to her, adorable Nellie Ann politely asked for more noodles in her cute little voice, declaring she would like seconds of that instead of dessert. But when Henry brought out the homemade vanilla ice cream with homemade hot fudge to dribble over it, Nellie Ann's eyes grew big and she quickly changed her tune. This made nearly everyone smile, and Junior put his hand over his mouth to squelch a chortle. When all was said and done, Nellie Ann was quite happy to feast on her dessert.

They spent the afternoon playing games

and, later, put on coats and boots to tramp through the snow to call Mamma at the old phone shed half a field away. It was a precious time, hearing her voice again and passing the phone around. Even little Nellie Ann expressed a Christmas wish for her grandma to come home. *"Kumme Heemet, Mammi, jah?"*

When it was Britta's turn, Susie noticed her eyes well up.

She misses Mamma more than ever.

Later, Susie enjoyed watching Henry and Polly give each of the children green-netting bags of hard candy, nuts, and oranges. Henry also read the Christmas story from the gospel of Matthew while the children sat attentively at his knee.

Afterward, as she gathered up her things to travel back to Hickory Hollow, Susie reflected on last night's short exchange between Henry and Britta, praying Britta would take it to heart, as Henry intended.

Three days later, the wind howled and snow flew horizontally during the van ride home from Saturday market. Susie was relieved when their stone house came into view, she felt that tense.

As soon as the van stopped at the end of the driveway, Britta got out and dashed over to the mailbox while Susie paid Rachelle for the ride. She then joined Britta as they trudged up the driveway together, leaning into the wind.

Inside, Susie didn't bother to remove her coat or scarf before stoking the coal stove, grateful for the remaining embers.

Meanwhile, Britta opened an envelope addressed to her and pulled out a pretty card. She read the greeting, then let out a gasp. "What the world?"

Susie frowned.

"It's a card."

"*Jah*, I can see that," Susie teased, edging closer. "But who from?"

"Kathleen Williamson . . . and she wrote her telephone number at the bottom."

Susie's heart fell.

"She says she's happy I contacted her and looks forward to talking to me," Britta said, "if I would welcome that." She glanced at the envelope again. "She didn't put her name with the return address. Maybe she wanted to surprise me. *Ach*, I'm so happy!"

Not wanting to put a damper on Britta's enthusiasm, Susie hardly knew how to react.

Britta held out the card.

Susie reached for it and noticed the lovely

nativity on the front and a Scripture verse inside. *Hearing from you was an unexpected Christmas surprise,* Kathleen had written.

"It's very nice," Susie managed to say, handing the card back to Britta.

"I think so, too . . . she didn't *have* to write back, or even this quick." Britta's excitement seemed to grow by the moment. "I might just run out to the stable and give her a call."

"Don't ya want to think it over first?" Susie wished she would—Henry's remarks on Christmas Eve must not have caused Britta to reconsider forging this connection.

"*Nee,* I'm gonna call her before I get cold feet." And with that, Britta got up and headed out to the utility room, where Susie could hear her putting on her snow boots again.

Why such a rush? Susie thought, feeling at a loss to know what to do. *If there was a way to stop her, would I?*

Don't be ferhoodled, Britta thought, her hand trembling as she dialed the number. She heard the ringing, and her throat felt like she'd eaten a ball of cotton. *O Lord, help me do this right,* she prayed, gripping the phone as she counted the rings.

At the end of the stable, one of the goats began to bleat, and she realized it was close to milking time. "I'll be right there," she called to the animal, then felt silly.

Kathleen's line kept ringing.

No one's home, Britta thought, disappointed.

Finally a man's voice came on the recording, directing her to leave a name and number and someone would return the call.

Quickly, Britta hung up. This was not how she'd imagined it. And now that she'd dialed and waited, she wondered what she would have said if Kathleen *had* answered.

Let down, she made her way to the shelf to grab the milk box containing everything she needed, including the clean stainless-steel bucket. As she worked, she wondered when the best time to call again might be.

While Britta was out in the stable, Susie went to her room to pray. At first, few words came to mind, and she tried to imagine what Mamma would pray in her position. Of course, Mamma *had* sent Kathleen's address to Britta, so that was something to ponder. *Why did Mamma seem to encourage her to reach out?*

After praying, she picked up her Bible, in its pretty quilted cover Britta had so beautifully made for her. Sitting in the chair between the two large windows, Susie read from Psalm 34, trying to calm herself. *I sought the Lord, and he heard me, and delivered me from all my fears. . . .*

"May it be so," she whispered, looking out at the rapidly falling snow. She could scarcely see the willow grove and the pond beyond. *It'll be beautiful once it stops. Maybe I can go skating again when the weather improves,* she thought, wondering what the forecast was for next week. First she'd need to get Britta to help her clear the pond of all this new snow.

Tomorrow was an off-Sunday from Preaching service, but she was certain they would not be traveling to visit any relatives. Not in this weather. *We'll have to stay put,* she mused, wondering how long Britta would be out there talking on the phone.

The snow had stopped in the night, leaving behind a glittering scene the next morning. The gazebo looked like a giant white muffin top, and the willows around the pond were cloaked in purest white.

After breakfast, Susie and Britta began to shovel out the back walkway, and it was only a short time before Jonathan Ebersol arrived to plow the drive.

Susie wondered if her sister would try

to call Kathleen again, but she decided to let Britta bring it up. *No sense encouraging her.* . . .

This being the Lord's Day, they would suspend all stitching, mending, and cleaning, and there would certainly be no sorting through boxes. As had always been Mamma's way, there would be little or no cooking, either. Susie had adhered to that practice, choosing to make Sunday different than other days. Rather, she and Britta would enjoy reading and playing checkers, as well as writing letters.

"I hope you're not upset with me for tryin' to contact Kathleen," Britta said during the noon meal of tuna sandwiches, potato chips, and fruit cup.

"Not upset, *nee.*"

"But you're concerned, *jah?*"

"Concerned is a better way of putting it." Susie reached for her sandwich.

Britta seemed to consider that. "I prayed last night, askin' God to help me have the courage to call again . . . and for the words to say."

Susie didn't let on that she really wondered how this potential relationship would benefit Britta, although she could understand how Kathleen might want to know the daughter she'd given away.

"Will ya pray for me while I call?" Britta asked, eyes pleading.

"When?"

"After dishes are done. Hopefully this time she'll answer."

Susie looked at her dear sister. "What would ya like me to pray for?"

Britta sighed. "God's will most of all."

It was obvious how much this meant to Britta. "*Jah*, I can pray for that."

Maybe it was because she had prayed herself, or maybe it was because Susie was praying even now, but Britta felt less nervous when she heard the phone ring this time.

"Hello?" came a woman's mellow voice on the line.

"Is this Kathleen Williamson?" Britta asked softly.

"Who is calling, please?"

Britta's heart beat fast. "It's Britta Mast . . . from Hickory Hollow."

A slight pause, then, "Britta? How wonderful to hear your voice!"

"*Denki* for the perty Christmas card and note," Britta said, pleased by Kathleen's enthusiastic response.

"And yours, too. It was so thoughtful— and such a wonderful surprise, too."

Britta mentioned that her Mamma had volunteered Kathleen's mailing address.

"Aquilla is very kind," Kathleen said. "Every year, without fail, she's sent me a lovely long letter to tell me about your life—your schoolwork, your hobbies, every imaginable thing my mother's heart longed to know. . . ." She stopped a moment. "Please excuse me, Britta. While I'm very glad you've reached out to me, I hope you understand I don't want to interfere with the beautiful relationship you obviously have with Aquilla. She's been a true mother to you in every way that matters."

A true mother, thought Britta, wondering how Mamma would feel if she could hear Kathleen say that. "I was . . . well, I've been very curious 'bout you," Britta continued, touched by her gracious words. "Do ya have other children?"

"Yes. My husband, Chad, and I have two sons, Trey and Randy, ten and eight." Kathleen mentioned that Chad managed an auto repair shop and that she and her family enjoyed winter sports: skating and tobogganing, but especially cross-country skiing.

Britta felt a little overwhelmed at this news, as well as how eager Kathleen seemed to be to share about her life.

"We're also very involved in our church. We host small groups in our home once a month, and Chad conducts a Saturday men's prayer group every other week, too." Kathleen talked of her sons' recent interest in rowing, and Britta mentioned the boat Dat had built years ago.

When there was a pause, Britta asked if she knew much about Hickory Hollow.

"Well, occasionally I take the boys to one of the farmers markets near there."

"Really?" Britta remembered seeing a woman at market who she'd thought could be her birth mother—at least as she imagined her—and with two young boys, no less. "I actually wondered if I saw ya there once," she told her.

"How long ago?" Kathleen asked.

"More than two years." Britta couldn't believe it. "To think we might've run into each other without knowing."

"No kidding." Kathleen paused. "Perhaps your mother told you, but I visited you several times when you were little. Has she said anything to you about those visits?"

Britta heard the note of hesitation in her voice. "*Jah*," she said. "I mean . . . yes."

"I've never been able to understand how Aquilla could forgive me like she did that first time we met," Kathleen said. "It was so immediate—I could tell that the loss of her little boy grieved her, yet she didn't seem to have to think about it. It was such a self-less gift to me." She paused, and Britta could hear her sigh. "I still can't forgive myself for Eli's death, though. And my own parents certainly haven't forgiven me for giving you up to be adopted. Thankfully, I made sure your mother had legal temporary custody before they found out about you. I granted her that even prior to your adoption."

Britta felt a pang in her stomach. "Well, *I* forgive you," she said, recalling all the times Mamma had shown mercy to someone, Britta included.

"Thank you, Britta. That means everything to me."

"Well, it seems to me that someone besides Mamma needed to forgive ya."

"You are truly her child," Kathleen said, her voice breaking.

"And you should know that everyone here in Hickory Hollow forgave ya long ago."

Kathleen was silent for a moment. "I'm so thankful. I hear what you're saying, but it's all so difficult to comprehend."

"The People believe in forgiveness. Mamma says it's about learning to let go. The Lord Jesus is our example, teaching us that if we seek forgiveness for ourselves, we must forgive others in turn." Britta stopped speaking, hoping she hadn't overstepped, but also certain that it was right for her to share this with Kathleen.

"I'd read that verse in the Sermon on the Mount, but I never experienced it until Aquilla forgave me. What a moment!" She sighed as if thinking back, then seemed to remember herself. "I assume you'll continue living there with your Plain community, once you're grown?"

Britta thought of the things Kathleen had shared earlier about her busy modern lifestyle . . . the kind of life *she* might have had. Truth be told, a part of her couldn't help comparing all of that to her own upbringing: the rewards of hard work, the simple pleasures of going to market, playing with the barn cats, learning to cook and bake from scratch, and sewing whatever was needed. She considered, too, her closeness with Susie and Mamma's unreserved love for her and the tender connection they'd always had.

Unexpectedly, Britta also recalled Aaron Kauffman taunting her years ago, and her own fretting over the name Britta, questioning her place in the community after learning of Kathleen's role in Eli's death. But most of all, she remembered the People's open arms to her, and she honestly doubted she could find such a warm reception anywhere else, in any other community.

Something rose up in her, and she said with conviction, "*Jah*, I *belong* here." The words sounded wonderful to her ears as tears sprang to her eyes. "In fact, Lord willin', I'll be baptized into the church this coming fall."

"You are quite a young woman," Kathleen replied. "I'm thankful you know your mind, and your heart most of all."

"I'd like to get to know ya better . . . exchange letters, if that's all right."

"Sure," Kathleen said. "I'll look forward to it."

"Oh—just one other thing. Is your hair wavy and hard to manage?"

"Is it ever!" Kathleen chuckled. "Why do you ask?"

Britta told her about trying to keep her own hair nice and neat under her *Kapp*, and they shared a little laugh.

Eventually, their conversation came to a pleasant end.

"I'm very glad you called, Britta. Happy New Year to you and your family."

"Same to you."

They said their good-byes, and when Britta hung up, she felt like a bird on a wind current, floating to the highest branch of their backyard tree. All doubts were gone, her burden lifted. She was free to be who God had intended.

Wanting to make the most of her
remaining days at her family's
old stone house, Susie had been
going out to skate on the pond after chores
during the final days of the year, no matter
how cold the temperature. Whenever Britta
was occupied with babysitting at the Ebersols'
or visiting Cousin Marnie or Hazel, Susie
would pull on her black leggings and snow
boots and don her coat, warmest scarf, and
blue mittens before picking her way down to
the pond, past the bare sugar maples and the
new silhouettes of drifted snow.

On this first morning in January, Susie
was grateful for Britta's recent decision to be
baptized into the Hickory Hollow church.
Her heart filled with joy, she decided to treat

herself to a nice long skate out in the dazzling sunlight. As she carried her skates to the brink of the pond, she was thankful for the waterproof mittens she'd purchased with Mamma's Christmas money. While sitting on a small boulder beneath the leafless willows, she removed her snow boots and pushed her stockinged feet into her skates, then took off her mittens to lace them up.

Glancing over her shoulder, she looked fondly at her childhood home, where Dat and Mamma had welcomed each new baby, where Dat's and then Eli's passing were deeply mourned, and where tiny Britta had been received with great delight. *And where Britta and I became close sisters,* she thought as she stepped onto the hard, shimmering surface.

She pushed against the blade, propelling herself forward, gliding over the ice. Facing into the sun, she crouched forward to gain speed, thankful for a new year, a brand-new slate. A year bound to bring big changes for her and Britta, although she still hoped Emmalyn's house, just up the road, would be the place where they might end up.

In thinking about the near future, she felt sorry about her unkind opinion of Allen. "I need to let my resentment go and forgive him," she admitted, the air cold against her lips. She had been too critical. After all, he was only doing what seemed best for Mamma while managing his own large family.

Why have I been so unyielding? she thought, doing slow figure eights now, the sun pleasantly warm on her back, then face . . . and now her shoulder. *What does it matter, as long as Mamma's content there and well cared for?*

Susie tried to imagine someday making the trip to visit her mother, and Allen and his family, too. *Such a reunion!*

Just then, the crunch of snow and the snap of a twig caught her attention. Startled, she turned and came to a sudden stop, her skates' blades scraping against the ice. She stared at the figure, her thoughts flying. *When did he get home? Was he in Hickory Hollow for Christmas?*

"Hullo, Susie," Obie called, waving to her.

She waved back, unsure what to say.

He sat down on the small boulder, removed his backpack, and took off his snow boots.

She felt *ferhoodled* at his presence. *How'd he know I was skating?*

Thinking she ought to head over to him to say something . . . anything, she pushed forward but simply skated the perimeter of the pond again. On the next time around, he was there by her side, matching her pace, as he often had when they skated together years ago. *Why is he here?* she wondered, bewildered yet so glad to see him.

He glanced at her, smiling. "Hope I'm not crashin' your party." He sped up, and she followed.

"Are ya home for New Year's?"

He nodded. "Have ya heard 'bout the bishop's upcoming retirement?" Obie asked, then said that he planned to buy out the business, taking over as Hickory Hollow's new blacksmith.

"Must be a recent decision. First I've heard it," she said, waiting for Obie to mention something about his girlfriend, thinking it was nice of him, though strange, to come skating like this for old times' sake. "Your family must be happy to have ya home."

"*Jah*, and I'm happy, too." He slowed and looked at her, a quizzical expression on his handsome face.

She breathed quickly and forged ahead. "Obie . . . I heard you were about to be engaged."

They were nearing the far end of the pond; then they curved toward the willow grove, the morning sun on their shoulders. "I was thinking about it," he admitted. "But it's never a *gut* idea, neither is it wise, to marry someone when you can't stop thinking of another."

She felt shocked that he'd ended things.

"*Nee*, certainly not," she replied, unsure what this meant.

A moment passed, and now they were practically flying across the ice. Then, as they were coasting, Obie spoke again, his voice softer, almost tentative. "I came close to askin' ya to court once . . . on your birthday, before I left for Sugar Valley."

So that's what he'd wanted to say that day. Just as she'd hoped. "I didn't know."

"And then I thought you and Del were dating. . . ." His voice trailed off.

"We weren't really together like that. Not seriously."

"I know," Obie said. "I heard that, much later on."

For a while, they skated slowly without speaking. When he drifted to a stop, she yearned to hear more.

"Susie," he said, his eyes searching hers, "I know it's been a long time since we've talked or even exchanged letters, but you've always been my best friend. No one's even come close."

She held her breath, waiting.

"Would ya consider bein' my sweetheart?"

She smiled and nodded. "S'pose a fella shouldn't have to ask twice."

His laughter filled the frosty air. "Then, you will?"

She really needed to ask him something first. "I hope it's not meddlesome, but do ya mind sayin' what happened to end your former relationship?"

"Not at all." He shook his head. "Plainly put, she wasn't you." His gaze held hers. "It's that simple."

Wonder filled her. "Then, *jah*, I'll be your girl."

He reached for her hand. And together, they skated in unison, her heart rejoicing as they accelerated.

When the cold had at last crept into their bones, Susie suggested having hot cocoa up at the house. Obie agreed, and once they'd skated to the shoreline to remove their skates and pull on their snow boots, he gazed up through the bare willow branches. "This, right here, was the spot where I first knew I loved ya," Obie said, returning his gaze to her.

Susie's merry heart recalled their many walks here, their rowboat rides, and the skating, too. And his first, unsuccessful attempt to ask her to court, on her twenty-second birthday. "The beginning of what we would become," she said, smiling into his dear face.

Obie's expression turned more serious. "If ya don't mind, I've often wondered what it might be like to hug my dearest friend," he said, opening his arms to her.

Overjoyed, she stepped toward him, surrendering to his loving embrace, never so happy as on this first day of the new year.

EPILOGUE

During the noon meal that day, I told Britta about every little detail of Obie's spur-of-the-moment visit. A mischievous smile appeared as she timidly revealed that she had been visiting Hazel and mentioned, in Obie's hearing, that I was skating.

Then tears glistened on Britta's face. "Oh, Susie, I'm so happy for ya!"

"I'm amazed at the Lord's timing," I replied.

"When's the wedding?"

"One step at a time, Schweschder."

"Well, Obie loves ya, just like I always suspected." Britta gave me a grin. "I've been waiting and waiting for this."

I laughed, enjoying her delight. "Somehow, you and Mamma always seemed to know, ain't so?"

"The only one who didn't was *you*." Britta giggled.

I shooed her upstairs to redd up her room,

still reveling in the absolute joy of Obie's return . . . and in our shared love.

Once the noontime dishes were washed
and dried, I sat at the table to write a long
letter to Mamma, telling my news. Every so
often, I glanced out the window at the gently falling snow—fine white feathers floating
from the gray sky.

As I finished the letter, it occurred to me
that Ella Mae's comment last fall—a reason
for Mamma to stay in Missouri—might have
been about freeing me to court.

Perhaps Mamma and Allen had been
looking out for my best interests, after all,
hoping I'd still have a chance to marry, even
though Obie was long gone. Of course, that
wasn't the only reason Mamma had remained
with Allen and family. Her health required
it. Besides, Mamma couldn't possibly have
known that Obie would change his mind
about his girlfriend, return to Hickory Hollow, and purchase Bishop Beiler's smithy
business! How could any of us have known?

Yet our heavenly Father did.

A week later, as the sun's rays began to
melt the snow atop the gazebo just beyond the

kitchen window, I began to wrap up Mamma's oldest set of dishes to box and store away, according to her suggestion.

Hearing a knock at the back door, I hurried to see who was there and opened it to see my darling beau, his smile so wide his eyes crinkled.

"Was just in the neighborhood and wondered if ya might have any more of that delicious hot cocoa," Obie said, his nose and cheeks red.

"Sure, I'll make some in a jiffy." I welcomed him into the kitchen.

He eyed the boxes and packing paper. "Looks like you're packin'."

"Mamma suggested what things to store, dispose of, and give away. This is a big house, so there's lots to do to get ready."

"True . . . and I heard it's up for rent."

I looked at him. "Oh, I didn't realize Allen had started advertising already."

Obie removed his hat and coat and went around the corner to hang them up. "It's a *wunnerbaar Haus*," he said, returning to the kitchen. "Who wouldn't want to live here?"

I poured milk into the saucepan for the cocoa. "Hopefully, whoever rents it will be a young couple with a family to fill up the rooms," I said, wondering how Obie even knew.

He wandered over to stand near the stove, watching me stir the milk. "Say, I was thinkin' . . ."

I caught his expression, a whimsical smile on his lips. "*Jah?*"

"How would you an' Britta feel 'bout stayin' on here?"

"But how?"

His face broke into an even bigger smile, and he looked down as he shuffled his feet. "Well . . ."

"*Ach*, did *you* rent it from Allen?"

Obie nodded. "With the option to buy . . . once we're wed."

My heart soared at his words.

"*Ach*, but I'm getting ahead of myself," he said, slipping his arm around me. "So . . . will ya marry me, Susie, and make me a very happy man?"

Overwhelmed, I nodded my answer, looking into his handsome face.

"I want to take care of you for the rest of my life, Susie. And I want to do it here."

"Obie . . ." I moved into his arms, unable to hold back the tears.

"Better stir the milk again, so it won't scald," he said, releasing me.

We laughed together, and later, when we were seated at the table, sipping our hot cocoa and eating frosted sugar cookies, I joked,

"Are ya sure you're not marryin' me just to live here?"

He chuckled. "Well, it *has* been like a second home."

"You're right." I nodded, remembering all the times he came to visit us as a schoolboy and beyond.

Later, he brought up the idea of Britta staying with us, after we were husband and wife. "Far as I'm concerned, she'd be welcome here for as long as need be."

Deeply moved by his kindness, I thanked him. "You have no idea what this means to me. And Britta will be so happy." Then I added, "I 'spect Roy Lantz may be interested in dating her once she starts attending Singings and all in July."

He reached for my hand, looking at me with the bluest eyes. "Whatever I can do to lessen your burden, Susie. You've worked too hard for too long."

"*Ach*, I'm just glad to help."

"Well, come fall, we'll be partners in every way, sharin' life's journey, with the strength of the Lord."

I appreciated that more than I could put into words and wondered about his agreement on the house. "Since Allen's consented to rent the house to you, surely Mamma knows, too."

Obie nodded. "In fact, Allen said she wanted *me* to be the one to tell ya."

"That sounds like Mamma, all right," I said, tickled at how everything seemed to be falling into place. "I can just imagine her joy over Britta and me getting to stay here . . . and havin' *you* in the family."

"The feelings are mutual." Obie finished eating his cookie. "I've had a soft spot in my heart for your Mamma for a long time."

I had an idea. "What if we give her a call right now?"

Obie slid his chair back. "I was hopin' ya might suggest it."

Together, we made our way through the snow to the stable, and the conversation with Mamma felt like a warm breeze, her love radiating through the phone line.

"All *gut* things come to those who wait," Mamma said sweetly. "The Wise Woman once told me that."

I smiled and looked at Obie, whose head was against mine so we could both hear. "And to those who wait on the Lord," I said.

"You didn't know it," Mamma went on, "but I prayed for the longest time that somethin' like this might happen."

Obie kissed my cheek. "I prayed for this, too," he said.

My eyes met his as Mamma said how

pleased she was that the house was staying in the family.

I agreed wholeheartedly and wished her a happy new year. And as Obie and I walked back toward the house, my heart was so full, I asked him to pinch me, to make sure I wasn't dreaming.

"Oh, believe me, you're not. But maybe this'll convince ya?" He stopped walking and leaned down to kiss me right there in the backyard before God and anyone watching.

I let a little laugh slip out, and he kissed me again.

"Well, s'pose I best be returning to work," Obie said, grinning now. "It was Bishop John's idea for me to take my break and come over to see ya, by the way."

"I'm so glad he suggested it."

Obie winked at me. "*Denki* for the tasty goodies, Susie. Blue-ribbon worthy." He waved. "I'll be seein' ya real soon."

I smiled, thrilled to hear it. Being newly betrothed, I looked forward to spending more time with him. It would be ten long months till November and the start of wedding season, but our courtship would be especially sweet, I was sure. After all, we'd been apart for much too long.

AUTHOR'S NOTE

One never can tell what will spark a novelist's imagination.

Two years ago, while visiting Lancaster County, Pennsylvania, I had a moment of reflection after my attention was captured by a placid lake surrounded by willows and a bundle of flowers placed along a country roadside—even a family tree wall hanging I'd seen in an Amish home. Although at the time I was researching aspects of my previous novel *The Stone Wall*, these three images sprang to life in my heart, lingering until I knew they were meant to be knitted together into *The Beginning*. I hope this story lifts your heart and offers a genuine and touching glimpse into a young Amishwoman's life journey through the challenges of loss to a hopeful new beginning.

As is usual, this book's cast of story people took time to form in my mind. Among them is a recurring favorite, Ella Mae Zook, whose endearing character continues to remind me of the sweet faces of two very wise women from my childhood—women who attended my father's church in Lancaster and who helped to shape my Christian view of the world. One was my mother's dear friend Edna, the wife of our music director, and the other, my best friend's mother, Helen. These women's insights and the way they honored God in word and deed made a lasting impression on my young heart. To this day, I am truly grateful.

I am additionally thankful to Dave Horton, my friend of many years, for acquiring this book and for his excellent insight into story and how stories are created. My heartfelt appreciation also goes to my meticulous and inspiring editorial team, headed up by Rochelle Glöege and including Charlene Patterson and Elisa Tally. Kudos, as well, to Steve Oates for his many years of selling and promoting my books, and to the Bethany House marketing department, particularly to Noelle Chew and Amy Lokkesmoe, for an outstanding launch campaign.

I offer special gratitude to my husband, Dave, for his helpful encouragement and editorial work, as well as to my sister, Barbara Birch, for her careful reading and checking of this manuscript. My appreciation to John and Cynthia Bachman for sharing the antics and unique personalities of their beloved felines. And many thanks to Amish and Mennonite consultants, research assistants, and proofreaders, as well as to faithful partners in prayer and my cherished family and friends, whose tender love and encouragement nurture my heart each day. And always to my dear, devoted readers—you continually amaze me!

My highest praise and thanksgiving are directed to God, the Creator of all things. *Soli Deo Gloria!*

Beverly Lewis, born in the heart of Pennsylvania Dutch country, is the *New York Times* bestselling author of more than one hundred books. Her stories have been published in twelve languages worldwide. A keen interest in her mother's Plain heritage has inspired Beverly to write many Amish-related novels, beginning with *The Shunning*, which has sold more than one million copies and is an Original Hallmark Channel movie. In 2007 *The Brethren* was honored with a Christy Award.

Beverly has been interviewed by both national and international media, including *Time* magazine, the Associated Press, and the BBC. She lives with her husband, David, in Colorado.

Visit her website at www.beverlylewis.com or www.facebook.com/officialbeverlylewis for more information.

The Orchard

The Next Novel from Beverly Lewis

For generations, Ellie and her family have tended their Lancaster County orchard, a tradition Ellie's twin brother will someday continue. Yet when Evan is called up for the Vietnam War, he makes a choice that shocks his Amish community—one in sharp contrast with that of Ellie's friend Solomon. As she struggles to make sense of the two very different paths taken by the most important young men in her life, Ellie finds herself increasingly drawn to Sol . . . yet wondering what tomorrow will bring.

AVAILABLE FALL 2022